THE
ADAM & EVE
PROJECT

By

Donna Dawson

THE ADAM & EVE PROJECT

ISBN: 1-897373-01-5

To contact the author, please email:
authordonnadawson@hotmail.com

Printed by Word Alive Press

WORD ALIVE PRESS

ACKNOWLEDGEMENTS

As always, I wish to thank my husband and children for patiently enduring the long stretches of time that I shut myself away to hammer out another book.

I offer a special thanks to my Dad and my brother Paul for their contributions in helping with the military information. I'm proud of their part in the Canadian military services and thankful for their advice and knowledge.

Thanks to Pauline and Bill, who share their busy days with me when I just need to get away.

Thanks to our Bible study group—you keep me accountable and in the Word.

Thanks to Eric and Lillian for befriending a couple of novice sailors.

TABLE OF CONTENTS

PROLOGUE

In the underground bunker the voices bounced hollowly, like floating apparitions of sound. It was 1940 and the German war machine was smashing its way boldly through Western Europe. Poland was occupied. The Germans had flanked the Maginot line entering Holland without as much as a warning. Britain sat itself squarely in Belgium, like a steadfast bulldog prepared to guard new territory. Japan turned its eyes on the vastness of the South Pacific, hungering for the expansion of her mighty empire, and Italy ceased waffling between the Axis powers and the Allies, firmly deciding to join with the nearest geographical might.

But in the bowels of the earth none of this was of importance at the moment. No one knew of this particular hole in the dirt. Far below the titanic conflict that threatened to destroy all that lived and moved in this European corner of the world nestled a conglomerate of rooms tied together by narrow and dimly lit halls. The rooms were proportionate only to the ability of their stabilizing structures in the effort to keep the tons of dirt above from swallowing them, but even still, they were large enough to host small groups of scheming and heavy-thinking men who enjoyed their strutting and crowing before the red and black banner of the Nazi movement. The thick language of the German people chopped through one room in particular, anger and dissatisfaction crashing against the steel walls like relentless mortar shells.

"What do you mean, you had to stop *The Project?* How do you know for certain that anyone is aware of the complex?"

The Fuehrer jumped to his feet, knocking the chair back in his tirade, a lock of unruly dark hair flopping across the tense forehead and spittle flecking the corners of his mouth. His eyes were wild with an instant fear and fury as he faced the possibility that his lifelong dream might be discovered by the enemy. Drawing a calming breath, the man struggled to control his infamous temper, and reached down to upright the chair. He sat slowly again, like a snake lowering itself into its coils before the strike. Glittering eyes scanned the faces in the room, noting with a strange satisfaction that no one would return his intense stare. That was good. They feared him.

The young officer who had brought the message stood straight as a rod, but Adolph Hitler could see that the lad was terrified. He wouldn't be the first one the leader of Germany had shot for delivering an unfavourable message. Hitler narrowed his eyes and looked closely at the young man. *Perfect. Beautiful. Foundation stock. Why is he not part of The Project?*

He eyed the second lieutenant like a predator would assess its next meal. The man was easily six feet tall and built solidly. Deep azure eyes drilled holes in the far wall, never wavering. Hair, so blonde—almost white—and silky, covered his head in a thick and wavy carpet. His skin was fair like a woman's and his cheeks were tinted with a bright red, telling all in the room that he feared the attention of his Fuehrer.

"What's your name, Leutnant?" He pronounced the German equivalent rank as '*loy*-ten-nant.'

"Eric, Mien Fuehrer. Eric Schneider," the young man said in an even, steady voice.

"What part do you have in *The Project?*" The words purred through the room and a few of the Generals shifted uncomfortably in their seats.

"I was in charge of security, Mien Fuehrer."

"I see." He was suddenly amused by the craftiness of *The Project*'s chief scientist. The fat old man was a genius in diplomacy and politics as much as he was in his particular scientific field. If the French had discovered the whereabouts of the experimental laboratory, it was because of this young man's inability to do his job correctly, and the aging scientist would make certain the punishment didn't land on *his* own doorstep. *Pity such a lovely specimen of the Aryan race had to be so incompetent.* He watched as the man swallowed hard, the fine forehead beading with perspiration.

"So, because of you…" Hitler rose to his feet, clamped a hand behind his back and, stroking his chin with the other, slowly circled the young man, eyeing him thoughtfully, "…my most prized project must stop?"

"Yes, Mien Fuehrer. I take full responsibility and await your decision on my discipline. I don't ask for mercy. That is weakness."

Hitler stopped his circling and looked directly into the Leutnant's hooded stare. He was surprised by the response, and strangely proud. *This is a true Aryan.* He remained brooding and silent for a moment longer and then he smiled. It sent a chill through the heart of the soldier standing at attention before him.

"You will not die today, young Leutnant. Your answer is the right one. You show true Aryan pride and dignity. For this I will reward you. Your genetics will be added to *The Project*, and your family line will live forever."

A muscle in the man's face twitched as he thought of some of the cruel and seemingly unnecessary experiments that were taking place in the name of *The Project*. Through his mind flitted a momentary thought of escape followed by defeated acceptance. He wouldn't get more than five feet from the door before being cut down by the guards in the room. Snapping his heels in resigned salute, accompanied by a raised arm and a strained "Heil Hitler," he turned sharply and marched toward the door, flanked on either side by two SS-Oberschutz.

The smile faded from the Fuehrer's face as he watched the brutal "black-shirts"—his elite killer soldiers—usher the next guinea pig for *The Project* through the chamber doors. *Let's hope the good doctor uses only the looks and bravery of this man and not his intellect,* the cruel leader mused.

He seated himself once again and remained still for some time, his mind working through the problem that had been laid out before him. Finally he roused himself, as a gentle cough shattered the silence of the room, leaving its harsh echo to fade into silence again.

"Yes, General?" he asked.

"I wish to offer a suggestion, Mien Fuehrer."

"Go on."

"The French have been a thorn in your side since the beginning," the General said, encouraged by the Fuehrer's silence. "You want to conquer France eventually, but if we strike now, perhaps we can speed up your supreme reign in Europe. If we can intimidate King Leopold of Belgium, maybe he will surrender. We can then enter Northern France and drive the French into the English Channel. Once we own France, your project is safe again."

The General sat waiting in silence, hoping he wouldn't be the next victim of *The Project*. Who knew where the whims of the mad leader would take them. Hitler dropped his chin into his hand and remained silent. The tension expanded. And then the Chief Commander of the Third Reich lifted his gaze to the General and smiled his stiff grin.

"Yes. It's a good plan, General. It will also advance our eventual conquest of England. And the rebuilding of the Aryan race won't be interrupted. Very good. Very good, indeed."

* 1 *

SHE WAS JUST OVER TWO YEARS OLD and sat abandoned by the side of the dusty road. Her dark ebony skin was a backdrop for the caked-on dirt that had been kicked up by the constant wind. Her stomach was bloated from lack of food and spindly limbs hung listlessly by her sides. A desperate mother had propped her against a rock and left her there. Eyes that would be nut brown couldn't be seen behind the hard crusts that glued the lids shut, and blistered lips had cracked and bled only to crack and bleed again. And yet, in spite of her frail condition, her lungs and vocal chords had expressed her discomfort and displeasure with a hearty and piercing wail.

The two men had heard her loud protests through the open window of the LKW Opel Blitz transport vehicle and pulled to the side of the road. That was nearly a day ago, and still she sat, occasionally bleating a small cry.

"I think we've seen enough. She will do. We can always get another if need be."

The man spoke with a precise British accent in spite of his German officer's garb. He scanned the horizon with squinting eyes, nervous that he had spent the last day in an active military zone. He was a portly, thin-haired man, and the uniform chafed his wattled neck as the sweat poured down his pasty face and into his collar. He hadn't enjoyed camping overnight in this God-forsaken land—if one could call sleeping behind the driver's wheel of a military truck "camping"—but the girl couldn't be overlooked. It appeared she had much in the way of endurance and that was the whole purpose of their foray into the eastern desert areas of Libya at the beginning of a world war.

Rommel had only recently come to the rescue of the Italian army, taking over the African regiment. The German General, known as the desert fox, was consuming North Africa in an attempt to satisfy his rapacious appetite for land, and the two men who sat in the shade of their truck shifted nervously, anxious to be away from the patch of barren dirt which would soon become a bone for two world powers to contend over.

Leaving the passenger side eagerly, the lower ranked officer scrambled over to the baby girl and tenderly lifted a weak and bony hand, cooing softly at the pathetic squawk that issued from parched lips.

"You'll be dead by sunset, but maybe that's a mercy," he whispered. Throwing a hurried look over his shoulder, he was somewhat relieved that his superior hadn't heard him. And then he bent over the small girl and gently scooped her into his arms. The life they were about to place before her was not exactly the kindest. But it was life. And by the looks of things that was better than the alternative for this small child.

He returned, toddler in hand, to the canvas covered truck loaded with supplies and a portable lab. The older scientist completely ignored the half-dead child as he shifted his rotund bulk in the discomfort of the scorching African heat. With reluctance, he left the cooler shade of the driver's seat to join his aide at the rear of the truck.

"Let's get the blood test done then and get out of here, Yngve. I can't stand this heat a moment longer."

"What if she tests positive?" The younger scientist dreaded the answer he knew would come.

"Well then, we leave her behind, of course. We can't be rescuing every abandoned child in Africa, you know. I thought you understood the purpose of *The Project* and the sacrifices needing to be made on its behalf." The sweating elder turned a haughty eye on his younger Swedish associate.

"I understood," Yngve said, "but I wasn't going to assume."

He could already feel the heartbreak of abandonment and ultimate death for the girl. But what were the odds that this child didn't carry the strange diseases that had been popping up across the continent?

Yngve laid the pathetic infant in the shade beyond the dropped tailgate of the olive green vehicle and opened a canteen of lukewarm water. He soaked a cloth with the precious liquid, sheltering it from the drifting clouds of tan coloured dust, and dribbled it across cracked and blistered lips, amazed when the child's tongue darted out to taste.

"Well, I'll be! Take a look at this, Sir Horace."

For some time, the kind man continued his work, slowly hydrating the young girl. His associate—for he refused to think of the callous man as a friend—paced impatiently in the shade of the truck.

"Would you hurry up, Yngve? We need to go or we'll be caught, and I dread to think of what could happen to us if we are found with a half-dead Libyan child."

Yngve clenched his teeth together, trying hard not to criticize the man for his shallowness. He reminded himself of the purity of *The Project* and its impact on the future of mankind.

"Be patient, Sir Horace. I can't draw blood if the child is too dehydrated. Even a finger prick won't bleed if her blood is too thick."

"It's been an hour since she started getting water. Do you think perhaps it's time for you to try?" Sir Horace asked.

Yngve threw an impatient glance at his associate, drew a lance from his store of sterilized instruments, and tapped it against a tiny black thumb. Both men turned a startled gaze to the child, surprised at the loud screech that accompanied the thumb prick, and Sir Horace smiled, hopeful for the first time since they had found the waif.

The younger man gently worked the small digit until a single drop of blood smeared against the glass slide, and then he covered the slide with another piece of glass to protect it from contamination. This he handed to Sir Horace, who had suddenly developed an interest in the child, and then he proceeded to clean and cover the miniscule wound on the girl's thumb while his superior tinkered with the offered slide.

"There, little lady. That's better now, isn't it?" Yngve said.

Sir Horace's smile broadened as he adjusted the microscope's eyepiece, bringing the sample into focus. The child's blood appeared to be clean; she wasn't infected as far as he could tell. She was simply malnourished and dehydrated. *Oh Glory Be!* he thought to himself, as he wiped the slide clean with alcohol and packed up the microscope amidst the foreign and unidentifiable bric-a-brac.

"I don't see anything that suggests the child is contaminated," Sir Horace said. "Pack up your things so we can get out of here."

Yngve grunted his agreement and began to gather a few things from the truck's supplies. Throwing a final look at the stock, he kept quiet his disgust of the selfishness that kept such advanced technology a secret. Not one piece of the equipment or serum that filled the truck had ever seen the inside of a public hospital. As far as the common man knew, the stuff hadn't even been invented yet. *And people continue to die unnecessarily because of it.* Again, he reminded himself of *The Project*'s mission and, gritting his teeth against the injustice of it, swallowed his emotions.

Sir Horace turned his attention back to the child and, for the first time, truly looked at her. Her wiry black hair had a bleached and singed appearance to it, common to one who hadn't seen proper food for some time.

"You've done wonders at cleaning that disgusting goop off of her eyelids, Yngve. By the look of things, they haven't been opened in a while. I don't think it's wise to rush that part of it, yes? The little sot is likely filled with parasites. Disgusting if you ask me."

Yngve wasn't asking. He would deal with the parasites, too—when the time was right. Patiently, he mixed a solution to be fed by dropper to the child, knowing that she would revive quickly upon ingesting the foul-tasting stuff. He had licked his finger once—and only once—after preparing a batch of the concoction. It had taken a day to get rid of the taste. But it *was* amazing stuff. Another invention no one knew about.

Sir Horace went to a file box and rifled through some papers.

"Where on *earth* did I put those bloody papers? Such a cluttered mess. Oh *there* we are."

Grunting with satisfaction, he pulled an official-looking document out and scribbled his name on it as adoptive father to the girl. Then he pulled out an inkpad and soaked the child's foot, applying a footprint to the document as a form of identification.

Yngve continued to drip the liquid into the girl's mouth, pleased by the grimace that accompanied each taste. *She might just live*, he thought as he shifted aside so Sir Horace could clean the ink from her right foot with an alcohol-laced cloth.

"What shall we call her?" Sir Horace's pen hovered over the paper as he lifted an inquiring gaze to his associate.

Yngve continued with his task while he quickly tossed ideas in his mind.

"Were she a boy, I would suggest Moses," he said.

Sir Horace looked at him strangely. Knowing the man to be an atheist, he was somewhat surprised by the Biblical reference.

"We didn't exactly find her among the reeds in a river, my good man," he said.

Yngve continued to feed his foul concoction, keeping an eye on the improving condition of the reclining child.

"Why not call her Eve, then? Since Eve was the first woman and mother of all mankind—so legend has it—it would be an appropriate designation, don't you think?" he said.

Sir Horace mulled that around for a moment and then settled upon it firmly.

"Eve it is, then. And her last name shall be Africa, since this is where she was found."

He scribbled the new name onto the document and stamped it with a seal, giving it an official and binding look. Once dry, he folded the new document and stuffed it into his breast pocket with his passport and letters.

"Hurry up, my friend. We must be gone. It shall be interesting to see how her cells compare to the young Prince's," Sir Horace said. The plump man packed up the file box and accessories and headed for the driver's door, hauling his bulk up into the shaded interior of the sturdy truck.

"This ruddy heat is going to be the end of me if we don't get out of here soon. I don't know how anyone can tolerate this place."

Tapping his fingers on the steering wheel, he waited while Yngve gathered a change of clothes for the tyke, water to sponge her with, a nappy and a bottle of powdered milk diluted with more of the lukewarm water. Yngve sidled up to the driver's door and handed the articles up to Sir Horace through the open window while he continued to cradle the girl in the crook of his muscular arm.

Sir Horace watched as the younger man circled the front of the truck, all the while talking gently to the young bundle, finally pulling himself easily into the passenger side. The older man started the truck, satisfied with the loud rev of the powerful engine, and kicked it into gear, turning the awkward vehicle in a large loop across the crusty soil.

He was a happy man. Never, in a million years, would he have thought they'd find what they needed so quickly. *Thank*

God for war, he mused, *it has a way of weeding out the weak and useless so the strong can survive.*

"The checkpoint guard might raise an eyebrow about this. It was a rather quick adoption, don't you think?" Yngve asked.

Sir Horace smiled a little.

"It doesn't matter. A letter from Adolf Hitler is never questioned. They wouldn't be so foolish as to search the truck."

He had all the necessary documents to legitimize the child. They would be waved through. His smile broadened as he savoured his position of power. He had similar letters from Heads of State in England and many other countries as well. And they were legitimate letters. *If the commoners only knew. If those who had signed the letters only knew.* But they didn't. They only knew what *The Committee* told them. And they did as they were told. Like he and Yngve did.

The girl began to cry softly and Sir Horace glanced briefly at her, amazed by the change. She had endurance all right. Yngve shushed her as he continued to strip away the filthy clothes, tossing them out the window in disgust. He had laid a plush towel across his lap and began the process of cleaning her, wiping her skin with a damp cloth as he removed each article of clothing. And then he deftly re-covered the gaunt frame with clean, new clothes—a simple top and a nappy.

He shook the powdered milk again, making certain it was mixed thoroughly with the water, and offered it to the child, unsure if she would have the strength to drink from the bottle. She lifted a weak hand and rested it on the glass container, pulling it greedily toward her sore mouth and ignoring the pain as she sucked slowly on the nipple.

"My, but you're a sturdy one, yes?"

The salve on her eyelids had done its work, easing the pain of infection and freeing the lids. Yngve couldn't see her eyes well through the film but he knew she had some form of vision as she turned her head enough to stare at his fair face, sunburned as it was. A faint smile spread across her countenance, causing her lips to crack and bleed, and then she concentrated on the task at hand and drained the bottle.

The truck bounced and jostled across the dirt track carved by the German Army in the desolate Libyan ground. Sir Horace was heading away from the horrors of warfare with its flame-throwers and thunderous artillery. Eve nestled against the white man's chest and dozed intermittently, grateful for the nourishment and cleansing.

Her young mind still grappled with the intense hurt of being left behind by her nomadic family, for although she was far into the severe stages of starvation, her extremely intelligent brain was more than aware of the departure of those who had brought her into the world. She had cried out to them, begging them, in her own childish language, not to leave her. But they had. And so she found herself, rocking with the rhythm of the noisy truck in the arms of a nice white man.

She looked up at him from time to time, wanting to see through the haze that blinded her to detail, allowing her only to differentiate between shapes and bold colours. After a time she sat up, realizing she had new coverings on by touching them with bony hands. A piece of tape covered her thumb and she rubbed it curiously. And then the man spoke. It was a harsh sound, full of consonants and completely foreign to her. Yngve spoke the German language to her as he had been instructed to do.

"So you are awake, little one? And how are your eyes? Here, let me."

She felt the soft cloth more than saw it as the sticky film was wiped from her face. And then it was gone and she lifted her lids again. For the first time in weeks her eyes focused, permitting her to clearly see her rescuer.

She lifted her slender hand and touched the white skin, marveling at its contrast to her own deeply chocolate-hued flesh. And then she reached farther and gently grasped a strand of the fine blond hair. The man chuckled, his bright blue eyes twinkling happily as he enjoyed her curiosity. He reached out with his own large mitt and touched her tightly curled close-cropped hair and she smiled at him.

"Well now. She seems to be a bright one, Sir Horace," he said.

The older man harrumphed and grumped his reply.

"That's all the more to our benefit then, isn't it?" He squinted his eyes tightly, trying to see the road through the growing swirls of dust and sand.

"Where is that blasted check point? We should be there by now."

They continued on in silence, the two passengers studying each other while the driver grunted his disapproval of the conditions of the road.

*   *   *

The German Obergrenadier stepped out onto the dirt road, shading his eyes against the setting sun, which was thinly veiled by the dust that was finally beginning to settle. He tried to identify the distant rumble of an engine. The vehicle was large—not a jeep—but he was pretty certain it was a German cargo truck. Still, it was wise to be safe.

"Stay alert, Grenadier! A vehicle approaches."

He planted himself firmly in the center of the track, machine gun poised across his chest. The truck slowed to a halt at the barricade and his eyes narrowed as he recognized the Oberfeldwebel and his Unteroffizier. *What were an Englishman and a Swede doing in German uniform?* He had asked himself that when they had crossed, going in the opposite direction, the day before.

"Tend to them but be on guard!" he said.

He tossed a brief glance at his subordinate. *Does he have enough brains to check the papers thoroughly?* The man was a fair bit older than he and dull as lead paint. He watched cautiously,

13

holding the gun easily as the Grenadier rifled through the offered papers and turned to him, shrugging. *Incompetent fool,* he thought as he shouldered his weapon and stalked over to the driver's window. *With men like this Grenadier, Germany will lose the war.*

"Let me see the papers again," he said.

He stared at the identification papers, Hitler's letter and the adoption certificate for some time, looking for a flaw that would allow him to arrest the two men. He could see none. Stepping up onto the running board, he glanced into the truck at the Swede and the black child nestled into the crook of his shoulder.

"That was a very quick adoption—*Sir.*" The two men in the truck stiffened noticeably. Perhaps they *did* have something to hide.

"Do you honestly expect me to believe these are authentic? I think I fell for that yesterday. I think you two are spies." He unshouldered his gun and held it at the ready while he barked to his private.

"Grenadier! Keep these men here while I call headquarters to find out if they really are envoys of the Fuehrer."

Grenadier Kurt Von Claus raised his rifle and shrugged again, offering a small smile to the truck's occupants. He'd been posted with this cocky young buck long enough to know that it was only a matter of time before the man learned not to question. Kurt, himself, had questioned once and received a demotion from the rank of Unterfeldwebel—or Sergeant—and a lovely vacation to this desert posting in Africa.

"You'd better do as he says. It should only take a moment, Sir," he said.

He cocked his head toward the small shack not five feet away, hoping to catch snatches of the conversation over the radio. Kurt needn't have moved at all. His smile broadened as he heard the screaming voice echoing through the receiver at his superior.

"How dare you question the orders of the Fuehrer? You idiot! Do you wish to be shot or would a court marshal be more appealing?!"

The younger man was a full five minutes receiving a dressing down and Kurt enjoyed the sideshow, discretely sharing his small humour with the driver of the truck who sat impatiently tapping his fingers, a smug expression plastered across his visage.

The Obergrenadier finally stepped from the shack, a sheen of sweat slicking his pasty face. He swallowed hard once and cast a quick glance at the Grenadier, noting his stern focus on the truck's occupants. He stepped back onto the running board and offered the papers back to the Englishman, his hand shaking enough to make the sheaf of documents jiggle and flutter more than the slight breeze warranted.

"I offer my sincere apologies, Oberfeldwebel. I was unaware of the importance of your work to the cause of the Third Reich," he said. "Please forgive my arrogance and stupidity. It will not happen again."

"I dare say. And so it shouldn't."

Sir Horace snatched the papers from the young man and folded them precisely, returning them to the breast pocket of his uniform. He harrumphed once, causing the excess skin on his neck to flop like a turkey's wattle. The First Class Private, soon to be Private, stepped down from the purring truck and flagged them on.

*   *   *

Sir Horace was hopping mad and muttered to himself for a good hour about the incompetence of mankind.

"I still don't see why they couldn't have given us the uniforms of Generals or at least a Captain. It's ridiculous to think that a Sergeant-Major and a Corporal would be direct envoys of the Fuehrer. It's no wonder we're stopped so often."

Yngve sighed, tired of hearing the same thing over and over.

"You know why they did it. A General—or even a Captain—is too valuable to an enemy. They'd never let us go. A private would be shot instantly. But a Sergeant-Major and his Corporal are middle ground soldiers. The enemy would hold us, hoping to gain information, long enough that a rescue would be possible, and yet we aren't important enough for the enemy to deliberately seek us out."

Sir Horace grumped a while longer and then grew silent. The sky eased into darkness and he switched on the truck's headlights, concentrating on the obscure track ahead. He was relieved that the dust storm had surrendered to the peaceful and eerie silence of the clear desert night. Somewhere out there was an airstrip, and that was his final destination in this rattletrap they called a vehicle. He couldn't wait for something with a smoother ride.

*   *   *

Nestled back against the firm support of her rescuer's chest, Eve had been gazing out the window for some time. She didn't understand the words the two men spoke and amused herself with the bleached and dusty scenery that skidded by in the quickly fading daylight. As night consumed the vast African sky, she watched the stars and the landscape, hoping for a change in the emptiness of the terrain.

They had traveled along in the silent darkness for some time when she pulled herself into a sitting position and rattled off a string of words in her native tongue. Yngve bolted awake, having drifted to sleep with the rocking motion of the truck as it bumped and bounced over the pothole-filled track. He looked at her in amazement.

"What are you telling me, little one?" he asked.

He followed the direction of her finger as it pointed into the darkness, targeting a small group of twinkling lights on the horizon ahead and to the right.

"Well, I'll be... It appears our new charge has found your airstrip for you, Sir Horace. I think we have truly discovered a treasure." He gave her a small hug and turned his attention to the approaching complex.

Sir Horace squinted his eyes again, making a mental note to have his glasses checked once he was back in Germany. Breathing a sigh of relief, he turned his vehicle off the road and onto the cracked and barren desert floor, heading directly for the cluster of buildings at the far edge of the smooth runway. A small twin-engine plane sat there, patiently waiting for its precious cargo consisting of a variety of medical equipment, two men, and an incredibly bright two-year-old African girl.

2

HE STALKED THE DEER SILENTLY, with a prowess that far surpassed his elders. The ten-year-old Native American boy was wily like the wolf, the bear, and the cougar. He had instinctively tested the air, finding the direction of the subtle current, and then slipped down-wind of the nervous animal to avoid detection. His father had taught him well. His father had taught him *many* things well and the boy remembered them all.

He settled onto his haunches patiently. He wanted the deer to relax somewhat. She would be less likely to flee while the arrow was still seeking its mark. His keen mind wandered while he waited for the perfect moment of interception.

His father had taught him much about the war that was taking place in another part of the world. He had taught him about the white man's God and how this war was a fight to protect the right to freedom—freedom to live where one wanted and to worship as one wished. His father had told him of the evil man named Hitler who wished to enslave God's chosen people and destroy Christianity and freedom. He brooded about it and wished he were old enough to fight the wicked leader. Some day.

The deer dropped her head to nibble on the greener grass near the babbling stream, presenting a good moment for the boy to nock the arrow and draw it slowly to his cheek. He hesitated, releasing his air slowly as he aimed at the thick body. He was shooting into the air currents so he drew a little farther, allowing the gut string to roll off his fingers with a mild whisper. The arrow plunged through the air silently, spinning ever-so-slightly with the angle of the fletching, and then it drove into flesh with deadly accuracy. The strongly beating heart jumped at the intrusion of the wooden shaft tipped with sharp metal—and then it stopped.

Convulsing once, the deer leapt a good ten feet before crashing face first into the underbrush alongside the stream. The boy stood with satisfaction, adrenaline pumping through his veins, feeding him with its euphoric juices as he let out a whoop of excitement. His father would hear the call and come running, he knew. He would be proud of his young hunter.

Lifting his foot to step from the foliage that had concealed him, the boy prepared to approach the cooling carcass in order to properly bleed and dress it. Suddenly he felt what he thought must be the sting of a hornet on his shoulder and turned his head to see. Before he could take another step, his vision swam and the boy pitched forward, not unlike the deer.

"That should keep the brat quiet for at least an hour." The muttered words filled the silence of the clearing.

Moving swiftly, his face smeared with mud, a man dressed from head to toe in muted greens scooped the young bundle from the patch of ferns and removed the dart, stabbing a piece of cork with the sharp end before dropping it into his jacket pocket. He tucked the boy under his arm like one would carry a small animal and started off through the brush, making as little sound as possible. And then he heard a man call the boy's name and he picked up his speed.

*   *   *

Andrew Grey Bear scratched his head as he read the wood signs. His son had been here, there was no doubt, as he picked up the hand-crafted bow and quiver full of arrows. He had made them for his only son, Hawk, and knew the lad would not have let them out of his sight if he could prevent it. But there had been no struggle. He looked over at the abandoned deer carcass and his concern grew. Hawk wouldn't have left the kill, either.

Grey Bear turned his acute gaze to the underbrush that surrounded him and studied it for some time. There. It wasn't much, but someone had passed into the thicket and it showed. Very little. His eyes narrowed and he and his brother, Peter, followed the faint trail, fear beginning to fill his heart as he prayed silently for the safety of his son.

*   *   *

No one saw the man stuff the boy into a cage in the back of the battered and rusty brown pickup truck, cover the cage with a tarp, and strip off his outer clothing. No one noticed him slip into the driver's seat and start the truck. No one else knew the logging road existed except the loggers who no longer used that patch of forest.

The truck roared to life and the man cursed profusely as the gears ground their objections to his rough handling.

"Come on, baby. If you don't get yourself into gear, we're gonna be cooked," he said to the sorry collection of bolts and metal. And then, as though consenting to the growled coaxing, the gears moved and the vehicle rattled off down the dirt track.

It was mid-afternoon when he arrived at the cabin by the lake. The man was waiting—the one who had offered him one hundred thousand dollars to kidnap the boy. What the guy wanted with the Indian brat, he didn't know. *He's probably some kind of pervert.* The kidnapper didn't care. He just wanted his money.

*   *   *

The man wore an expensive, well-tailored black suit and he waited patiently for his guest to pull up to the cabin. Leaning against a stolen Buick—also black—he kept his expression unreadable. Beside him on the ground was a black leather suitcase, and he stooped to retrieve it as the approaching vehicle groaned to a stop. He watched as the driver—a disgusting cretin—pulled himself from the pile of trash held together with twine and prayers that he called a truck and sauntered over to stand before him.

"Did you bring the money?" the kidnapper asked. He was a foul-smelling man who cared little about what the world thought of him. That made him perfect for hire since his accountability was limited by the strength of his closest friends' stomachs.

The suit turned, placing the case on the hood of the pristine car. He popped open the twin latches and stepped back, allowing the woodsman to lift the lid. Gaping at the mound of bills stacked neatly in rows in the square case, the kidnapper smiled. He would have snapped the lid shut, pulled himself back into the rotting vehicle, and left, but the man in the black suit stepped up behind him, syringe in hand, and plunged the sharp tip into the muscle of the thickset man's neck, whispering quietly into his ear as he accompanied the sliding body down the hood of the shiny car.

"I hope you have friends. Otherwise, you'll rot here where you land. *They'll* call it a heart attack. But *you* and *I* will know differently, won't we?"

He pulled the needle from the man and allowed him to crumple onto the ground, knowing that his heart had already stopped. Capping the needle, he placed it into the suitcase with the beautiful crisp bills and clipped the lid shut once more. With calm deliberation, he placed the case into the trunk of the car and headed to the truck, pleased that it had gone as well as it had.

The boy was awake and curled into one corner. His eyes looked mean and wary. Yes, this one would be perfect. He marveled at the keen intelligence apparent on the lad's face. The boy pulled his feet up under him, ready to spring when the cage opened.

"I don't think so, my young friend. I think you're going to enjoy another little sleep. Trust me, it's better this way."

The voice was soft and oily and the man drew a small blowgun from his inner pocket. The instrument had been a gift from a tribal leader in some obscure country in Africa and he knew it was an effective way to tranquilize an animal. He'd watched the African demonstrate it just before he killed him.

Pulling a dart from the metal case in the same pocket he slipped it into the end of the wooden tube. As he brought it to his lips and took aim the lad covered his head in protection. He understood the weapon.

"Well, I'll be... You certainly are a smart one, aren't you?" he commented.

And then he took a breath and blew hard, pushing the dart from the gun through the wire cage into the boy's hip. Within seconds the lad slept again.

The man returned the weapon to its hiding place, opened the cage, and lifted the limp bundle from its prison. He carried the boy to the car, lowering him onto the leather bench. Carefully, he removed the dart, placing it back in its case. Opening the glove box, he drew out sturdy cord and deftly secured the small hands and feet, stuffing a wad of cloth into the sleep-pursed mouth.

He shut the car door and turned back to the corpse, which lay stiffening in the afternoon shadows. He'd almost forgotten one small detail that could have raised a few questions with the local law enforcement officers—if they ever found the man. Rifling through pockets, he found the twin to his own crafty weapon and withdrew it, placing it next to his more ornate version. And then he stood, scanning the scene for missed details. None.

"Good, then," he said.

Straightening his jacket, he made one last sweep of the surrounding area with eyes that missed nothing. Satisfied, he rounded the vehicle and slipped behind the wheel, starting the engine and shifting it into gear. The boy would sleep for hours. The man—forever.

"You're just going to leave it there?"

"Yes."

"Aren't you worried that someone will find it?"

"I don't really care if they do. They can't trace it. You worry too much."

The black car sat abandoned on the sparse and rugged track that ended at the edge of a small northern Canadian lake. The sleek Lake LA-4-200 Buccaneer drifted slowly across the water's smooth surface, gradually gaining speed, and the man in the black suit shifted in his seat to take one last glimpse at his young cargo, trussed up and tossed on the floor between two of the four seats of the light Float Plane. The boy was still asleep, blissfully unaware of the drone of the Avco-Lycoming engine that lifted the twenty-four foot craft from its cradle of frothing and churning lake water.

"I don't see anything special about him," the pilot said.

"You weren't privy to his blood work analysis. I was."

The pilot threw a brief glance at his dark-suited co-pilot before returning his attention to the many buttons and gadgets that aided in the plane's function.

"I'd love to know how you managed to get a hold of that," he said.

"No. No you wouldn't."

As the flying boat leveled out and the single engine chewed through the air until it settled into its 150-miles-per-hour, the man in the black suit reached into his inner pocket again and pulled out a small band of material, slipping it over his arm and working it up the sleeve of his suit coat. It would never do to arrive in Germany without his favourite form of identification. He glanced down at the swastika and smiled. *Sir Horace will be pleased.* He paused in his thoughts. *Adolf Hitler will be pleased.*

Sighing audibly, he revealed his impatience to be back in his Nazi Germany. He stared into the cloying gloom, which concealed all landmarks below the thirty-eight foot wingspan.

"This is going to be a long night, I think," he said.

It was an understatement, and the pilot grimaced as he began the long task of dodging the British, Canadian, and American forces that swarmed over North America's east coast and into the Atlantic Ocean. He worried a little, hoping the plane would not be detected as it climbed to 14,000 feet. Somewhere out in that vast collection of icy saltwater, a German U-30 awaited them, and it was only a matter of time before the combined Allied forces discovered its presence.

"Do you think they'll find us?" the man in black asked.

He looked out the window through the dark, slowly relaxing as the pilot deftly maneuvered the craft through the air currents.

"Nein, Herr Obersturmfuhrer," he said. "Our ship lies just off the coast and they don't even know it's there. Besides…who cares about one small floatplane? No one will even know we were here."

The boy moaned in his sleep and struggled briefly with his rough bindings, and then all was silent but for the hum of the small plane. The hours ticked on, interrupted by a handful of stops on lakes holding small caches of fuel hidden for this very mission. The Buccaneer sputtered and chugged its way to its destination, finally gliding down onto the choppy water of the North Atlantic Ocean to await its rendezvous with the submersed U-Boat recently pulled from the killing grounds of the British Coast.

*   *   *

"What do you mean, 'We'll be heading directly to the island?' I was given direct orders to deliver the boy to the complex in Germany."

The Obersturmfuhrer was a master at masking his impatience. He had left Germany in the late 1930's, fired with the importance of his mission. It had taken him years to find the boy, verify that his genetic code was the one wanted, and capture him—and now he was being diverted from his course. It irritated him to have his plans interrupted, but irritation was not a luxury one could express in the current circumstances.

"I realize that. However," the ship's captain said, "Sir Horace contacted his superiors informing them that their position had been compromised. They have been moved down to the island. I'm sorry, Herr Obersturmfuhrer, but those are *my* orders." He watched the SS officer with caution, knowing the man's reputation for brutality.

The Obersturmfuhrer gritted his teeth, resigning himself to the inevitable. Upon accepting his new orders, he locked himself in his quarters aboard the submersible fighting machine to wait impatiently while they proceeded south. It was more than an inconvenience to have the ship carry him and his cargo to the island hidden deep in the warm and hospitable waters of the Caribbean. He had, only once, seen the complex planted firmly above the caves that twisted and wended their way through the rocky foundation. He had no desire to return.

"What I would give to wring Sir Horace's neck," he said. How he loathed the man.

*   *   *

The boy blinked his eyes rapidly in the bright light and tried to open his mouth. It was stuffed with a damp rag and he knew a brief moment of panic. Forcing himself to stay calm, Hawk pulled a breath of air in through his nostrils, slowly and quietly spat out the rag, and allowed his vision to adapt to the intense glare.

He lay on a tarp tossed carelessly on a sandy beach. Crates and kegs were stacked neatly around him and off in the distance a great ship rested on the smooth waters that quietly lapped the shoreline. Men in uniforms grunted in their efforts to move the abundant cargo from a craft draped with netting and sailcloth. The bulky boat rested in the shallow water, its hull brushing gently against the wet sand.

Hawk sat up slowly and looked around him, allowing his foggy brain to clear. His hands and feet were snugly bound and he immediately set to the patient work of freeing himself. A small hand worked its way down his pant leg to his knee-high buckskin boot. Surprisingly, his captors had overlooked the large hunting knife hidden on the inner side of the stiff and tight-fitting boot. If the boy hadn't been drugged through the entire trip, they might have had a chance to experience the edge of that weapon. No one seemed to notice his initial movements so he lay back down and focused his attention on the task at hand.

Please, God, keep them from seeing me. He sawed at the coarse ropes between his ankles with tiny movements until the binding relaxed around one foot. As much as he wanted to stretch his legs to work out the cramps, he remained still, slowly and patiently eating up time while removing the rest of his restraints. And then he lay there a moment longer, allowing the blood to return to tingling hands and feet.

His father had taught him that it was possible to move without moving noticeably. It was a necessary thing to do when hunting. One wrong sound could frighten away the next supply of food. Keeping the same position, he clenched and unclenched each muscle, tightening and releasing until he could feel the strength return to the unused limbs.

Piercing eyes discreetly surveyed the surrounding terrain, assessing the landscape for the best escape route. Behind him was a forest of some sort. The trees were unfamiliar, but there was thick undergrowth there and he was intimate with the knowledge of how to best use it in whatever form it presented itself. He knew he could conceal himself quite nicely—it was one of his many talents.

They had dumped him with his chest facing the beach and he dared not turn too quickly for fear of drawing attention from the men at the water's edge. To his right was a rough and narrow road, at one time hacked through the jungle for the few vehicles busily trundling supplies away from the beach to some unknown destination. Following a steady incline, the sorry track curved to the right into the obscurity of the fan-like plants which clustered around the tall umbrella-shaped trees. To his left the beach became rocky and he assessed it with new interest.

If he could slip behind the crates, he might be able to sneak his way into the rocks and disappear amidst the thick dense growth beyond. Slowly and carefully he re-sheathed the knife, rolled over, and eased around the tarps and cases and crates. On his belly, the boy shimmied his way behind a large wooden box to give himself one more layer of concealment. Once there, he balled his bindings into his hands and slowly slipped his way back along the soft sand to its brief joining with the coarser and more challenging gravel.

*   *   *

"Where's the boy?" The man in the black suit looked in every direction, panic rising in his chest. He had no intention of becoming one of the many experiments that went on behind the heavily sealed doors of the huge laboratory nestled near the center of the island.

"How could you lose a ten-year-old boy?!" he screamed at the Grenadier, and then cuffed him on the back of his head.

"I just saw him, Mien Obersturmfuhrer. He was asleep among the crates, where you left him." The man stood at attention, taking the cuff without question, hoping that was all he received.

"Well he can't have gotten far. You men—spread out and find that boy!"

*   *   *

Hawk chuckled to himself. *Stupid soldiers. Don't they know a ruse when they see one?* His father had taught him about ruses and how wild animals used them to hide or escape from predators. The Killdeer was a perfect example. She dragged her wings in the dirt, as though injured, to lure any intruders away from the nest. He had remembered that and made several small tracks in the other direction, tossing the wad of rope discreetly out onto the sand.

Backtracking, he covered his prints until he eased onto the rocky shelf and then, inch by painful inch, worked his way into the forest behind the rocks, climbing a tree to wait until nightfall.

They had discovered he was missing just as he was entering the forest, forcing him to duck lower and move slowly, watching them the whole time. He knew he could never outrun them. Camouflage was his only hope. His father had taught him to climb trees by hugging them with arms and legs, alternating his grip between the different limbs. He had done that while the soldier men scrambled around on the beach like ants.

The tree was tall and thick with smaller rope-like tendrils dropping from its branches to anchor in the sandy soil. Hawk carefully eased his way into the upper canopy and wedged himself into one of the tree's many crotches. Thank the Lord he still had his buckskins. His father always let him wear the tan-coloured animal skins on the hunt. He would blend beautifully with the brown tree trunk if he sat very still.

A crashing in the forest edge brought his attention to the ground far beneath him. Two soldiers were scouring the ferns and thick and luscious greenery, expecting any moment to find a scared little Indian boy hovering amidst them. They spoke their strange harsh language and Hawk could sense the fear behind it. He pushed himself against the smooth bark, waiting until the noise faded away, and then he leaned forward just enough to watch the goings-on down on the beach.

*   *   *

"If we don't find him by nightfall, Sir Horace will have our heads, Mien Obersturmfuhrer." The younger pilot was anxious and continued to scan the tree line with his blue eyes while he waited beside the man in the black suit.

"Don't worry about it. I have an idea. Come with me."

The officer left the jumble of boxes and headed back to the beached boat, barking orders as he went. Stepping up to the vessel, he snatched the radio from a young soldier who stood nearby and addressed a voice at the other end of the radio's signal.

"Get me Sir Horace. Now!" He paused as he waited, mentally forming his words with caution, knowing that, if he were not careful, the next five minutes could change his course drastically—and not for the better.

"Yes, Sir Horace. I got the boy onto the island. It appears my observations and studies were extremely accurate. The lad is unusually cunning and talented for a ten-year-old. He managed to escape into the forest." The Obersturmfuhrer pulled the phone-like radio away from his ear while the old scientist bellowed his dissatisfaction.

"Sir Horace, does it really matter?" he asked. "The lad is exactly where you want him. He's on the island in an environment that will help him feel at home and at ease. Isn't that what you wanted?" He waited, letting the idea settle on the old stuff-shirt.

"I suggest you allow us to get off the island so the boy can't sneak back onto the U-Boat somehow. It wouldn't surprise me if he were able. *You* know he's strongly capable of survival, so just leave him and let him survive. You'll find him eventually. I do have another suggestion, though," he paused, allowing Sir Horace to absorb all he had said thus far.

"Find the girl who will be his mate and let her loose here. He will find her. He'll want to protect her and may even fall in love with her. You can always find their child when the time is right. True?" The man smiled and wiped a bead of sweat from his cheek with a nervous hand. He nodded his head as though Sir Horace would see him, offered a "Heil

Hitler," and signed off. The Obersturmfuhrer turned once again to the men on the beach and shouted to them.

"Leave the cargo for the islanders to retrieve. We are to leave now. Rouse! Rouse! Hurry!"

Someone blew a piercing whistle repeatedly, drawing the scattered soldiers back to the beach. They pushed at the bulky fishing boat, forcing it from its cradle in the sand, and piled on as it drifted in the gentle waves, waiting for the pull of the several manpowered oars to direct it back to its briny anchorage beyond the shark-infested reef where it met with the larger ocean-going ships.

*   *   *

Hawk watched it all from his perch, not understanding. They had left him. Abandoned him. Suddenly he found himself alone in a strange forest without his father and uncle. A fat droplet of water formed in the corner of his eye and spilled over onto a dirt-smudged cheek as the reality of his situation settled upon him. And then another fell. And another. Soon the boy was sobbing uncontrollably, frightened by the seeming emptiness of the island. Time passed, allowing the lad to empty himself of the emotions that roiled inside. And then he remembered something his father had told him not so long ago.

"Hawk, I may not always be with you but you need to know two things. **Jesus** *is with you no matter where you are and* **I** *will always love you."* A strange peace settled over him then as he savoured the wisdom delivered to his memory by the deep and rich tones of his father's voice.

Hawk had never known his mother. She had died in childbirth. It could have crushed a lesser man, but his father was strong. When the boy had asked about the woman who had brought him into the world, Gray Bear had clenched his jaw and looked into the heavens.

"God allowed it. I don't understand it and it hurts me a lot sometimes. But some day, I'll be in Heaven with her and that's all that matters to me. Remember that, son. Don't ever walk away from Jesus just because you don't understand. Someday, he'll make *all* things right."

The boy heard a faint rustling to his left and turned his head slightly, focusing his eyes beyond the tree's thick leaves. Quietly, stealthily, a huge snake worked its way down the stumpy branch toward him. Hawk was amazed by the mass of the creature, knowing that he could never win in a battle against it. He would need to be crafty and quick to survive the crushing coils of the serpent as it moved, like cold molasses, ever closer.

Again the boy sought the assistance of the heavy blade and carefully, he waited, his eyes never leaving the hypnotic progress of what he hoped was his next meal. The snake's tongue flickered in a quick and erratic attempt to taste the air for the boy's fear, but the boy wasn't afraid. The adrenalin pumped once again, filling him with energy and clarity of mind. And then he struck. Quickly and accurately. Bringing his knife down, he neatly impaled the giant creature's head to the tree limb.

The offended snake thrashed violently, cuffing the boy across the face with a mighty coil as it convulsed, throwing him back against the trunk once again. Hawk had aimed true. As always. His arm was strong. As always. And while the boy massaged the bruise rising on his cheek, the jerks and spasms of the snake slowed and ended. Each coil relaxed, slipping slowly, one-by-one, from the tree branch as the knife firmly held the broad head against the smooth and sturdy wood.

Hawk marveled at the length of the snake. It had to be ten feet long. He would have to store the meat somehow. Maybe if he smoked it like his father and uncle did with the deer meat he could make it last for quite some time. He knew how it was done. But he also knew that smoke attracted attention. He thought for a few moments and then shrugged. Right now he was hungry and it was soon going to start to get dark.

Working the knife back and forth, the boy finally pulled it from the branch, allowing the snake to drop to the ground with a heavy thud. He shimmied down the tree quickly and scanned the forest with an inbred wariness, looking for predators that would steal his meal and on the lookout for stray soldiers at the same time. Prying the mouth open, the boy cut the large fangs from the boa constrictor's jaw. It was a trophy that he would prize. He then removed the head—just in case.

It took Hawk an hour to skin the creature and carefully work the meat off of the long spine. His father used oak bark to tan hides, but he didn't know if the island had oak trees. Ashes would have to do. Deftly, he rolled the long skin into a bundle and tied it with a piece of his buckskin fringe. He then repeated the action with the long strips of meat and wrapped each bundle in a huge fern frond to protect it from flies. He hurried. The smell of death would drift on the air currents, drawing scavengers. Digging a small hole, the boy buried the remains of the huge snake, satisfied with how much of his father's teachings had been remembered.

Scouting around the clearing, he spied a clump of young trees with branches that were green and springy. Sawing with his knife, he cut down a couple of the thin saplings and began the tedious job of stripping the bark off. He needed the long inch-wide strips if he wanted to take the meat and skin with him. Working quickly, he braided three strands of the bark to make a sturdy rope. Bending a sapling into a u-shape, he tied the ends with the braided bark, forming a frame to tie the meat and skin to. This done, he fashioned a harness of the remaining braided strips and slipped into the weighty contraption, pleased that it functioned properly.

Hawk was sturdy at ten years of age. Where another wouldn't have attempted to carry so much, he struggled with determination, pulling himself and his load up the steady incline toward the dark spot on the hillside that he hoped was a cave. Briars and thick scrub brush blocked his way as he

Donna Dawson

neared the rocky outcropping that had formed the shadow he had seen earlier.

He looked at the twisted mass ahead and smiled grimly at the natural defense that blocked his path, forcing him to work his way through the tangled and clinging twigs to the scooped out clearing just before the cavern's entrance. Collapsing upon reaching the hollow indentation, he allowed himself time to renew his spent energy.

After a while, he unshouldered the awkward bundle and pulled another braided rope from it. He tied the rope to a piece of the frame and tossed the free end over a low branch, pulling the meat into the waiting arms of the nearby tree and securing it there until he was ready for it. No sense having wild animals eat it on him.

Drawing his knife again, he ventured into the cavern that he hoped would become his temporary home. His young mind would not allow him to dwell on the permanency of his situation. He leaned against the wall, keeping low as he worked his way slowly into the darkness, pausing often to allow his eyes to adjust to the dim interior. Light filtered sparsely into the cave, allowing him only a muted view of its contents, so he moved with caution.

The room was almost completely round, the walls smooth. At some time in the distant past a fierce rush of water had attacked the sandy surface, washing it smooth as it swirled deeper and deeper into the cave, finally hitting rock solid enough to end its quick and efficient appetite. The place stank. Like death.

He squinted his eyes and leaned forward, gagging as he identified a cache of bones and rotting remains at the far end of the room near a darker shadow that could only be a tunnel. The cave had been a den for some predator. He would find a way to fix that. For now, it appeared empty and he stepped further into the hollow, satisfied that he could make a good home of this place. He would have to bury the carcass—or burn it. With that thought in mind, Hawk left the foul-

34

smelling confines, grateful to draw in the sweet fresh air beyond the cave's entrance.

He had a lot of work ahead of him yet. Lifting his gaze, he was pleased by the abundance of trees that spread their long and twisted branches overhead and formed a thick canopy that brushed against the rock wall. The naturally formed lattice would filter the smoke of a fire, preventing someone from tracking him down. He set out again, scavenging deadfall for his wood supply. Back and forth he trekked until he had filled one side of the room with a large quantity of different sized branches. And then he gathered a small bundle of dried leaves and grasses, hoping they would light easily with the piece of flint he carried in his boot beside the knife sheath.

He placed his small tinder on the opposite side of the cave from his woodpile and added a few thin twigs to it. Drawing his knife and the small chunk of flint, he began striking them together over the grass, holding his breath as he watched sparks jump from the stone to the kindling. And then he smiled and blew gently on the small tendril of smoke rising from the edges of the crispy foliage.

It took a long time to burn the carcass. Initially, he had thought to drag the rotting animal to the fire, piece by piece. But then another thought overrode that one as the stench increased upon his approach, and he decided to stack a small pile of firewood against the foul mess. When the bundle was sufficient, Hawk pushed glowing coals into the wood, lighting the whole pile aflame. A few times he had to turn away or leave the cave, but eventually the smell faded as the fire worked its way into the dried muscle and cartilage. He might have been smarter to bury it, but the ground there was rocky and he couldn't hide the stench any other way.

Keeping vigil, Hawk spent most of his night tending the fire or pacing in the open air. Morning approached gradually and the fire crackled on, meticulously consuming all that it touched that wasn't made of stone. He was exhausted, but he pushed on until the carcass was gone and the stench with it. It was time to prepare the meat—and secure the cave.

He once more stepped out into the forest, selecting young saplings and more firewood, driving himself to complete the work. By noon he had a tidy frame fashioned that he could lay the excess strips of snake meat over. It looked like a table of sorts and he set it above the fire, high enough to be in the direct path of the smoke without being affected by the flame's heat. Green foliage was added to the fire to induce the smoking effect and Hawk sat back and allowed the meat time to cure.

Sharpening a stick, the boy skewered another large chunk of meat, creating a rotisserie of sorts closer to the fire where the coals glowed red with their intense heat. While the meat cooked, he doggedly scraped the flesh from the snakeskin, stopping on occasion to turn the meat. Once the skin was clean, Hawk stretched it over another frame he had fashioned. He had separated a large portion of ash from the fire earlier, allowing it to cool on the stone floor. This he spread over the inner side of the skin, bleaching it and making it more workable. It wouldn't preserve the skin as well as oak but it was better than nothing.

And then he ate. He devoured the meat, washing it down with water he had retrieved from a spring nearby in a cup fashioned from a broad leaf—another skill taught by his father.

Hawk was beyond tired at this point. Leaning his back against the stone wall away from the fire, the weary boy stared at the open door through bloodshot eyes. Survival instinct told him he should secure the narrow opening and explore the small tunnel before he slept, but reality told him he wouldn't. His father had told him once that, in life, a man should do all he could do and trust the rest to Jesus. Well, he would just have to do that then. Closing his eyes, he whispered a brief prayer.

"Jesus, thank you for keeping me safe and providing me with so much. Help my father and Uncle to know I am safe and alive. Protect me while I sleep. Amen." And then, he slept.

* 3 *

SHE WAS EIGHTEEN AND BEYOND BEAUTIFUL. Her parents owned a large ranch in California, allowing them a number of luxuries unavailable to the common man. They had made it quite plain to their daughter that they didn't trust the young man, Dennis, at all. They were wise, he mused as he waited for her to approach him. He knew Carolyn couldn't understand why they didn't like him. She simply thought her parents were over-reacting—again.

He smiled sadly, his eyes hidden behind the sunglasses he wore. She was so naïve and innocent. He watched as she laid her bike against the tree at the far end of the runway. The sun had only just peaked over the eastern horizon and by the time they knew she was gone, the plane would be somewhere over eastern America. Once they hit the coast, she would be off-loaded into the submarine and trundled off to the island.

She drew closer, a picture of purity interwoven with little flames of stubborn fire. He swallowed hard as the sunlight caught the golden glints in her waist-long hair and the breeze rifled the silky strands enticingly. Eyes as blue as sapphires looked deep into him, filled with untainted infatuation, and his smile widened.

He stepped away from the Lockheed 5 C Vega and adopted his best cowboy twang as she wrapped her arms around his waist.

"I told you I had a plane. Are you ready for a small tour?"

She smiled her dazzling grin and nodded, her eyes shining with excitement.

"My parents didn't believe me when I told them you had a job flying planes."

He sighed, feigning hurt.

"I don't understand why they don't like me. I'll tell you what—why don't we go for a quick run and then we'll take them to dinner tonight? I got my paycheck and it would be fun. What do you think?"

She nodded again and scooted into the plane, prepared to settle into one of the seats of the small luxury craft. Carolyn never felt the pinprick. Dennis jumped, startled, as she tumbled limply into the cushioned chair just past the aircraft's entrance, a small, feathered dart protruding from her fine neck.

"Sheesh! I wish you wouldn't sneak up like that. It scares the tar out of me."

He heard the dead chuckle drift to him from the tail of the expensive private plane as his boss approached the still figure and pulled the fine tipped dart, pocketing it along with the small blowgun.

"Would you rather I introduced myself out there on the tarmac?"

Dennis shook his head, exasperated, and helped the Obersturmfuhrer move the girl into a more comfortable position in the seat. Using soft braided chord, they secured her and moved forward to take their own places.

"You'd better ease down to the end of the strip and we'll pick up her bike. It's best not to leave anything behind. I'm sure someone on board ship will buy it." Again the dry chuckle and Dennis felt his hackles rise. He detested the man but made sure to never show it. He detested the job—and again—didn't show it. And he hated himself for the depths he had sunk to. No amount of money was worth losing his soul. And he had.

He started the aircraft and buzzed his way to the end of the smooth private strip. This piece of land and its private plane belonged to a very important, influential man, and

Dennis shook his head a little at the screwy nature of the war. An American banker providing a German pilot runway space so an SS officer could kidnap an American citizen was a bizarre and bold act of treason if one got caught. All in the name of *The Project*. The salvation of the human race. Baloney. Again—he would never let his boss know how he felt.

He watched the cold-hearted man hop from the plane and walk the remaining distance to the tree. Dennis turned the plane slowly, with ease, and waited until the First Lieutenant of the SS lifted the bike into the spacious craft, climbed in after it, and closed the heavy door.

Carolyn woke long after she had been smuggled aboard the newly commission U-505. It had waited, hiding in the Atlantic's depths just off the New York City coastline while its fragile cargo had been delivered to a private airstrip outside the large city. From there, she was transported to a small yacht—also private—and loaded aboard the deck of the IX-C German submarine only moments before it turned its two-hundred-and-fifty-two feet of heavy steel and weaponry onto a southeasterly path toward the mid-Atlantic ridge.

Her first impressions were of her own throat-clenching terror. And then her eyes adjusted to the dimness in the small storage room, lit only by a small lamp hung from the wall. Dennis sat nearby, watching her with a strangely forlorn expression on his face. He reached across and gently ungagged her.

The scream came of its own accord, working its way past her tight neck muscles to explode through the small amplifier of her mouth. Dennis' lips lifted in a sad and crooked smile and he sat back, waiting until she was finished, all the while trying to ignore the piercing sound as it bounced repeatedly around the metallic room.

"They will only think I've raped you if you continue."

Carolyn clamped her mouth shut instantly, grimacing as she heard the faint sound of laughter from behind the heavy steel door that held her captive. And then the door flew open and an unfamiliar man in a black suit peered in, anger dying in his eyes as he noted the distance between she and Dennis.

"Is he bothering you, young Miss?" His voice was smooth and thickly accented and Carolyn's eyes bugged with incredulity.

"Are you joking? I'm tied up in a closet in a floating tin can who-knows-where with a man I thought I could trust and someone else that I don't even know. You're *both* bothering me. Now let me go and I won't report you to the police," she said.

He answered her with an amused smile, nodded to his pilot, and closed the door again, leaving her flabbergasted and frustrated. She tried to sit up, jerking her shoulder away when Dennis rose and offered assistance.

"Don't touch me. I thought you cared about me. I thought we…" and then the tears came and she turned her face away, refusing to let him see her cry.

"Look…" he inched forward and began to untie her wrists. "You and I can throw insults at one another, or I can explain this to you and help you to understand." He sat back again, watching as she massaged life into her tingling hands.

"Fine. So what is it all about then?" She snapped the words out, her fear poorly hidden by a saucy bravado. No wonder he liked her. He waited until she settled on a small stool and then the brief smile left his face.

"Years ago, a group of people—important people—came together for the sake of preserving mankind. These people have money at their disposal like no one else on earth. They live in different countries but owe loyalty to none. They've manipulated governments, the media, the economy—you name it—so they could meet their final goal, which is to create the perfect human race and preserve balance economically, politically, and financially.

"Long ago they discovered that mankind was falling apart. Decade after decade produced more disease and deformity and they came together with the purpose of regenerating the human line. Adolf Hitler has been the only one bold enough to actually take their ideas and try to make them a reality."

She was interested but still wary.

"So what does that have to do with me?"

He looked at her again, the wistful sadness in his eyes.

"You're beautiful. Beyond beautiful. Your parents are beautiful. Your siblings are beautiful. Your bloodline of beauty is strong. Beauty is part of the human factor. You're needed for it," he said. She was stunned.

"Let me get this right, Dennis—if that's really your name. You lied to me, acted like you loved me and kidnapped me so I could be a laboratory rat for a scientific experiment— just because I'm...beautiful?"

He nodded. "That's where it gets a little touchy," he said. "It was supposed to happen that way but I actually do like you...a lot." He looked away then, staring blankly at the solid door. "I can't change what's happened and they'd easily kill me if I tried."

Bringing his gaze back to her he stared soberly at her perfect face.

"We have a choice here, you and I do. I can pretend that I don't love you and I'm a hundred percent behind their stupid project. You can resign yourself to the fact that you're about to become part of a program to create a disease-free line of human beings. Or...we can both try something heroic and stupid and we'll both die. There you have it."

Dennis watched, heartbroken, as the lovely young woman processed all he had told her. He saw her brave front crumble and fall. And then he went to her, cradling her in his arms tenderly, crying with her as he acknowledged to himself that she would be given to another and that he had been one of the evil people behind it all.

*   *   *

The door opened again and the Obersturmfuhrer cleared his throat, clearly annoyed at finding them huddled together. He would have to reprimand his young pilot for this. The girl was to bond with the young German Leutnant. The Fuhrer would be furious if he saw this. His curt nod gestured to the couple that the ship had broken through the clear waters of the ocean near the Antilles Ridge where the warmer Caribbean met and mingled with the icier Atlantic and indicated that they should be prepared to disembark soon. Their journey to the island would end in a matter of hours. The Obersturmfuhrer glared angrily at his pilot, hoping the young man would take the hint and move away from the girl.

Dennis returned his look, a silent refusal in his own hooded gaze. *Later.* The First Lieutenant would deal with it later. The girl pulled away and wiped at her face with her sweater sleeve. She was stunning. More beautiful than any he had ever seen. Maybe it wasn't wise to show her off to a shipload of sailors. He shrugged. He would shoot anyone who tried to touch her. Even the ship's General, if necessary.

*   *   *

Carolyn stepped hesitantly from the small room and straightened her long skirt. For the first time in her life, she was grateful for her mother's insistence on modesty. Normally her hair was coiled up in a tight roll but she, in a final act of defiance, had maliciously pulled the pins from the knot and flung them across her bedroom.

A dozen such rebellious moments flashed through her memory and bitter regret brought tears to her eyes again. Lifting her chin, she wrenched her elbow free of the Obersturmfuhrer's mild grasp and stepped forward, walking, with resolve—alone.

Row upon row of sailors stood at attention on the narrow, water-slicked deck, watching her with a mixture of emotions. Desire. Lust. Adoration. Pity. Not one man moved as she marched before them, but all silently acknowledged the incredible beauty of the girl who, chin lifted defiantly, passed through their ranks. The First Lieutenant stepped up to one side and Dennis eased to her other. Together, they ushered her to where the Admiral stood, awaiting his formal introduction to one of Hitler's special guests.

After a brief conference, in which she participated with minimal effort, Carolyn found herself escorted to a plainly furnished single occupant's room where she was left locked in—alone. For her own safety—so she was told. She wandered around the cabin aimlessly, bored to tears. It didn't take a lot of thought for her to realize she was in an officer's cabin as she noted its size and the few extra luxuries she knew crew of lesser rank would not be privy to.

She thought of home. What would her family be doing at that moment? If only she could find some way to tell them she loved them. She looked at the room forlornly. Pictures of ancient battles covered the otherwise bare walls. A black and white photo of Adolf Hitler stared down at her from its prominent place on the wall opposite the door, his gaze stern and imposing as if to say, "I will conquer everything in my path. You shall see." Turning her head from the unnerving portrait, she looked at the desk with its paper and pen. Throwing a brief glance at the heavy steel door, she allowed a thought to form in her mind.

Leaving her perch on the plain single cot, she began to rifle through the few shelves looking for something—she wasn't sure what. Moving to the cupboard on the far side of the room, she pulled open the metal door and gasped with pleasure at its meager contents. Various sized bottles were intermittently scattered upon the shelves, some full, others half-drained. She pulled a tiny medicine bottle from the top shelf and closed the door.

The bottle had only an ounce or so of some foul-smelling liquid left in the bottom so she emptied it onto the floor under the bed, shaking the bottle to dry it as best she could. Carrying it to the desk, Carolyn picked up the pen and began the process of composing a letter.

> *July 13, 1943,*
> *Dear Mom and Dad,*
> *I'm fine. I've been kidnapped. I'm on some kind of submarine but I don't know where I'm going. There are lots of soldiers in funny uniforms and they speak a different language. You were right about Dennis. He was part of the kidnapping but knows now that it was wrong. He told me all about a secret group of financial leaders that are trying to recreate the human race by taking people from all different countries and matching them up. I am supposed to be one of those people. I love you and will try to escape.*
> *Love Carolyn Stillwater*
> *San Francisco, California, USA*

She blew on the paper, making sure it was dry before stuffing it into the bottle and sealing it with its cork. Looking around the room, she placed the bottle into her skirt pocket and scurried to clean up her mess just as the loud clang of the door shattered the silence.

"And how have you been spending the morning, young lady?" The Obersturmfuhrer eyed the paper and writing tools, obviously used. When she never answered, he stepped into the room and lifted the pad.

"Where is the letter, Carolyn?" he said. His voice sounded cold and dangerous, causing her to turn, her chin lifted stubbornly. She looked around her and tried to sound convincingly bitter.

"I never got it started. You interrupted me—quite rudely, I might add."

He smiled.

"Sir Horace will like your strength of character. But that is another matter," he said. "Right now, I wish for you to meet someone. He once was a Leutnant...ah...Second

Lieutenant…in the Third Reich. Now, he's a prisoner—like you. I thought you might like some company on deck. For your safety, of course."

She turned her back on him.

"Or is he to be my partner in this project of yours?" she countered.

The SS officer narrowed his eyes. He would definitely have to have a word with his pilot. The man was revealing far too much information and that could be dangerous. He mentally sighed as he weighed this new tidbit. Did it really matter what she knew? She couldn't tell anyone. Not now. He reached for the paper and pen, confiscating them.

"If you don't mind, I will escort you to the deck where you will meet your new friend," he said. She snorted and turned back to him, marching past him into the hallway, ignoring his dry chuckle.

Out on deck, the wind caught her hair and whipped it about her face. Carolyn leaned against the ship's rail, trying to look casual as she removed the small bottle and allowed it to slip into the churning waters below her. She shrugged to herself, feeling as though she had wasted the effort in such a vast ocean, but knowing that she had at least tried.

She turned her back to the rail, trying to ignore the attention she attracted, while she worked at capturing her long hair to braid into a rope.

"Don't do that." The voice was deep and rich and she whipped her head around to see its author.

"You startled me," she said. And then with as much nonchalance as she could muster, Carolyn ignored the tall man and turned back to the rail to resume her pleating. "I have to braid my hair in this wind or it will be a mass of knots." She paused and looked at him again. "What do you care?"

The man glanced at Dennis, who stood fifty feet away, eyeing them with his own unreadable expression.

"It appears that you and I are to get to know one another. I just thought your hair looked better flowing in the wind. I understand now."

Carolyn watched him from the corner of her eye as he leaned his elbows on the steel rung that surrounded the deck of the large floating weapon. Bright blue eyes, distant and angry, looked out over the choppy water. He was tall, muscular, and incredibly handsome—and she wasn't interested, she told herself. He could have been her brother, so closely matched were their colouring and looks.

"So you're the one I'm supposed to fall madly in love with. Good luck. I don't think so." She waited, hoping to read his response.

He turned his blue eyes on her and assessed her again. She might easily be the most beautiful woman he had ever seen, but she was certainly no pushover. He admired that. He looked back to the ocean, silent for a time as he thought about what to tell her. She was young. What would she understand? He sighed. Did it really matter if she understood? He was alive only because he was beautiful—as was she.

"I was a Leutnant not so long ago. It's a position of honor, of decent rank. Men looked up to me and I wanted their respect. I worked hard, never questioning our insane leader and his strange ideas—it was never safe to do so. I was assigned to the security of *The Project* in an underground bunker in central Germany. No one knew of its existence.

"And then one day we heard that the French were sending out scouts to record the German activity. It didn't matter, I thought to myself. We were underground. Impregnable. But I had overlooked a flaw. I had allowed radio operations to continue and a message was intercepted. Then another. And another. I didn't know until my own people intercepted a French transmission to the British telling about a secret underground facility near the German border. They didn't know what we were doing, but they knew we were there.

"The Fuhrer was unimpressed, to say the least. For the past two years, I have undergone more blood and tissue tests than I care to mention. And now, I, and many others, must be moved to their island because the war has jeopardized the work in Germany. If I hadn't had the looks of the Aryan people of the past, I would be dead now."

He stopped and a muscle twitched in the side of his face.

"I am on this ship for you and only you."

Carolyn threw a distracted gaze toward Dennis, who still stood guard, watching them from a discrete distance. His deception cut deep and she suddenly found it easy to ignore her betrayer, no longer willing to be understanding. Turning once more to the man beside her she gave him her full attention, recognizing quickly the similarities of their situation.

"You mean to tell me that you're German…but you're a prisoner?"

He merely nodded.

"So what's with this Project and this island? I understand the whole concept of trying to restore the human race, but why the secrecy and why the kidnapping?"

He turned to look at her again, surprised by her interest.

"You don't know?" She shook her head in reply. "No…I suppose not many do," he said. "Have you ever heard of *The Committee?*" Again she shook her head.

"They are the leaders behind the world leaders," he said. She nodded then, remembering Dennis' description of the world's power brokers.

"After the first world war, Germany was devastated," he said. "The world was thrown into chaos. The free countries had their stock markets and they went wild. People made millions of dollars on speculation. And then the stock markets crashed followed by your depression. Too many countries were lying in ruins and that was a bad thing for the world economy.

"*The Committee* knew that a war would revitalize the battered economies. A war would need soldiers, machinery, and food. People would be needed to provide all of these things. If war were to break out again, there would be plenty of jobs and those sagging economies would live once more. Only the countries who lost the war would suffer—and the innocent, of course.

"So they started their political maneuverings. I only know of this because my father was an important man in Germany in the '30's. He was there when the North American and European members of the committee gathered to speak with the Fuhrer, offering—in private, of course—to help him revive the economy.

"They knew Hitler was mad. They also knew he was brilliant. A frightening combination. They loaded him down with money, helping him conquer the German world. My father was shot and I changed my name so I would not die with him.

"Then they switched sides, pouring more money onto the British, Canadians, Americans and French. But Hitler has become stronger than they thought he would. And crazier. He has changed their precious project from trying to restore the human race to trying to refine it. He wants to take it back to the original Aryan people. The first Germans."

He stopped then and continued to look into the distance.

"Why are you telling me all of this?" she asked. She waited for his answer, afraid of it and yet knowing it already.

"I told you already. I am on this ship for you. If we are to become man and wife, we might just as well get to know each other first."

* 4 *

THE BOY WAS ARROGANT. That could be cured. It didn't really matter at this point. He was smart, and that was what really mattered. Come to think of it, his father was arrogant too, so perhaps it was understandable. He would certainly need to learn a newer method of treating women, mused Sir Horace. The lad's future wife must be comfortable with her mate or she might not produce at her optimum.

He watched as the guards pinned the nine-year-old to the wall. The nurse clenched her teeth angrily as she swabbed the bite mark on her arm. The foul little monster had attacked her for speaking to him. *Bloody Middle Eastern traditions*, he sighed.

"Put him in isolation. A few days alone may help him to come to terms with his opinion about women." The nurse nodded her thanks and translated the orders into German.

The older soldier picked the lad up and carried him by his shirt collar, watching with sadistic pleasure as the boy choked and gagged. He swung his fists and chopped the air with his feet, fury fuelling his wrath until his oxygen supply petered out and he grew limp. The burly Unterscarfuhrer set him on the ground and nudged him with a toe.

"Get up, you spoiled brat. You can walk to the isolation cell," he said.

The boy gasped in the precious air, waiting for the dizziness to pass, and then he whimpered, confused as to why he was being treated with such dishonour.

"When my father hears of this, he will cut your skin from your back and feed it to the palace dogs." He bared his teeth as though to bite again and the man reached a meaty hand toward the boy's collar. The young prince cowered.

"Your father abandoned you to us," the soldier said. "He's ashamed of you. You're mine now, you little dumkopf, and I'm going to teach you respect for the weaker gender."

"But women are property," the boy said, his disdain earning him a cuff to his ear.

"Women are gifts to be handled gently." The soldier gave the boy a shake as if to drive the point home. "True, they're for our pleasure, but they're humans, not property, and you'll learn to treat them with respect and with gentleness."

Stormy eyes looked up at the Unterscarfuhrer with a challenge. The boy was not afraid of the SS man. Lifting his chin he spat the single word.

"Never!" He received another cuff for his impudence.

The man smiled thinly and tossed a look over his shoulder at the British traitor who was his commanding officer. If it weren't for the soft Brit he'd have this young pup cowed in an hour, but he had been given strict warnings not to break the lad's will. *What the foolish old man doesn't know won't hurt him.*

"We'll see, young prince," he whispered loud enough for only the boy to hear. "We'll see."

The Prince spent four days in a lightless, rat-infested cell. He was fed decently enough, but he had to eat quickly to keep the rats from stealing his small portion. His cramped nook was nothing more than a damp hole with only the filth encrusted floor to sleep on. By the end of the fourth day, he was seriously reconsidering his views on the treatment of women. They weren't nearly as offensive as the man he'd been presently dealing with. The heavy metal door clanked open, spilling light into his dim world, and the boy whimpered in fear.

"Get up, boy. You're to be bathed and given responsibilities."

He was confused and frightened but the lad obeyed, trailing docilely behind the Unterscarfuhrer along the narrow hall that led to the room he had been dragged from four days earlier. The same nurse sat in his quarters beside a tub of steaming water and he stopped in his tracks when he spotted her.

"Come here." Her voice wasn't exactly pleasant but he knew she was at least trying to be kind. Tradition and upbringing fought for the upper hand in the young mind and he swelled with indignation once again. Women weren't to speak unless spoken to. Even his mother was becoming more careful about what she asked of him.

"Asad. Come here," she said.

How *dare* she call him by his given name? He was a *Prince* and should at least be addressed as one. He remained rooted to the floor, unable to convince his strong will that this woman had any rights at all, let alone the right to mistreat him this way. He shook his head, receiving the all-too-familiar cuff for it. The woman looked up to the man who stood guard beside him and he picked the lad up and escorted him, kicking and screaming again, back to the foul cell.

It took two more days for the boy to call to the guard and tell him he would obey. Minutes later, the key clicked in the lock and he found himself, again, following the cruel SS man to the waiting bath and the stern nurse.

She merely pointed to the water and this time, though his eyes rebelled, he dropped his filthy and rank-smelling robes and stepped into the soapy bath. The nurse lathered his jet-black hair, pouring water over it to rinse away the dirt and suds. She scrubbed his back with strong-smelling lye soap and then handed him the bar and cloth to finish his own bath.

The nurse stood then, holding out a large fluffy robe, and looked away while the lad slipped into it. And then she spoke again and he worked hard to pretend she was just a man—with a few alterations.

"Asad, do you understand why you are here?" she queried.

He shook his head, saddened suddenly and feeling abandoned and lonely without his family. The nurse turned to the soldier again and Asad felt his stomach tighten. He was relieved to see her nod a dismissal to the large surly man. The Unterscarfuhrer pinned him with one final warning look and then smiled briefly at the nurse before he turned to leave.

"Just call if you need me, miss," he said before stepping through the doorway.

"Asad, I know your father is a man of great importance. I know he's a king, but he's also a wise man. He willingly gave you to us because you're so smart. We all understand that you can think far beyond your years and this is what makes you valuable to us. But you must learn that the world outside your country is very different. You must learn that women aren't possessions, they're people, with feelings and thoughts of their own."

The boy looked at the floor and mulled the new idea around in his mind. He had never heard a woman speak this way before and knew instantly that it was because they were afraid to, not because they were incapable. Returning his intelligent gaze to her face, he nodded.

"Go on."

"You're probably the smartest person in the world. Not many nine-year-olds have learned the game of chess, let alone mastered it. We know you understand physics and algebra and that you've mastered several languages. Your father was kind to give you to us."

Asad shook his head then, a large tear squeezing from lowered lids.

"No, nurse. My father is ashamed of me. He thinks I spend too much time with books and not enough time training as a warrior prince should. He told me this thing. He was glad to be rid of me."

And then the tears flowed and the wall between nurse and captive crumbled. Asad leaned his head against her shoulder, allowing her to comfort him as he had always longed to be comforted, permitting the silly traditions to slide away for the moment. He had worked so hard to please his father, but if he weren't killing something, his father would be angry. Perhaps he would be accepted in this place for who he really was.

Finally the nurse sat him up and wiped the tears away with the washcloth.

"My young prince, this will be our secret. No one will know you and I have had this talk, but from now on, we'll treat each other with respect. Agreed?" She offered her hand in the western-style handshake. He looked at it for only a moment and then firmly clasped it, feeling a new affection for the nurse.

Later that day, after his trip to a massive library where he was left to roam, Asad and his nurse found themselves in another's quarters, and the boy tensed again. A tall, blond man in a doctor's lab coat sat quietly talking to a small child—a pretty black girl—and Asad wondered if he was expected to submit to this child, too. He stood straight and kept emotion from his face, waiting.

"Asad, I would like you to meet Dr. Yngve Sigverd and his friend, Eve Africa. I don't know if you're up to the task, but Eve is quite a smart young girl herself and she needs someone willing to teach her. I'll be here with you each day— if you're willing—to teach you the proper ways of dealing with a young lady, and you must assess her capabilities and teach what you can. Is it a deal?"

Yngve watched the nurse deftly manipulate the nine-year-old prince and marveled when the boy pursed his lips in thought, pulling on the bottom one, much as the lad's father had done. Asad slowly nodded his agreement and then lifted uncertain eyes to the doctor. Yngve's heart warmed to the lad and he offered him his most encouraging smile.

"Is this the teacher you told me about, Papa?" Eve said.

Yngve was amazed, as he had been many times in his recent interactions with the child, not only by the content of the question asked him, but by the flawless German it was spoken in. He had not once encouraged the girl to call him Papa, and yet the title seemed to fit and gave him a strangely pleasant feeling. He hugged Eve with a small squeeze and answered in the same language, thrilled that she had begun to understand it so quickly.

"Yes, my little flower, this is your new teacher," he said. "His name is Asad." He watched Asad stiffen and raised an eyebrow in the boy's direction. Asad looked at the floor quickly and forced himself to relax, cringing only a little when the sweet voice addressed him.

"Hello, Asad. Are you going to be my friend, too?" Large chocolate eyes swallowed the boy with their innocence and he remained still and quiet, choosing not to respond. Eve looked up to her new father with small concern and wrinkled her dark forehead.

"Papa. Asad didn't answer. Does that mean he can't speak the way we do?"

Yngve's eyes danced as he connected with the nurse's own amused look.

"I can so! I just don't know what I'm supposed to say to a girl yet," he said and turned his back, leaving Eve confused, lip trembling from being snapped at. The nurse touched the boy's arm and shook her head, a stern warning on her face. Slowly, he turned back and bowed to the girl.

"I ask your pardon." This he choked out and the nurse bit her tongue, so as not to laugh. "I am your tutor and for now—that is all."

* 5 *

"HE'S BECOMING A LIABILITY."

"Yes, I know. What do you want me to do about it?"

"Let's place it before the others and let them decide."

*   *   *

There were eleven men in the room. It was a secluded place—a chateau in Switzerland—and no one knew they were there. They sat in a library of sorts, around a large hardwood table where thick velvet draperies and the massive accumulation of books deadened the sound of their voices.

An older gentleman sat at the head of the table, and off to his right shoulder stood a tall, blond-haired man dressed in a black suit. The swastika had been removed from the man's arm and he stood at ease with the group of financiers. The old man motioned for silence and then waited while the other men settled in their seats and brought their attention around to him.

"Gentlemen..." his voice rasped with the combination of age and cigar smoke and his watery brown eyes swept the room one last time.

"I have asked the First Lieutenant to join us. We have a problem that needs to be dealt with and I feel he would be the best man to assist us in this."

The man in the black suit smiled and bowed slightly, his eyes soaking in the detail of everyone in the room. They shifted uneasily, each recognizing the deadly hunger of a born killer. And yet, he could very well serve their purpose. The old man looked up at him and nodded, urging him to speak.

"Our Fuhrer has gone quite mad," the First Lieutenant said. "He is obsessed now with creating the perfect race, only he wishes to exclude all peoples other than Germans. It goes beyond this. He has fashioned himself as a god over these people that he is to create. He intends to rule the world. Alone."

The ten men began to mutter, disturbed by the news. They weren't unaware of the leader's quirks, but to have one of his own people so boldly announce it was more than a bit unnerving.

"He has engaged in the mass slaughter of the Jewish race and has even created crematoriums and torture chambers to experiment on the Jews," he said.

A gasp echoed throughout the room as the SS officer continued.

"I am not adverse to killing in the name of war, but I understand the idea behind *The Project*. He has taken your dream and changed it. He has his own secret laboratories across Germany, and when it is found out that this august group of gentlemen financed him, you will find yourselves in a very difficult situation."

"Are you threatening us?" A middle-aged man jumped to his feet, his florid jowls flapping with indignation. The old man who had introduced the SS officer to the group lifted his hand in a placating way, cutting into the conversation.

"Gentlemen, you must excuse my friend here. He is a soldier first and foremost, unused to diplomacy. Please allow him to finish and then we can discuss it further." The muttering calmed somewhat, but the soldier had their full attention.

"I do not make threats, gentlemen. I'm merely stating facts. There are those who know you funded Hitler just so the world economy could receive a boost. People aren't so foolish. You must stop the man."

A large man sitting halfway down the table leaned back in his plush chair and tipped his black cowboy hat back on his balding head. A cigar sat clenched between his teeth and bounced smoothly with each word he spoke.

"What all do you propose, my friend?" he asked.

The Obersturmfuhrer formed his words carefully, knowing that these men had the power to make him great—or to make him disappear—if they chose to do so.

"Hitler must die. You must win the war. This will keep people from caring about your small *faux pas*. They'll be so happy that it's finished, they will not remember. And all the evil that has been done across Germany will sit squarely on the shoulders of a dead leader."

He waited, allowing the group of men to digest his ideas. The cowboy shifted his cigar from one side of his jutting jaw to the other.

"So how do y'all plan on killing Hitler?" he said. "We've been trying to do that since Pearl Harbour brought America into this crazy war."

The First Lieutenant waited for a full moment, his eyes moving from man to man, assessing their resolve.

"One of you must convince the German Generals of the value of disposing of Hitler. If they assassinate him, it will end any speculation and accusation. It will also give the German people a way to explain the mass murders. Once the war is over, this fine group of men," he waved his hand to include those seated at the long table, "can resume *The Project* out on the island without anyone being the wiser." The Obersturmfuhrer stopped and stood at attention once more.

An economist from the Soviet Union dropped his gaze to the highly polished table, deep in thought, allowing his mind to filter through all that had been said and how it would benefit or hinder *The Project*. He looked up at the cowboy and nodded, his confidence growing.

"It's a good plan. I think I can reach the Generals; I have a few strings to pull. Can we agree to offer them a nice sum of money—quietly of course?" he asked.

Heads nodded all around the grand table and a plan was formed.

*   *   *

He had always hated Hitler. He didn't need the money offered to him to assassinate the buffoon, but it certainly would help in building the newer, more liberal government that he and his associates longed for. There were many within the German government—if you could call it that—who despised the madman.

The Standartenfuhrer, or Colonel, as the Americans called him, shrugged into his overcoat quickly as he strode down the hallway and away from the conference room. Hopefully those in the room who were on the side of freeing Germany from the clutches of Nazi dictatorship would be able to get out of the way of the blast which would tear through the conference room any second, ripping the Nazi leader to shreds. If they couldn't, it would be a small price to pay for the rescue of Europe.

The Standartenfuhrer left the building as the bomb erupted through the confines of the briefcase he had left on the floor to the right of the Fuhrer, and the man turned to watch the effects of his own handiwork. As the debris settled, he smiled, satisfied, turned again and made his way to a waiting airplane, the plans of his overthrow of the German government rolling around in his mind.

*   *   *

"Hitler didn't die in your little blast."

"What?!"

"You heard me. He didn't die. Someone moved the bomb. He only suffered damage to his eardrums and got knocked about a bit. Four others were killed, though."

The Standartenfuhrer thought over the information and how it would affect his world.

"You failed. I would suggest you find a very deep hole to bury yourself in and I will finish the job."

*   *   *

1945 came and went in a series of titanic clashes. Germany was crushed. Japan was crushed. Italy was cowed. And France was free. As of an hour earlier, Hitler was no longer a problem. Soon the world would rejoice at its newfound freedom.

The blond man in the black suit skirted around a pile of debris. What had once been a beautiful city was a mass of destruction. He glanced around uneasily. It wouldn't do at all to be recognized, although it wouldn't really matter in a few hours. The Fuhrer and his new wife were dead. Would anyone really care about a mystery man at the scene of their death anyway? He smiled and slid into his waiting staff car, the Nazi flag still dangling from its perch on the radio antennae. He sat still for a moment, playing the past hour over in his mind, looking for flaws before he drove off.

Hitler and Eva had been holed up in their bunker and the Obersturmfuhrer had found it easy to gain access. It helped that he had been discreetly given all the proper codes and passwords. In a few hours, the world was about to discover the shocking news that the two had committed suicide. He smiled pleasantly to himself. Several nations had been unable to do in six years what he had accomplished in a matter of moments. He savoured the euphoria that always came to him after a kill.

Shooting the Fuhrer in the head had not been difficult. The man hadn't seen him open the sealed door and aim the pistol. Eva had been another matter. She had gone into hysterics, giving him no option but to force the cyanide capsule down her throat. It had to look genuine.

When her convulsing had ended, all signs of interference had been removed and then he left, resealing the bunker. No one would ever know the difference. The war was over and the crazy man could do no more damage.

* * *

"The job is finished, gentlemen." The old man coughed heavily, the rattle working its way through his weakened lungs and throat.

"So, now what do we do about Roosevelt's death? Does anyone have a voice with the new President?" he queried.

"That's not going to be a problem, Sir. He knows nothing of *The Project*. So far, we've been able to keep the island concealed. I have a man who has influence with him if we need it," the cowboy said.

"That's all fine and well, but is this man going to open a can of worms if he finds out we had a hand in financing Hitler?" the old man asked.

"No, Sir, we've been able to downplay that quite a bit. Those who have brought it up were warned and we've silenced those who didn't heed the warning." The cigar bounced around in the cowboy's generous mouth, garbling his words from time to time.

"Good. So the work must continue now that the war is over. We have attained most of our genetic material, but there are a few specimens left which need to be tracked down. I would suggest we ask our friend from Germany to take over those responsibilities. He's been quite efficient thus far. Agreed?"

"But he was an SS officer," the Russian argued. "How do we keep him from going through the trials and being hanged?"

"That shouldn't be too difficult. I'm sure we can find some form of documentation that clears him. He's never been one to present a high profile, at any rate, so I don't see a problem." The old man's voice shifted into a wheeze as the conversation strained the frail lungs. "Do I have agreement on placing the Obersturmfuhrer at the helm of *The Project*? Of course, we'll have to call him something else. I don't think his German title would be a benefit. What say we give him the same rank in British documentation?"

One by one, ten men raised their hands in the air and the unity of *The Committee* continued unhindered.

* 6 *

MAY 14, 1948 HAD USHERED IN A NEW ERA. Israel was a recognized state, and the surrounding Arab nations were furious. Rachel Samuels celebrated her thirteenth birthday that same day, but no one really cared that an orphaned Jewish girl, brought over to Israel from a Nazi concentration camp, had entered her teen years. Even Rachel shrugged it off as a passing thought, although she did mention it to her gunmate as they hunkered down in the dirt while the Arab forces fired their rifles at them.

That had been six months earlier, and Rachel was sick of hunkering down in foxholes. She had become a very efficient marksman since then—thirteen years old and able to shoot a man in the heart at a fair distance. She had acquired quite a reputation among the ragtag group of desperate soldiers.

As if surviving the death camps wasn't enough, she thought miserably. She checked her rifle one last time, always wary for the next attack. Looking out behind her at the group of young men and women scattered amidst the rocks, she felt pride swell in her young chest. They were a feisty unit, working efficiently to keep the road open for the supply caravans that brought much-needed food and medical equipment to the city beyond.

It was discovered early in her warring career that she was a genius at tactical maneuvers—even at such a young age— and she found herself welcomed into the meetings of her superiors. She still felt shy when the older leaders approached her to ask her opinion on a particular terrain or the best positions to take up in an upcoming battle. They had, long ago, forgotten she was only thirteen. Many things had to be overlooked when one was fighting against overwhelming odds.

She allowed herself a small smile, her sad eyes studying the landscape laid out before her. She should be learning how to be a wife and mother in a good Jewish family. Instead, she was fighting for the very existence of her new nation and her own right to live—and was discovering that she was quite good at it.

Dark slowly descended on the rocky and seemingly barren landscape near Jerusalem, and Rachel was growing weary. She had been forced to stay in the same hiding spot for two days, allowed only brief breaks as the fighting continued almost nonstop. Had Daniel not brought a small bowl of goat meat soup and a strong cup of coffee, she would have been unable to stay awake no matter how loud the enemy got.

She allowed a tender thought of her friend to linger in her mind. He was eighteen and liked her—a lot. He had already informed some of the other male soldiers that she was off limits, and that was okay by Rachel. She liked him, too—at least a little. But she was uncertain if her mind could wrap itself around the concept of love after she had witnessed so much violence at such a young age.

Her eyes gradually adjusted to the dimming light and she slowly and quietly stretched her aching muscles, grateful for the lull in the battle. Israel was hanging on with a tenacity that rivaled the most persistent Arab fighter, much to the surprise of the nations across the world. Her thoughts grew angry as she reflected on the lack of help her new country had received in defending its beleaguered borders. It was almost as though the world wanted the Arabs to finish what Hitler had started.

Above her and to the right, a pebble skittered down the gradual slope and she swung her ever-ready rifle in that direction, sighting down it with keen and wary eyes. She could see nothing, but her hackles rose just the same. There.

Another pebble dislodged. She cocked the old rifle, prepared to fire, looking through the growing blackness for the shape of the one who approached with stealth.

Suddenly her arms grew heavy and her vision swam. And then all feeling and awareness abandoned the young soldier. A small dart had found its way through the dusky evening air and embedded itself in her thigh. The rifle clattered noisily to the rocks below as a limp hand released its grip and an accented male voice swore in the stillness. Then a shot fired, pinging off a nearby outcrop. And another. The night sky split once again with the thunderous sound of artillery as the weakened Israeli forces stood their ground—again.

Amidst it all, under the cover of night, a man in dark clothing, with great caution, found, secured and carried away a thirteen-year-old Jewish warrior, knowing she would not be missed until the next day.

*   *   *

Rachel woke, dizzy and nauseated, in the hold of an ancient fishing boat. It rocked and creaked with the swelling motion of an oceanic storm. The dimness of the cargo area restricted her ability to define detail, but it was not so dark that she couldn't see the stacks of supplies. She sat up slowly, working to get her equilibrium stabilized, and her stomach rolled with the bucking vessel. A wooden bucket lay nearby, its accompanying rag mop propped tenuously against a massive oak barrel that she hoped held water.

With much effort, she worked her way over to the bucket as sweat beaded on her forehead. Making it just in time, she proceeded to throw up the meager contents of her unsettled stomach, leaving her mouth dry and bitter tasting. She spat a few times as she worked at the barrel's lid, hoping to pry it loose and rid herself of the after-effects of the drug that had subdued her.

"So you're finally awake?"

Rachel spun around, the sudden movement pitching her off balance, and she found herself sprawled on the floor again. The silhouette left the muted daylight of the hold's entrance and made its way cautiously toward her. Her eyes burned with anger as she tried to steady herself. Recognizing the German language and the formal poise of military training, the girl spat at the man's feet in answer.

"Oh come now, Rachel. There's no need to be hostile here. I'm not going to hurt you."

"Nazi pig!" She threw the words at him in Yiddish, refusing to speak the language of those who had destroyed her world. Watching him as a cornered animal watches its tormentor, her hand slowly worked its way toward the bucket she had used moments before. Her temper flared more as the man chuckled his quiet, lifeless laugh.

"Rachel, I haven't been a Nazi since I assassinated Hitler."

"That evil monster killed himself. The whole world knows that. And it was the best thing that could have ever happened."

The man cocked his hip and leaned against the nearest stack of crates.

"The world *thinks* he killed himself. In reality, a very important group of men requested that I remove him from power in any way that I could. It's nice to know that I was successful in making it look like a suicide."

He pushed away from the crates, preparing to assist the young teen to her feet just as her hand clasped the edge of the bucket. The Obersturmfuhrer barely dogged the missile as it sailed toward his head, spilling its contents around the room. He cursed, more at the foul mess that dripped from the front of his black suit than from the quick escape as the girl slid past him and up the ladder into the daylight.

He shook his head, uncertain whether to be angry with her for soiling him or to admire her quick thinking and actions. Grabbing a rag, the blond man dampened it and followed the path the girl had taken, dabbing at his suit as he slowly climbed from the hold.

She stood, rooted to the deck, gripping the rail at the bow of the vessel. The wind and rain lashed at her short-cropped brown hair and her gray eyes matched the hue of the storm-churned ocean. She still wore the men's clothes she had been given months before, worn with use and multiple hand washings, now flapping furiously in the gusts that whipped across the waves and over the deck.

The Obersturmfuhrer approached the shivering girl, his Aryan-colored hair slicking with the increasing rain. He stood beside her in silence for some time, assessing this frail-looking daughter of Zion. Eyeing the partially revealed tattoo on her forearm, he found himself surprised that one so young had survived the concentration camps. Leaning over, he shouted to the girl, fighting to be heard over the thunder that echoed across the roiling waters.

"Please, Rachel. You and I need to talk. This is no place for you to hear what has to be said. Please."

She stood like stone for moments longer and then turned her resentful eyes to him. Staring boldly up into his face, she abandoned the rail and staggered her way back to the hold. The blond man in the black suit followed carefully.

Together, silently, they cleaned up the mess Rachel had made in her attempt to flee. It was enough to make the close confines uncomfortable if left unattended. The old rag was rinsed and the bucket emptied over the rail before the two of them settled onto crates for the necessary explanations.

"Why did you kidnap me?" Her voice was laced with bitterness and accusation and she leaned back against the ship's ribbing, wary but willing to listen.

"It's a long story, Miss Samuels, but since we have a long journey, I'll share as much as I can with you." He settled back against his own prop, trying to get as comfortable as he could.

"There's a group of men called *The Committee*. That's all I know to call them. This committee consists of ten men from the wealthiest families in the world. For centuries, this group has existed, choosing its members from within the various families. Their goal has always been to keep worldwide balance. They have worked behind the scenes, causing nations to rise and fall, all in an effort to keep that fragile world balance.

Over the past sixty years, they've become aware of an alarming occurrence in the populations across the globe. Disease and deformities have risen drastically and, if their projections are correct, will continue to do so until mankind no longer exists."

He paused then, allowing the drama of the moment to grab and hold her attention. Her mind was quick and she immediately jumped in with her own thoughts and suspicions.

"So, in essence, you're telling me that this...committee...put Hitler in power?" She pinned him with her angry gaze as he nodded his assent.

"Then they don't really care for the safety of mankind, do they?"

The Obersturmfuhrer smiled sadly, meeting the glittering eyes.

"They didn't know how evil the man was," he said. "It was the same risk that *The Committee* takes any time they support a potential leader. You must understand that they didn't know he hated Jews until it was too late. That's why he is dead. That's why Germany is broken and your people have a nation of their own."

Rachel snorted and looked away, her jaw clenching as she tried to control her anger.

"Some nation. No one will help us protect it. It's held only because we're through with being pushed around. We're determined to survive," she said.

"No, my dear," the Obersturmfuhrer said. "It's surviving because, ever so quietly, *The Committee* is filtering money into your new government. Call it an act of atonement." He nodded at her startled expression and continued.

"It's true. I can promise you that your fledgling nation will survive and thrive. Doesn't your God sometimes use your enemies to accomplish his will? At any rate, on the surface, it will be a difficult battle, but *The Committee* will make certain the Nation of Israel comes into its own," he said.

"Now, where was I? Oh yes. Mankind is quickly becoming extinct and doesn't yet know it. Ten years ago, *The Committee* decided to take drastic measures in order to revitalize the human race. They began what we refer to as *The Project*. Not a very creative title, but it works.

"During that time, I, among others, was chosen to study and capture people who showed extreme talent in different areas. You, my dear, for one so young, have an amazing skill in tactical warfare. You've been studied over this past year, and we've been in awe of your marksmanship skills, your ability to learn and take advantage of any terrain, and your mental capacity toward advanced military maneuvers. Thirteen is quite young to be so inclined. For that reason, you were chosen. You bear the genetics of a true warrior and, although we hope this new race to be a peaceful people, these are skills they will need to survive against the elements.

"We have numerous others, all collected on an island hidden deep in the Caribbean Sea. Some came willingly. Others were coerced. It was necessary in order to get the dominant genetics for each trait required to rejuvenate mankind. Each person will be paired for life with another who carries an equally dominant set of genes in a complementary area.

"The young man we have chosen for you is a Native American boy from central Canada. He's known as Hawk and has lived on the island for the past five years. He has the run of the island and chooses to live in the wild. On occasion he visits one of our younger doctors, but doesn't stay long. Obviously, his skill is in surviving and he's quite good at it.

"We have those gifted with endurance, intellect, extremely good health, longevity. We even have one young lad who managed to build the basics of what he calls a 'computer' at the age of nine. *The Project* has drawn people from every continent and we've worked hard to make certain that all races are represented. By combining the peoples of this world, we return to the origins of mankind, creating a species of people who will, once again, live for a thousand years."

He stopped, the quiet passion settling in the deep shadows of the damp hold, and cocked his head to the side, waiting for Rachel's reaction. She sat still, deep in thought, as her quick brain weighed all the factors surrounding this astounding information. Absently, she stroked the dark tattoo with her thumb, her thoughts bouncing in all directions.

"I have no say in this?" For the first time, she looked young and uncertain, and the Obertsturmfuhrer smiled. He used his most gentle voice.

"No, my dear, I'm afraid not. *The Committee* offers you the chance to have a husband and a family and to live relatively free. You have what is needed. I hate to say it, but within the next few decades, the nations as you know them will cease to exist. Your family line will continue on— whether you are willing or not. I only hope you can resign yourself to this without forcing us to render you unconscious and take what is needed. We do have the means to create a child outside of a mother's womb."

She gasped then and he held up his hand.

"The world currently knows nothing of these methods, but they will be 'invented' soon enough. But it *is* a last resort for us. We'd prefer that all of our special people recognize the importance of *The Project* and submit to what's necessary. Who knows? You may, some day, actually love Hawk. And you will, no longer, be alone."

He rose then and headed to the ladder, leaving her with her thoughts. One brief glance told him that she had lost her anger and was thinking deeply about all he had laid before her. He smiled again and threw back the hatch, intent on sharing a coffee with the captain of the sturdy vessel. He would have to pay closer attention to his airplane pilot's methods. *Sometimes a tender word* **does** *bring better results than violence,* he mused, as he closed the trapdoor to leave her to come to her own conclusions.

* * *

The air was sticky and hot when the boat stopped in a large lagoon of crystal blue water that lapped gently against a beach. Rachel feasted her eyes on the beautiful white sand that stretched in a thin line along that whole side of the island. She stood at the rail as the Captain continued to blow the foghorn, signaling that they were there. She offered a stiff smile as the Obersturmfuhrer sidled up beside her.

"Warm, isn't it?" He kept his voice light and pleasant.

"Yes." The horn blew again and she looked back at the cabin with a frown.

"Why does he keep sounding that blasted thing?"

He chuckled and turned his back to the rail, tipping his face toward the warm sun.

"It's to let the workers in the facility know that we're here—that you're here. They'll meet us on shore."

"Ober—Ober—what is it that the Captain calls you?"

"Obersturmfuhrer, but please call me Lieutenant. That is the equivalent in British rank, and since the Third Reich no longer exists, neither does the SS."

Rachel pulled in a harsh breath and took a step back. The Obersturmfuhrer raised his hands in a placating gesture and stepped away, allowing her the space she suddenly needed.

"I had nothing to do with the death camps. I was put in the SS by *The Committee* to monitor the madman. I have not killed a single Jew, my dear, so you need not fear me. I'm no longer SS and you must remember that it was I who aided Hitler on his journey into his next life."

The girl turned back to the rail, her jaw twitching as memories of the camp's horrors floated through her mind. Swallowing hard, she tried to sound casual.

"Lieutenant—why doesn't the Captain just pull the boat as close to shore as possible? We could wade in and be halfway to the facility by the time they hear us." She was sick of living on the floating tub and wanted to feel the hot sand on her feet.

"Have patience, Rachel. We stay here until they arrive. This is so we don't lose any of those who are chosen. Not all have resigned themselves to life on the island. We don't want one single person in this very important project slipping aboard a ship and setting the work back."

She grunted and turned her sharp eyes to the tree line enveloping the small sandy track that cut up the side of a steep hill. Somewhere in all that dense foliage was a fifteen-year-old boy who was to someday become her husband. Strangely, she felt the heat of a mild blush creep up her neck, ending in her cheeks, and she turned away, hoping the Lieutenant had missed it.

* 7 *

"HOW ARE ALL THE CHILDREN DOING?"

The question came from the Russian sitting at the opposite end of the heavily draperied room. The ten were seated in the plush and cozy drawing room of an old mansion on the outskirts of St. Petersburg, Russia. A snowstorm howled and whistled around the stone towers of the ancient building, but the occupants were warm and comfortable as they sampled their wine and smoked their cigars.

The man, who was once known as the Obersturmfuhrer, and who recently answered only to his English title of Lieutenant, coughed in the heavy haze of the drawing room and stood to attention out of habit.

"They're adapting well. We have hundreds of them now. Needless to say, we have repeats of different traits, but it was necessary in order to include every people group. We didn't concern ourselves with remote dialects since some of the races are close enough in genetic makeup, but we did try, as much as possible, to find people from different countries who excelled in different things. We do, however, continue to search for specimens of spectacular quality among the nations in order to keep the gene pool from become too narrow, so this should swell the numbers even more over the next few years.

"I have some more excellent news. You'll be pleased to note that we will be celebrating our first wedding on the island."

This tidbit of information rippled around the room and the men beamed at one another, offering light applause. The old man wheezed, his lips blue with the effort of breathing.

He was a shadow of his former self as he lifted his hand weakly to draw the attention of the others.

"Dare I guess that it is beauty about to be reproduced?" he asked.

The Lieutenant clicked his heels together and bowed with respect, smiling as he did so.

"You have guessed correctly, sir. A young woman by the name of Carolyn Stillwater has finally succumbed to an errant German Lieutenant named Eric Schneider. But it gets better than that. Does the name Von Straussler mean anything to anyone in this room?

A lean middle-aged man swathed in the trappings of a sheik sat up and set down his wine goblet. His face was a mask as he threw his own question back at the ex-soldier.

"Why do you ask this thing? Everyone in this committee knows the name Von Straussler. He was one of the richest men in Germany before Hitler came to power. He was shot shortly after. He wouldn't support the Third Reich." The man sat back and absently remarked more to himself. "It appears he wasn't so foolish after all."

The Lieutenant nodded.

"Yes, and our Eric Schneider, whom the Fuhrer sent to the island, is none other than his only son, Eric Von Straussler. He doesn't know that his father was part of your secret group. Nor does he know that you had him assassinated because he didn't support your move to place Hitler in power."

The Lieutenant was enjoying the buzz his little speech created. The American jumped to his feet in agitation, angry that one of the identities had been revealed.

"How did you find out? Don't even think of blackmailing us. You won't last a day outside this room if you think you can."

The Lieutenant gestured with his hands to calm the group as he pushed on.

"I have known for years and, as you see, have said nothing—not to you gentlemen—not to anyone. No, good sirs, it's not my intention to reveal anything. I only want to be welcomed within this group as a peer, but not as you may think." He began pacing, one arm tucked neatly behind his back.

"I have worked for years alongside that buffoon, Sir Horace Wellington. He's becoming a nuisance, losing track of information, hoarding research from the other scientists. I wish to dispose of the man and replace him as ultimate head of *The Project*.

"I realize I don't have the scientific knowledge, but I do know that this project needs someone who's not afraid to maintain an efficient program or cross moral barriers in order to accomplish the work. I propose to put the Swede, Dr. Yngve Sigverd, in charge of the island so that the children will adapt better. He's a far superior scientist and the subjects adore him and will do anything he asks.

"I'll continue as administrator of research and development. There are new areas that must be explored and Sir Horace isn't willing to do this."

"Such as?" The old man rasped the question, spittle trickling from the corner of his mouth. He dabbed daintily at it with a scrap of linen tucked in his veined and trembling hand.

"There are a few adventurous workers who wish to break down the elements of the unborn child. They're certain there are cells that, when stimulated, can be duplicated. Through this duplication process, we can strengthen the desired traits such as immunity, intellect, survival instinct, et cetera. Sir Horace knows that there are elements of society who think nothing of aborting an unwanted child and yet he won't take this offered bounty to further the work.

"If we work in co-operation with discreet doctors, we can have plenty of subject material to work on in all developmental stages. This will allow us to speed up the process of genetic manipulation and help us achieve the end result of a resilient and perfect race of people far more quickly than the traditional method of reproduction and cross-reproduction."

He stopped and waited, tasting the response in the room. Some looked concerned, tossing the morality of the plan about in their uneasy minds. Others fastened onto it like a starving dog with a meaty bone. And then he fanned the interest with one last morsel.

"Just think, gentlemen. This could speed up the process by two or three generations—or more. Once we've discovered all there is to know about the unborn, we could draw samples from our next generation and create their offspring in test tubes. From those offspring, we could create others, cutting out years of wasted time. The choice is yours, my friends. I will leave it to you to decide."

He saluted with utmost respect, turned, and strode from the room, leaving them to make their own conclusions.

*   *   *

It was far too sunny a day for a funeral. Ten men stood silently amidst a somber crowd, sweating in their formal attire. No two stood together, but all spread themselves out among the gathered to say their final farewells to the old man. Some were annoyed that the Lieutenant was among them, but they didn't show it. Others were relieved—and also didn't show it.

The old man had no heir and his estate would be filtered into the vast holdings of *The Committee*. Someone needed to replace him. Each man assessed the Lieutenant cautiously, trying not to be noticed. The nine would meet secretly—as always—and decide from there.

The casket was lowered into the tastefully concealed hole, the complimentary words of condolence spoken, and the crowd thinned. The birds continued to sing and the flowers filled the thick air with their heavy fragrances. *The*

Committee would go on, as would *The Project*, but the old man would be missed.

*　　　*　　　*

Sir Horace fumed as he stalked around the room, throwing books and papers in every direction.

"How dare that upstart replace me? I'm the one who gave him his job in the first place. Retired? I think not!"

His anger left as quickly as it came and he settled his portly frame into the plush office chair. Steepling his fingers, he mulled over the new twist in the plans on *The Project*. Resolve settled deep into his active mind. He would make contact with *The Committee* and find out what was really happening. They would put a stop to this man's ambition.

The calendar on the wall caught his eye and he smiled at the bold reminder printed in black ink. October 19, 1949 at 3:00 p.m. Carolyn and Eric were getting married. One week. It would start the beginning of stage two. She was twenty-seven and he was thirty-one. Far older than they had hoped, but it was necessary for them to be at ease with this.

He marveled at Yngve's way with the island's inhabitants. He had even managed to draw out that wild young Indian, Hawk. The boy was still uneasy without his skins and the jungle undergrowth but he was starting to show interest in Rachel. Things were moving along nicely.

He rubbed his hands together and picked up pen and paper. He would jot a note down and send it off to the special postbox *The Committee* used for correspondence in such matters pertaining to this secret world of his. In a matter of weeks, the Lieutenant would be out of his way and the work would resume the way it should.

*　　　*　　　*

Eric Von Straussler stood straight and handsome in his formal clothing. His suit, along with Carolyn's gown and the wedding party's clothes, had been brought in by ship for this occasion. The collection of fine wool and cotton garments chafed and felt heavy and clinging in the humid air. He had been so long in simple peasant-type garb he had forgotten how uncomfortable formal wear was.

Yngve Sigverd stood beside him, equally uncomfortable trussed up in the tropical sun, and beside the scientist was a young lad named Charlie Wong—one of the island's technological wizards. All three men beamed with excitement as they stared down the aisle that split through the ranks of their friends and associates.

Earlier that morning the young teenage girls had attacked the clearing with eagerness and romantic excitement, decorating anything and everything with flowers gathered from the tropical wilderness. They were in awe of the beautiful older woman and wanted her wedding day to be magnificent.

All eyes faced the back of the clearing, waiting for the imported record player to begin churning out the strains of the "Moonlight Sonata." And then the haunting melody began, filling nature's cathedral with its smooth flowing waltz. A gasp rippled through the ranks as Carolyn stepped into view. Eric swallowed hard, unable to believe that the world's most beautiful woman could take her beauty to even greater heights. But she had.

Fine lace covered her face to her chin, leaving the rim of her perfect jaw to hint of the beauty hidden beneath the shimmering curtain. The remainder of the dainty veil flowed down her back, covering the satin of her train with a delicate shadow. The dress was made to fit her form and drew up to her neck in a high, modest collar. It was a good thing the ceremony was a short one or Carolyn might have fainted in such an over-abundance of satin and lace. The skirt was wide and flowing, full of flounces and frills, and yet it became her in its extravagance. The one fleeting thought that brought a dark cloud over the moment was that her parents couldn't be there to see her in all her splendor.

No one thought that it would take so many years for Carolyn and Eric to fall in love. The first few years were a miniature copy of the war which had continued to explode across the world. She was American. He was German. And they fought with the same volatility and temper that the two nations had.

And just as the world discovered peace, they, too, had decided to call a truce. A friendship developed, and still, they both felt nothing more. Then one day, Eric awoke to find that he didn't want to live without her, and from that moment on, he began courting her with persistence. She seemed confused at first—and then distant—and then not distant. This day, they would be married. He was a happy man. And she glowed with the beauty of a bride-to-be.

*   *   *

Rachel scanned the crowd of people sitting on blankets on the grass. *He should be here*, she thought with distraction. *He should see this.* She forced her mind to focus on the arch made from strands of twisted vines and festooned with fragrant flowers of all colours. The delicate structure demanded one's attention and drew consideration to the couple who stood beneath, lost in each other's eyes.

She admired the ethereal beauty of the older woman. The elegant gown, with all its frills, somehow became her. *Not me*, she mused. *I want a wedding in the wild. Somewhere up on a cliff.* As if to validate that thought her eyes wandered up the side of the sheer wall to her left, groping for the spot where it met the sky. *Yes. Up there.* And then her gaze scaled back down the smooth surface and skipped over to the arbor again. She focused, once more, on the wedding, chastising herself for allowing her mind to wander. What was wrong with her?

The Reverend droned on. He was a nice enough man but he sure knew how to make religion sound dull. She shifted her weight quietly, well practiced at moving without drawing attention. Once again, without conscious effort, she had chosen the most tactically advantageous spot from which to view the ceremony.

After surveying the area, she had found a knoll near the back of the clearing and spread her blanket. With the rise in the land, she had an uninterrupted view. The backdrop of the cliff, which curved from behind her around one side of the clearing to the end where the couple stood, made a perfect amplifier, directing the voices along its smooth surface to where she sat. Rachel heard and saw everything.

"Did I miss it?"

Rachel nearly jumped out of her skin as she whipped around to face her friend. Leave it to Hawk to find the one flaw in the terrain and to find a way to use it. Behind and to the right of her, the cliff faded back into the jungle and the thick undergrowth moved in. He was skilled enough to move into that undergrowth without making a sound, bringing him directly into her blind spot, where he could surprise her. He did that often. She gave him a playful swat in reprimand.

"No, but almost. Papa Yngve would have been so mad if you had."

"Aw. He would have just told me that it wasn't nice of me to ignore such a special day. But I would've felt bad. I did want to be here."

"So what took you?"

Hawk settled himself comfortably beside Rachel and watched the ceremony as he answered her with a neutral voice.

"I was making something for you."

She perked up and turned a questioning glance at him, receiving only a shake of his head. She knew better than to push it. Hawk was stubborn and would show her when he was ready. She didn't understand him sometimes. He could be so distant one moment and then do something so kind and thoughtful the next. She shrugged and turned back to watch the kiss that sealed the commitment the two had made.

Something in her chest fluttered and expanded as she watched the gesture which brought the ceremony to a close and she tried to see Hawk's reaction from the corner of her eye. He showed none.

*   *   *

The party that followed the ceremony was primitive in its trappings, but the joy and happiness that accompanied it more than made up for it. All on the island were invited. Most came. Even Sir Horace looked as though he was enjoying himself. No one mentioned the small group of people who refused to attend. These were the ones who still suffered the loss of family and home. They had not yet learned to find joy amidst trial.

Yngve sighed as he helped himself to another glass of the fruit punch made from the island's own produce. He was pleased that Eric and Carolyn had finally chosen their fate, but it saddened him that he needed to manipulate people's lives in such a way. If it weren't for the noble purpose behind *The Project* he would never have been party to it. He scanned the crowd and his eyes settled on Hawk and Rachel.

Those two were coming along nicely. That had been blind luck, really. The moment they met, the lad had befriended the forlorn Jewish girl and now Yngve seldom saw one without the other—that is, when they didn't disappear into the jungles that were more home to both of them than any of the cottages would ever be.

It had been a difficult time for the boy that first year on the island. He thrived in the wild but despaired over the loss of his family. It had taken Yngve months to even find him, never mind get a chance to make contact. The lad had reverted back to his native language, choosing to ignore the English dialect Yngve had spoken to him.

He knew Hawk understood, but the boy refused to speak anything but his father's tongue for over a year. That gave Yngve an opportunity to learn a new language and it was that effort which won the boy's trust. The lad mourned the loss of his father and uncle and gradually shared the lessons and adventures that he had experienced throughout his childhood with the Swedish doctor. His had been a heartbreaking story. *The Project* had not rescued this boy. It had taken people and places he loved away from him.

Rachel's was another tale entirely. Immersing herself in the peace and solitude of the island, the girl began the process of healing from the traumas of World War II. She made it very plain, once she had settled in, that she was exactly where she wanted to be and had no intention of leaving. Her experience with *The Project* gave Yngve the small taste of hope and justification he needed from time to time. He smiled as he watched the two slip silently into the jungle away from the noise and ruckus of the wedding celebration.

A screech broke the happy atmosphere and his attention was drawn to yet another couple, not quite so thrilled with one another. Eleven-year-old Eve Africa stood, her tightly curled black hair dripping with fruit punch, a glare of intense hatred directed at—who else—Prince Asad Mohammed. The eighteen-year-old stood nearby, a smirk covering his face as he crossed his arms, satisfied with the retaliation he deemed necessary. *Perhaps a little isolation would be good for that couple,* Yngve thought as he headed in their direction.

*   *   *

Rachel slipped into the jungle behind the stealthily moving boy. Excitement coursed through her veins as it did each time he led her into his domain. There were so many incredible things he had shown her in the year she had been on the island, and so many things he had taught her.

With everyone else he seemed distant and reserved, standing solid, like a rock, while the world moved around him. Sometimes he spoke to the others, but more often than not, he merely crossed his muscled arms over the quickly expanding chest and stared at them with his unnerving brown eyes.

When he was alone with the girl, however, he rattled on unceasingly, pointing out this plant or that cave, explaining the animal skin tanning process he had discovered or a new wood to make a sturdy bow with. She was content to listen, absorbing all he shared with her, happy with the feeling of belonging.

Rachel watched the figure ahead of her as he moved lithely through the ferns and vines. The snakeskin vest that he always wore was getting far too tight for him. She knew he had made it when he first came to the island and was surprised when he had allowed her to re-stitch the seams that had begun to fall apart. The increasing breadth of his shoulders was becoming a distraction as they pulled and stretched at the worn vest. She would have to ask him for some skins so she could make a new vest for him.

*   *   *

The girl never failed to express her pleasure in the cave and its contents. For some strange reason, that made Hawk want to do more with it, adding a small carving here or another chair there. He was nervous around her. Normally he would shy away from those who made him uncomfortable, but this was a different kind of nervousness.

He could hear her slightly elevated breathing behind him as she struggled to keep up, and he slowed his pace for her sake. He was always tense like this just before he gave her something he had made for her. He didn't understand why, however, because she always exclaimed over each gift, admiring the skill and work that went into whatever he made.

Papa Yngve had teased him gently that perhaps there was some interest there. Hawk frowned. Of course there was interest there. He had come to the conclusion that he adored Rachel. But the lad had never really had a woman in his life and didn't know how to go about showing her. So he continued with the little gifts and the silent suffering as he agonized over how to express his feelings.

He had come so close when Eric had kissed Carolyn, but then Rachel had become still. He had watched her from the corner of his eye. He didn't know whether it was good or not that she had frozen all movement. He hoped so. And then he had chickened out.

*   *   *

It always surprised Rachel when they reached the row of shrubs that shielded Hawk's hideaway. They were so dense and overlapped but the lad had found a way to enter on a diagonal without disturbing their growth. One minute he was there, facing the shrubs. The next minute he was gone without so much as a broken twig to indicate where he had entered. She was impressed, and not much in the line of camouflaging skills impressed her after seeing all that she had seen in Germany and Israel.

She followed, trying hard to duplicate his quiet movements. Anyone else who entered the thicket would easily lose their way, but she had memorized the trail the first time he had shown it to her and repeated it the next day, catching him by surprise .

That day all thoughts of leaving the island had disappeared as she had stared into the boy's face, which revealed a grudging admiration. And from then on, they were inseparable. But she didn't know whether it was because she could keep up with him or because he liked her. She sighed, wishing there was a way to find out.

They broke through the thicket and Rachel settled herself in the bark and stick hammock that Hawk had fashioned and strung up months earlier. It was surprisingly comfortable with its mattress of woven grasses. That had been her contribution, and he had beamed at her when she showed him. Hawk didn't beam often, so she knew she had accomplished something that day.

She stared at the bright sky through the tall canopy of trees, content to wait while he went in search of whatever it was he wanted to show her. He did that often lately, and she mused over the increasing offerings of gifts. Maybe he did like her. She smiled and blushed. She sure liked him. Someday she would marry him. It wasn't wishful thinking. It was fact. And she was happy about it. She would be a good wife to him.

Rachel sensed Hawk's presence more than heard it and tipped her head back to gaze up at him. He stood awkwardly, with his hands behind his back and she sat up, looking at him questioningly.

"I told you I was making something for you. I finished it," he said, with a shy quietness in his voice.

He stood there, hesitant and awkward, and she giggled.

"Can I see it, Hawk?" she said.

The boy's darker-hued skin flooded with a red undertone and he thrust a leaf-wrapped package in her direction. Rachel rose and approached, wonder and excitement dancing in her eyes. She knew it would be incredible. It always was.

Hawk watched nervously as the girl carefully unwrapped the gift. His anxious eyes searched her face when she gasped. And then she looked up at him, and he drowned in the steely depths of her marvelous gaze.

She said nothing as she unfolded the tunic. That was all she could think to call it. It was made of the skin of a large cat of some sort and she shivered when her hands made contact with the luxuriously silky fur. It was short and smooth, and black as the depths of his cave home. Simply crafted, the V-shaped collar was rimmed with small beads made of wood of different colours. He had formed patterns from the beads and the overall effect was intricate and delicate looking.

Rachel ran her hand over the fur and then turned a portion of the inner skin so she could examine it. It was light—almost bleached white—and soft. She looked from the tunic to Hawk, wonder on her face.

"You did it, Hawk. You found a tanning agent that works. It's beautiful."

Impulsively, she reached up and hugged him, thrilled with the gift and the work he had put into it. The lad's arms circled her awkwardly and she enjoyed the feeling of safety his clumsy embrace offered.

Hawk almost cried when Rachel broke away from him. His mouth opened and then closed as she slipped the tunic over her head. He must tell her. He couldn't let it go further without her knowing. He cleared his throat, overcome by the vision of the brown-haired girl in his bridal tunic.

"It's for our wedding."

She froze and he rushed on in his quiet voice.

"Where I come from, so my father told me, when a man likes a woman, he makes her a bridal tunic. If she accepts it, it is her way of saying she will someday become his wife. If she rejects it, he will burn it, and when another comes along to become his bride he will make a new one. This allows him to keep his dignity without the rest of the tribe knowing how they feel about one another.

"She only wears it once before her wedding day. She wears it the day she accepts it to show the elders that she has been spoken for and has accepted. She will then wear it on the day that she is joined to the man and any time she wishes after that. It is his way of showing her he will provide for her."

Hawk stood silently, waiting, his heart pounding as he watched her absorb all he had said. He was sixteen. She was fourteen. Some would say they were not old enough. He didn't agree. He could provide for a family. For that matter, so could she. They were the same. Somehow that made it right. And he couldn't imagine life without her.

He didn't care one whit about *The Project* that Papa Yngve had told him about or that they would choose a wife for him. None of the girls on the island had ever interested him—until last year when the Lieutenant brought Rachel. In that single act, the wicked German—the man who had destroyed his life—had earned redemption from the horrible death the boy had, for years, planned for him.

Rachel continued to stroke the soft fur while she listened to him talk, her eyes staring sightlessly at Hawk's bare feet. And then he stopped talking and she was afraid to look up for fear he would take it all back. The silence stretched out and she continued to search for words in the repetitive movement of her hand on the fur. And then she lifted her eyes, tears brimming on the thick lashes, and she smiled and nodded, her constricted throat preventing spoken words.

Hawk let out a yell and swept Rachel off her feet, swinging her around him. She laughed then, all of her relief and excitement released into the joyful sound.

"Hawk, let me down. You're making me dizzy," she said, her words laced with giggles.

Together, they walked back to the wedding celebration, he sporting a smile of happiness and pride, and she, her bridal tunic. He would give it a week, maybe two, and then he would tell Papa Yngve to bring the Reverend back to the island as soon as possible.

✳ 8 ✳

"BRING THE BOY TO ME." The voice still carried the same dead, cold tones that separated it from any other voice, and Yngve shuddered. He nodded to one of his laboratory workers and the man scrambled to obey.

"I think you are right, Doctor," the Lieutenant said. "I think isolation will do him good. Prepare a valise for him. He'll be coming with me."

"But I meant for both of them…"

"Doctor, do as I ask, please. Believe me, Asad will be more than willing to treat his future bride with a little more respect when he returns. He will work on the barge until the girl is fourteen. In the meantime, you had better teach her to be a little more careful with her tongue. There is only so much provocation a man can take."

Yngve gasped.

"But that's three years! He'll never survive on the barge. They'll destroy him."

The Lieutenant smiled again and turned as the sullen teen entered the room.

"I think he'll do alright, Yngve. Asad, you will be accompanying me to the barge. There you will remain in the hold, scouring every inch of it with a brush and a bucket of water. When that is finished, you will repair and wash each sailor's clothing. You will be our guest for the next three years so you might want to think about the pleasantries of life on the island while you work for me. It might help you view your relationship with your future wife a little differently."

Asad blanched as two security officers flanked him.

"But you can't do this. My father…"

91

"Your father has not made contact since he gave you to us. Take him away, gentlemen."

Yngve cringed as the boy's yells echoed down the hall of the massive complex, his mind instantly jumping back to that first meeting, years ago when a much younger Asad had been treated to a similar punishment. He sat waiting, anger simmering below the surface. He could sense the shift in power between the Lieutenant and Sir Horace without needing to be told, but he didn't like the rough treatment this man was known for. He spoke in his soft voice, taking a risk in order to verify his suspicions.

"What do you think Sir Horace will say to this, Lieutenant?" he said.

The man chuckled and rose from his chair, drawing a letter from his breast pocket.

"According to this," he tossed it onto the desk for Yngve's perusal, "our good Sir Horace has been officially retired. There will be a celebration in London honouring him for his tremendous work in science—although most of the world doesn't know anything other than that he *was* a scientist—and then he will settle back into the life of a country gentlemen on his family's estate. As a matter of fact, I am going to present this document to him now," he said.

"You will be stepping into his position at the facility but you'll take your direction from me. Did you never wonder why you were brought along in the first place? Sir Horace was never the real goal for *The Committee*, Yngve. You were. But we knew we would have to have him because of your incredible sense of loyalty, and the partnership worked so well that it was simply left that way. But it's time for Sir Horace to step aside and allow the true genius to do his job."

He retrieved the document as Yngve thought through this promotion and what it meant. He wasn't certain if it would improve his own situation or make it into a more dangerous one. He didn't see eye-to-eye with the Lieutenant on several levels and the blatant flattery did nothing to improve his level of trust for the man. He watched the man leave his office and sighed as thoughts of doubt continued to flood his mind.

*   *   *

"You cannot fire me!"

"Sir Horace, you aren't being fired. You are being retired to your country estate. *The Committee* has appreciated all you've done, but it's time for you to enjoy the fruits of your labour."

"We'll see about this. I'm not finished yet. *The Committee* will be hearing from me." The old man slammed the door as he stomped from the conference room and the Lieutenant crumpled the document angrily and tossed it aside.

*   *   *

"He won't keep quiet."

"No, Sir Horace has never been one to practice prudence."

"So what do you suggest?"

"I have a nice compound that, when administered, causes the symptoms of a heart-attack and kills the victim quickly. He'll only feel a moment of discomfort. He can be buried in great pomp just as he would have wanted. No one will know."

"We don't care how you do it. Just do it—and quickly, before the whole world knows what he's been working at for the past few years."

*   *   *

It rained the day England buried Sir Horace Wellington in the tiny cemetery on his country estate. The cause of his death was attributed to some unknown disease that he had contracted during the war, leaving him a withered shell of his former rotund self. No one seemed to know what the disease actually was, but they all agreed that it had to have been an awful way to die.

The cathedral was packed with people from all walks of life. Most came out of curiosity, eager to know who would be there, for few actually liked the man. Fellow scientists and government officials gave flowery eulogies, but all that was said remained vague in substance. The choir lifted hymns of sorrow and hope to the ancient wooden rafters, their haunting and rich tones bouncing through the dim and high-ceilinged church, a compliment to the many multi-hued vitric portraits lining the dark-paneled walls. The cloying scent of the many floral bouquets prompted an occasional sneeze or cough, and the shifting of restless bodies only mildly distracted from the solemn affair.

At the back of the church sat a blond haired man, streaks of gray mingling in the wavy locks. He wore a black suit and showed no sign of emotion, but the keen eyes scanned the crowd, counting, making note of those who attended with the intent of paying their last respects to the occupant of the lavishly ornamented, closed coffin. Finally he nodded, satisfied that all who had been asked to attend had indeed come. After one last perusal he rose and exited the aged building, breathing in the afternoon's damp spring air.

*   *   *

For ten years, the political and economic world experienced a series of upheavals. Russia developed an atomic bomb while China converted to communism, promoting the expansion of its population along with submission to the good of the state. The Cold War was at its peak, America and Russia vying for the affections of the various Third World countries. The North Atlantic Treaty Organization— NATO—was formed, and the United Nations continued to struggle in their feeble attempt to attain world peace—a dream which seemed as unlikely to be fulfilled as any.

The Korean War broke out, proving the impotence of the UN. Nikita Khrushchev became leader of the Soviet Union and sent a ripple of fear across the globe with the Warsaw Pact, a military alliance with Eastern European countries. The Suez Canal was caught in a crisis of its own as Gamal Abdel Nasser attempted to control the shipping lanes, denying Israel rights. The Eisenhower doctrine was approved in American congress, allowing the US to come to Israel's aid.

Ghana became the first African nation south of the Sahara to attain its freedom. Upon crushing the Hungarian Revolt, the USSR launched Sputnik, the world's first manmade satellite. Cuba turned to communism as the new leader, Fidel Castro, became the iron fist that the citizenry hadn't been prepared for. In the free world, under the cover of an exploding population and sudden prosperity, bomb shelters were built and food was stockpiled.

None of these events meant a thing to those inhabiting a small island lost in the wide and protective embrace of the Atlantic Ocean. Only one small event tugged at the undercurrents of their placid lives, and the small community wasn't even aware of its existence until much later.

With Castro's reforms sweeping Cuba, those with the financial means gave everything to find a way to escape to the shores of America and the freedom she offered. Some built their own crafts. Others purchased passage in the holds of rotting and foul-smelling fishing vessels.

It was in the depths of one such craft that a small child, Patricia, came across a seaweed-encased bottle. It had come aboard ship in the rope nets that hauled in whatever meager bounty the oceanic waters offered. Entwined in the green grasses that had stretched from the depths of the ocean floor, snagging the nets that dragged behind the boats, it had been missed and the entire mass was tossed aside while the fisherman sorted through the catch of the day. Somehow, with the pitching of the currents, the slimy glob shifted and worked its way to the deck opening that provided the only source of air to the passengers below.

The glass container should have shattered on impact, but the black-green foliage cushioned the fall and it remained intact. The girl was curious and had no qualms whatsoever about poking and prodding the clump of smelly stuff, in spite of her mother's reprimands. That was how the bottle was discovered and Patricia secretly hoarded it to herself, wiping it on her skirt hem before slipping it into her coat pocket.

The journey ended several days later on the shores of Florida in the middle of the night. No one saw the fishing boat lay anchor and drop five people over the side. Only the quarter moon watched as the boat maneuvered around quickly and headed for high seas again while the silent figures waded onto the warm beach, disappearing into the streets of the small port town.

Had Patricia known the English language, she could have read the note that lay folded in the amber bottle. But she didn't know the language yet and was content to treasure the find as it was, valuing it as a memory of their flight to freedom.

*   *   *

The American President was Roman Catholic and took his beliefs seriously, jumping at every chance to attend mass in whatever town his entourage settled in.

So, when a determined mother approached the Presidential party outside a Cathedral in the heart of San Francisco, begging him, in the name of God, to hear her plea for the rescue of her child, the President stopped to listen. The media closed in, eager and hungry for a new story, and the mother protectively pulled her child's photo to her chest. With a nod, a secret serviceman took the flustered woman by the arm and ushered her into the church ahead of the President and his entourage. The heavy oak doors boomed firmly closed behind them.

The young man sat and listened to the tale of a Cuban girl who found a bottle in a fishing boat. The bottle had been sealed with a cork but carried a note penned by the woman's daughter. It was amazing the note had survived nine years in the briny depths. The mother handed the worn letter to the President and he frowned as he read its contents:

> *July 13, 1943*
> *Dear Mom and Dad,*
> *I'm fine. I've been kidnapped. I'm on some kind of submarine but I don't know where I'm going. There are lots of soldiers in funny uniforms and they speak a different language. You were right about Dennis. He was part of the kidnapping but knows now that it was wrong. He told me all about a secret group of financial leaders that are trying to recreate the human race by taking people from all different countries and matching them up. I am supposed to be one of those people. I love you and will try to escape.*
> *Love Carolyn Stillwater*
> *San Francisco, California, USA*

The President blew out a heavy sigh, unsure how to help this hurting mother. So many years of waiting and wondering only to have this thrust at her. He raised his tired eyes to her anguished face and the bland words of condolence died on his lips. He looked at the note again and then handed it to one of his men.

"I can't promise you anything, Mrs. Stillwater, but I will look into this. No mother should be made to wonder what has become of her daughter. And no American citizen should be abandoned by her country. I'll see what I can do."

*   *   *

"Your new young President is asking some rather embarrassing questions."

"Yes, I know. None of us thought he would carry it so far."

"What has he discovered?"

"He knows the girl was kidnapped by Germans during the war. He has mentioned that he has a contact who has told him there is some secret project going on involved with restoring the human race. He doesn't know the details."

"There isn't much more than that for him to know. He must be stopped. If the media gets wind of this..."

"Don't worry. I have an idea. And just the man to carry it out."

"Do I want to know the details?"

"Probably not. Just keep your eyes on your television. You'll know when it happens. *The Project* will be safe. Trust me."

"Good. And for pity's sake, get rid of the contact who passed the information to the President in the first place."

*　　*　　*

It was November 22, 1963, and the motorcade, led by the President of the United States of America, his wife, and two guests, puttered its way through the streets of one of the country's major cities. People waved and cheered with excitement at seeing the American royalty. But not everyone was smiling. Somewhere along the route stood a man with an umbrella and another man with a two-way radio.

These two searched the crowds cautiously, avoiding eye contact with each other as much as possible. Across the grassy knoll beyond the fence another two men waited. One carried a rifle and the man with the umbrella squinted his eyes to better focus on him. The man was middle-aged and wore a black suit. He held the rifle with a steady hand. It was amazing that no one had spotted him and his partner as they waited.

The antsy crowd shifted and murmured as the limousine pulled into the busy plaza, and a cheer erupted as the

President's vehicle turned down the narrow street that filtered off of the city's square. They were a beautiful couple and waved with affection to the crowds that had gathered to pay them homage. And then several things happened at once.

As the vehicle passed a large freeway sign, the chuttering of rifle fire erupted. Later, some would say they had heard three shots, others—four. It didn't matter, really. The President was dead. That was all that would be remembered with certainty.

The crowds dove for cover, all but two men. The man with the umbrella and his associate with the walkie-talkie sat down and waited. And then they rose and left the scene, each going in a different direction. The plaza turned into a field of chaos as people processed the moment's events. The President was dead. The graying blond man in the black suit carrying the rifle smiled to his associate and then walked away. The job was finished.

*   *   *

"All you've done is open a can of worms!" The American was furious and ranted as he paced the room. The Lieutenant sat and watched him through hooded eyes. He would let the man pace and he would say nothing. The kill had been a joy to him and no one—not even *The Committee*— could take that away. And the men he had hired were now the scapegoats—the men who knew nothing but were paid well to do nothing more than carry a walkie-talkie and an umbrella.

"What are we going to do about all the agents involved and the witnesses? How do we silence them? Answer that, Lieutenant! Are you going to kill them all?" he asked.

The Lieutenant smiled and nodded once, shocking the American into silence.

"As I need to—yes. I have paid some, threatened others. Don't worry. There are enough who believe in *The Project*— and those who believe in the ones who believe in it—that it will be safe. I offer my guarantee. I promise you that this little demonstration will act as a reminder to those who would otherwise whisper of our little project to keep their lips tightly sealed."

Another voice—a calmer voice—joined in and the chaos in the room settled some.

"Listen to the Lieutenant, gentlemen. For these past twenty years, he has served *The Committee* well. Although I don't approve all his methods, he usually ends up being right in the end." The eighty-year-old Russian turned to his associate and leveled a steady eye on him.

"As for you, I think it wise that you retire your killing skills. You are fifty—something? Don't you think your time could be put to better use at this age? Clean up this last mess and then focus on what is important. You promised us stem cell research and cloning and it has only begun to take baby steps. It is time to move on, comrade. Don't you agree?"

The Lieutenant gritted his teeth but nodded at the chairman of *The Committee*. Little did the old Russian know that the Lieutenant had made headway in other directions. He had an arsenal of untraceable narcotics that would kill an old man quickly. He just needed to clear up this mess and he could be the next chairman.

* 9 *

"BUT YNGVE, YOU'RE TRYING TO REDO what God's already done. Forgive my boldness, but don't you think that's a bit arrogant? He has a purpose for mankind and all you're doing with this whole project is telling him that he's not all-powerful."

Yngve chuckled at Hawk's fervor, but deep down his dormant conscience stirred.

"Come now, Hawk. Do you really think that this God whom you believe in cares all that much about the small machinations of mankind? Wouldn't he have intercepted somehow to stop our destructive ways?"

Rachel smiled a small grin. She knew what was coming and couldn't help but feel sorry for Yngve. Hawk was formidable in his persuasiveness—especially if he believed something to be true. It was that very persistence that had won her intellect over to the Bible and her heart hadn't been long to follow.

"That's what I've been trying to tell you for months, Yngve. He *did* intercede. And mankind hung him on a cross to die for it."

"And that's why I've been reminding you, Hawk, that he couldn't have been much of a God if they could do that to him." Yngve sat back, allowing the silence to punctuate his logic, and yet his face spoke of a subdued eagerness to be proved wrong.

Normally, Rachel would have said nothing, letting Hawk share God's word as he felt led, but she could sense a hesitation and frustration in him, something he experienced only occasionally and only when speaking to the few older inhabitants of the island. And now, it seemed compounded by the parental influence Yngve had had on Hawk during his formative years, leaving the Native American with a feeling of inequality.

But Rachel had no such inhibitions. She had come to the island as a teen, glad to have a home, but grown up in her own right. Yngve was simply another adult to her, and to her now twenty-eight years that made him of equal standing.

"Yngve, would you say I had a reason to believe there was no God?"

Rachel's soft voice broke into the conversation and Hawk threw her a grateful look. She always seemed to know when he was floundering, and on those rare occasions she came to his rescue with her redeemed past.

Yngve frowned in thought.

"Come to think of it, yes you would."

"Would you like to know how an orphan girl from the concentration camps of Germany could live with such horrors and, against all odds, overcome them and acknowledge that not only is there a God but that he's deeply involved in the human race?"

Yngve paused, uncertain for the first time. He had seen the change in the young family since Hawk had requested a Bible for his twenty-fifth birthday. It was a consideration that the scientist had thought would be harmless, so he had acquired one from the Reverend who performed the island's weddings. When Yngve asked the young man why he wanted the book, he simply replied that his father would have wanted him to have one.

"Ok, Rachel, why *do* you believe in God now?" he inquired.

Rachel settled herself further onto the soft chesterfield in the doctor's office. She massaged her expanded belly, feeling the kicks of her seventh and eighth children. Yngve absently smiled at the gesture and Hawk's eyes glittered with the pride of a father.

"I began my life in a traditional Jewish home in Germany. I was four when the war started and knew nothing of the horrors to come. We went on with our spoiled and wealthy lives, certain that nothing could touch us. We were God's chosen ones. He would protect us. When the Nazis came to our home, I remember Father being so indignant that he began to argue with the soldier who told us we were to leave our wealth and our home.

"The soldier allowed my father to yell at him for about ten minutes and then he pulled his gun and shot him in the head. Right there in front of us. Just stood there, saying nothing, and shot him." Rachel's throat tightened with the memories and Hawk came to settle himself on the sofa arm beside her, stroking her shoulder as she pushed on. He had heard it all before but he knew it was one of those wounds that would take a lifetime to completely heal.

"We children, our mother, and all of the Jewish servants were shuffled off to the train station. We were only allowed one suitcase each. That was such a cruel joke in itself because they took that from us when we entered our first concentration camp. I remember that camp well.

"We were all herded into dormitories that were already overcrowded and stinking of human filth. My mother and I shared one bunk with my four older sisters, huddling together each night to keep warm, hoarding our small rations so we wouldn't starve. I watched women I knew who were, in another time, gentle people, become thieving bullies, taking others' food for themselves. I saw some of them shot or brutalized and others die of horrible illnesses. I saw despair and defeat eat away at the hearts and souls of people whose only offense was to be born of the Jewish race. I watched them give up hope and faith and I, too, wondered where God was in all of it.

"As the war moved on, we were taught that we were animals and as such, must be treated as animals. One by one my siblings died or were taken away until Mother and I were the only ones left. Then a day came when we were told to gather what few things we had because a bunch of us were going to another camp called Auschwitz.

"Mother knew we would die there. We had heard the rumours of the infamous death camp and its crematoriums. I was so small and thin by then that it was a miracle that had I survived at all. But it was my very thinness that saved my life.

"We were herded onto a cattle train and left in the station with no food or water for a whole day. I was the only child on that car since all the others had not been able to survive the camp. People were beginning to faint and the smell was horrible." Rachel's eyes grew distant and cold as the memories washed over her. "Sometimes I'm sure I can smell the stench again and I have to pray for help to carry on.

"Slowly, Mother worked her way over every inch of that car, pulling gently on boards to see if any were loose. Others watched her and knew what she was doing. Some joined her. After a time, they managed to pry a floorboard loose. It wasn't much, but she knew I could squeeze through. I can still see her bleeding hands and I remember being afraid to touch them for fear I would hurt her. But she ignored the pain and held me close for the rest of that day.

"We waited. The train moved from the station and for another day it traveled across Germany, stopping regularly for more and more people, as if any one else could fit into the already crowded cars. It was growing dark as we made our last stop for yet another group of Jews intended for Auschwitz. Mother watched through the slats as the soldiers circled the train, their machine guns ready to cut down any who broke free. And then our chance came.

"I remember it so clearly. She knelt in front of me and held me to her while she whispered instructions in my ear. I was eight by then. Far too young. And yet old enough. I listened as she told me to be careful and not to trust just anyone. The train would begin to pull from the station. Since our car was near the front this was a good thing. The soldiers would be watching the back cars and might not notice one small girl.

"I was to be lowered through the hole and should lay flat on my back until nightfall or until there were no soldiers to see me. Hopefully, I would be far enough down the tracks that I could slip into the ditch unseen. It all sounded so easy. She was crying when she pulled away from me and it was then that I realized I would never see my mother again. She told me to be brave—for the sake of our family line—and then she and a few others lowered me, feet first, through the hole.

"It was the most painful and frightening thing I had ever faced. My heels dragged on the ties as the train pulled away. Still they hung on until they felt I was far enough to be safe. Then they let go and I dropped with a thump, cracking my head as it hit the dirt.

"I lay like that—my arms stretched straight above my head—for what felt like hours. Car after train car passed over me as my Mother and others I had known for years were taken farther and farther away. I was frozen with the terror and pain of the ordeal and remained there for some time.

"It was the distant blow of another train's whistle that finally roused me, and I lifted my head to look both ways down the tracks. I could see the train light in the distance and only then realized that it was dark. The soldiers had moved inside the station long ago, not aware of my presence. The coming train would bring them back onto the platform and I would be discovered.

"I remember my heart pounding with fear as I cautiously rolled over the rail and down into the ditch. I crawled to a patch of scrub brush and curled up in its brambles, not feeling the stinging barbs as they tore at my arms and legs. I stayed there while the train pulled up to the station. I listened to voices and dogs barking and machine gun fire and I never moved once.

"When the train was gone and all was quiet, I began to travel along the ditch, working my way east as Mother had told me to do. It was during that time that I began to get an inkling of how to use the terrain. I'm still amazed that I made it to the home of a German man who hated Hitler and what he had done. This man helped me find a woman he knew could help me.

"The woman took me in and had papers forged for me. I and another Jewish woman were sent to Holland with Dutch passports where we spent the remainder of the war. My mother died in Auschwitz, leaving me alone in this world. All of my relatives and friends were killed in that hellish war.

"When the news spread throughout the world that Israel had become a nation, I was already there, having gone over with my 'Dutch Mother' a year earlier. We were getting pretty good at being smuggled around the planet and managed, once again, to go where no Jew should have been able to go. At that point, I decided God was dead—or powerless—or a dream. Or that he just hated me.

"And then I was kidnapped and brought here to my husband. I was told that I would be valued for my Jewish blood and that excited me. Having no beliefs, the morality of *The Project* meant nothing. Hawk and I fell in love quickly and—well—you know the rest." Rachel reached for her husband's hand, clasping it in an affectionate grasp, drawing strength from the love bond they shared.

"When you brought the Bible to Hawk for his birthday, I was furious. All I could think was, 'How dare you bring such a book of hypocrisy into my home!' But I love my husband and it was what he wanted. I tolerated him spending hours reading and rereading passages and I even listened with half an ear when he began to tell me the things his father had taught him and how he had found the verses to go with them.

"I love my husband and I listened out of respect for him. But I rejected it all in my heart of hearts. God didn't care. If he did, Auschwitz would have never happened. I remember mentioning that to Hawk once and was surprised at his answer. He had studied the book well because he took me right back to Genesis to the Garden of Eden.

"He showed me where God had created a beautiful place for man to grow and prosper—much like here on the island—and he only made one stipulation. Man was not to eat from the tree of good and evil. Hawk told me that it was not unlike you warning us that the whole island was ours but we were to stay away from the cliffs on the south side. Just as the rocks and riptides were deadly to us, the knowledge the first people gained from that tree would bring death to them.

"God gave them plenty of other trees to eat from and I can't help but think they were probably more beautiful and had better fruit. But he also gave man a free will, leaving him with the ability to choose. God only wanted them to choose him over a dumb tree. Instead, they were deceived and ate the fruit, bringing sin and death to our world.

"Hawk then led me, step by step, through the Old Testament, showing me how, time and again, God reached out to bridge the gap between mankind and himself. And each time man failed, God tried again. Oh, he punished. And he disciplined. He tried pretty much everything a parent will do to keep their children going in the right direction. But mankind chose to be rebellious, and with each rejection, with each act of rebellion, with each sin, the gap between God and man widened.

"I'm sure it broke his heart to see the beautiful creatures and the incredible planet he had made slowly giving in to corruption. It became a breeding ground for monsters like Hitler and the innocent became victims, seemingly without hope.

"In one final effort to fill in the gap, God poured all his anger, disappointment, and punishment on his own Son, allowing Jesus to take our place so that we would no longer be separated from him. And then after he had allowed his

Son to die on our behalf, he raised him from the dead, conquering death and evil once and for all times.

"I told Hawk that was a nice fairy tale but he couldn't prove a thing." Rachel stopped for a moment and her gaze grew distant and misty once more.

"He took me to the Old Testament again and showed me prophecy after prophecy about Jesus—of how he would be born, crucified and raised again. It still meant nothing. And then God led Hawk to the one part of the Bible that was relevant to me.

"When he turned to the book of Ezekiel it was as though time had ceased and I was there, hearing the very things I had seen. I have memorized that portion to remind myself of God's faithfulness in the moments when I doubt." She raised a questioning brow to Yngve and he nodded, suddenly caught up in her tale.

"Ezekiel 37:15 says:

> *The word of the Lord came to me: "Son of man, take a stick of wood and write on it, 'Belonging to Judah and the Israelites associated with him.' Then take another stick of wood, and write on it, 'Ephraim's stick, belonging to Joseph and all the house of Israel associated with him.' Join them together into one stick so that they will become one in your hand.*
>
> *When your countrymen ask you, 'Won't you tell us what you mean by this?' say to them, 'This is what the Sovereign Lord says: I am going to take the stick of Joseph—which is in Ephraim's hand—and of the Israelite tribes associated with him, and join it to Judah's stick, making them a single stick of wood, and they will become one in my hand.' Hold before their eyes the sticks you have written on and say to them, 'This is what the Sovereign Lord says: I will take the Israelites out of the nations where they have gone. I will gather them from all around and bring them back into their own land. I will make them one nation in the land, on*

the mountains of Israel. There will be one king over all of them and they will never again be two nations or be divided into two kingdoms. They will no longer defile themselves with their idols and vile images or with any of their offenses, for I will save them from all their sinful backsliding, and I will cleanse them. They will be my people, and I will be their God."

Rachel stopped then, wiped a tear of joy from her cheek, and looked pointedly at the older scientist, forcing him to digest all she had told him.

"Yngve, we have lived in the time of that one prophecy's fulfillment. Israel has its own nation for the first time in several thousand years and it is under *one* king and under *one* name. The last time it was under one name was during the reign of King Solomon. You have seen fulfilled what we had read. Even if this document were only one hundred years old it still predicted the prophecy in every way. And that is only one of many. It was that one prophecy that made me see that there really is a God and he is very actively involved in this world. It didn't take me long to realize that if this part of the Bible was true, the rest had to be. That meant all God's promises of love and hope and mercy could be mine.

"For this reason this project is wrong. It's a noble thing to want to save mankind, but when we take over God's job we're walking on dangerous ground. He *will* have his way whether we agree or not, and his word says that the illnesses and disasters will only increase—in spite of your best efforts."

Yngve leaned back in his chair, his mind full of everything the young woman had spoken of. He had never had time for the illusiveness of religion, but when he could see—had seen—the substance of it in a logical and orderly way, it caught his attention.

"Thank you that you both had the courage to come to me with this thing. I think I will do some research as you've done and see what I can find out for myself. I'm quite a skeptic, I'll warn you, and I won't hesitate to try to prove you wrong, but I must say, I have never read the book so I can't really judge it fairly, can I?" He smiled at Hawk, a twinkle in his eye.

"I do so like a challenge, though, so you had better study that book too, young man. I think you're about to become involved in some very strenuous debates."

*   *   *

He paced back and forth, an arm tucked behind his back and a perplexed frown puckering his forehead.

"This religion thing is getting out of hand. It seems to be spreading like a plague on the island. Only a handful of people have rejected it. I have no idea how Christianity was introduced but I'm at a bit of a loss on how to deal with this one."

"Has it affected *The Project*?" The Sheik adjusted himself in the comfortable office chair.

"I don't think so. For the most part, everyone's getting along quite nicely. It's just strange that I hadn't thought of a spiritual element and yet they're all drawn to one. I'll put a stop to it if it causes problems. I do have another situation to deal with, however," the Lieutenant said to the group of men once again spread around the polished table.

"Oh? What is it?"

"I'm having trouble with the young prince. We have a few others involved in *The Project* from the Middle East, but they seem to have adapted quite nicely. That tells me that it's more than just a cultural thing. The older the lad gets, the more unhinged he has become. Asad has never liked Eve— and I have to say—the girl has tried hard to please him. I'm concerned with her safety if the prince doesn't stabilize. He's grown quite sullen and violent lately and we've taken to keeping a watch on the couple for her sake."

"Is there anything you can do? I'm sure you didn't bring up the subject without having a solution, if my guess is correct," the Canadian committee member said.

"True. You know me well, my friend. We've decided that it's time to put into practice what we've been experimenting with for so long. Since Asad and Eve don't seem to be in such a hurry to procreate we'll help them along. She will be our first to try embryo implants.

"We'll sedate them both in a fortnight and collect the samples we need. We've had much success with test tube conceptions, so once we can create her child, we'll sedate her again and impregnate her. We'll watch carefully to make certain the pregnancy takes. Neither of them will have a choice. I've been patient enough with them."

"Won't it affect the purity of the samples?"

"I don't think so. As they will be sedated without their knowledge, they won't experience stress in any way and eventually I can rid the island of Asad's negative influence. I think—not unlike putting down a distressed animal—it would be a kindness to the boy."

"Just make sure you don't dispose of him too soon. You might need him again."

"Leave that to me.

10

IT WAS THE FIRST FUNERAL the island had experienced and the inhabitants were uncertain and frightened. Everyone had their doubts as to the validity of the story passed around by the island's cold and unfeeling leader. The Lieutenant made a show of the loose rocks at the south cliff's edge where they had found Asad's body.

Yngve was certain it had begun with the young man's discovery of his wife's pregnancy. To coin a phrase—all hell broke loose. He had gone wild with accusations and begun to slap Eve without mercy. Had it not been for the concern of one of the scientists who had verified her pregnancy test, she might have died.

The whole island knew of Asad's dislike for his wife. He was quite vocal about it and about his unwillingness to give her his children. The woman physician sensed the girl's fear and followed her home. When the screaming and shouting began, she quickly interceded with a call for help from some of the other young men. What followed was a scene that would come back to haunt the islanders in the weeks and months to come.

It took several men to subdue Asad, but none could stop the foul stream of cruel and evil words from pouring from his mouth as he hurled them at his weeping wife. She sat crumpled in a heap on the cottage's packed dirt floor, her hand pressed against her split and bleeding lip as she cringed under the verbal assault. Bruises and welts grew more apparent across her swelling face and her ankle showed signs of a bad sprain.

"I knew you didn't love me. No one loves me. You aren't carrying my child. Who have you slept with? May Allah grant me vengeance against the man who has defiled you. I knew years ago that women weren't to be trusted. My father was right. You're all just property and if I find the man you've been with, I'll kill him!"

"That would be me—in a manner of speaking." The cold tones cut through Asad's frenzy, rendering him into shocked silence as the Lieutenant stepped into the chaotic gathering. He nodded to the men gripping the prince's arms and came to stand before him.

"Release him. Asad, I know you haven't slept with your wife. You've never touched her once. It was quite a surprise for our scientists when they tried to harvest her eggs and discovered she was still a virgin." He began to circle the young man, eyeing him with disdain.

"I'm rather surprised that you've continued to carry such bitterness against your father and yet still took on some of his ridiculous and outdated traditions. But that's of no concern to me, really. What does concern me is the lack of interest you have for your wife. She's tried hard to please you and answer to your every whim. In exchange, she only wanted your children. You shamed her by refusing.

"Because of this, we took matters into our own hands and harvested her eggs and your seed—so I suppose, it is my fault that she's pregnant and I would love to see you try to kill me." The crowd gasped at the bold and challenging words of the older man. Husbands pulled their wives closer, anger hovering at the surface as they wondered if they, too, had unknowingly received similar interference.

Asad clenched his fists in fury, his eyes darting from his downtrodden wife, huddled in the protection of the woman doctor's arms, to the man who had dominated him from childhood. With a scream of pent up frustration, he threw himself at the fifty-four year old ex-SS officer.

The battle was quick but effective. In spite of his years—or maybe because of them—the Lieutenant had an enduring fitness about him, allowing him to move quickly to the side as Asad charged him. The younger man, meeting no resistance, stumbled past, his arms flailing. Like a snake striking its victim, the Lieutenant's arm darted out, grasping the windmilling limb as it passed, allowing the lad's momentum to carry him in an arc. He snapped Asad's body around and slammed him against the outer wall of their small hut, knocking the wind from the weaker man. And then the Lieutenant stepped in quickly, wrapping his free hand around the vulnerable throat and squeezing slowly to make his point. The younger man gasped and groped for air, vividly reminded of his first experience with that other brutish German guard so many years earlier. The Lieutenant stood still, muscles coiled, as all the killing experience and military training pumped its own adrenaline through his veins.

"Don't fool yourself, Asad. You're here for *my* purpose and you'll fulfill *my* will, not the will of some impotent god. Your wife will bear your children, one way or another, because this project must not fail and your genetics are necessary for its success."

He released the choking man then and stepped back, raising his voice for all to hear.

"Let this be a lesson to all of you. You will complete the mandate laid down by *The Committee*, and when the time comes for you to have children, you'll have them with the one we have chosen for you. When it's your children's times, we'll choose their mates as well. If you're willing to cooperate, all will go well. But please remember this—there are other ways for us to accomplish what must be accomplished. The choice is yours."

He turned then and stalked away with a military stiffness, leaving behind him a stunned silence. Resentful thoughts of physical interference and manipulation filled each person's mind, fighting for dominance over the feelings of shame that accompanied them. Accusing eyes turned to Yngve and the gentle man lowered his head in remorse.

Later, he would insist, in a conversation with Hawk, that he knew nothing of the abductions and harvestings and that the Lieutenant was giving him less and less work in the genetic manipulation laboratory—a new addition to the work of *The Project*. Sensing Yngve's reluctance to cross certain moral boundaries, the heartless leader had shifted the doctor's workload to consist more of dealing with the island's inhabitants and their social lives and less with the actual experimentation of genetic code and DNA. Nevertheless, the scientist was disturbed by the revelation and determined to do some quiet sleuthing of his own.

Eve was watched closely as the weeks ticked by and it was no surprise when her screams echoed through the small valley that cradled their fresh water source—a deep pond of sparkling blue. Hawk was her rescuer this time, knocking Asad into the water and off of her drowning form. They fought ferociously while Rachel dragged a spluttering and crying Eve from the shallows.

Rachel left Eve and the younger children of her brood with her oldest twins, Isaac and Jacob, boys of sturdy frame and keen intellect, and ran like the wind for assistance. Later, as Eve stuttered out her story, Asad was subdued and bundled off to the science complex, swearing vindictively as he struggled against his restraints.

She had come to the pond's edge with her bucket, intent on retrieving water for her washing. Asad had followed her discretely with the idea of drowning her. He'd forgotten that Hawk and Rachel had their home in the cave not far up the hill and he hadn't anticipated his wife's panicky struggle, which gave her one small chance to scream for help. He had calmly laid out his plan to her, holding her in an iron grip, one hand clamped tightly across her mouth, while he spat the words at her.

"I'm going to drown you and that evil creature that is no child of mine. Then I will be free to choose a wife on my own and no one will be able to stop me." And then she bit him and let loose a blood-curdling screech. Hawk, who had been gathering firewood nearby, had effectively ended the vicious threat with his blind charge, and Asad cursed his retribution as he was heartlessly dragged from the clearing.

No one heard from or saw Asad for days and then he was back in his little cottage, quiet and meek. His face was a map of bruises and cuts and his arm hung useless in a sling. He limped the few times he left his chair and completely ignored Eve's offers of food. For four days he moped about, saying little and eating less. And then he disappeared.

That night a small fire broke out in the new wing of the genetics lab where only a handful of people knew the samples were kept. The fire was slow moving, having very little to feed it, it's weak and sluggish flames drawing attention instantly from those whose job it was to keep the complex secure. It was a useless fire—easily controlled. And three days later, Asad's body washed up among the rocks by the cliff. He was smashed to pieces.

*   *   *

The islanders mourned as they buried Asad, not just for the young man, but for all that had brought him to this point. They mourned their own isolation and the freedom that had been snatched from them. They cried for the brutality that forced them into a life in which they had no say. And they wept for Eve, who stood, desolate, defeated, and swelling with a pregnancy brought on through research and manipulation—not of love.

*   *   *

He had always thought that Hitler's spiritual curiosity was his biggest downfall, but perhaps the lunatic knew more than the Lieutenant gave him credit for. He was amazed at how the community members had begun to seek out, for spiritual guidance, the young native man and the five other men referred to as elders. It was as though some part of them was missing and they needed to fill it with the unknown. Foolishness. And yet already he was seeing a positive change in those who were adopting the formal Christian religion that the six men were teaching. Perhaps it was time to resurrect some of Hitler's ideas.

He scanned through the Bible that he had taken from the musty collection of books left behind by Sir Horace in his hurry to leave. Such rubbish. He had enough trouble deciphering the archaic language but once he got past that, he was appalled at the whole core of the strange religion.

The Lieutenant had gone to the state church as a lad, but he had little recollection of its doctrines and traditions. Now, he felt that by understanding this book he might understand the growing band of "believers," as they called themselves. And if he understood correctly, that meant loving one's enemies. *But that's weakness, and the purpose behind this whole project is one of strength,* he thought as he absently stroked an eyebrow—a mindless, repetitive gesture meant to soothe the growing headache that had begun to penetrate his concentration.

He read further, his anger and scorn at the teachings of God's love, forgiveness, and freedom from sin growing with each word he absorbed. It eluded him. Why would anyone lower himself or herself to a position of vulnerability on some vague promise of a paradise after life? Fairy tales. How could anyone with any sort of intellect rely on such fairy tales?

With frustration, he snapped the book shut. It was beyond understanding. Resting his elbows on either side of the dusty tome, he steepled his fingers and lowered his chin on to them in concentration. Forgiveness. Freedom. Love. He paused. Freedom.

That's it! He thought to himself, *these people are looking for freedom, and this religion offers some abstract form of emotional and spiritual freedom that they feel they've been robbed of.* He chuckled quietly, amazed at mankind's ability to delude itself, and then he pushed the Bible aside and pulled out a worn, leather-bound notebook, opening it to its first page.

Hitler's diary. A book that the world would love to discover and never would. The man *was* a genius. He had to admit it. If he hadn't gone insane, the world would likely be shouting "Heil Hitler." But he *had* gone insane and the Lieutenant was curious to find out why. Would the ink scratchings in the small book reveal it? Would he find out what it was about the cults that fascinated the dead leader of the dead Third Reich? He was determined to try.

He settled back into the overstuffed chair and forced himself to concentrate once again, pulling the words of a madman into his own cruel and wicked mind. In the depths of the spirit world, an evil chuckle crossed the chasms of time and an ethereal being felt a gleaming of satisfaction as he yearned after one more soul ripe for destruction.

*   *   *

It was a shock to Yngve when he discovered that his role in genetic work had become obsolete. He didn't know when the locks had been changed for the genetic manipulation wing of the huge complex but it alarmed him to know that he had been effectively shuffled aside from the more advanced genetic work. The most frightening thing was the fact that it had happened and he hadn't even noticed. Was he that dense?

He sighed quietly, not wanting to draw attention to himself as he furtively looked down the hall to the so-called nurse's station. How would he gain access? He needed a plan. He jumped as a loud cough erupted from around the corner and wiped at a trickle of sweat on his cheek. What would happen if he were caught there? He remembered the look of maniacal hunger on the Lieutenant's face as he had held Asad by the throat and Yngve felt his heart speed into a churning flutter. He really didn't want to be on the receiving end of that man's anger. Turning, he walked with purpose to the nearest exit, giving the impression that he had recently been in that wing.

The nurse glanced up from her work at the desk and nodded, eyeing him carefully as he passed. Yngve smiled and returned the nod, hoping she wouldn't ask for his identification. In spite of his level of authority, there were still many nurses, doctors, and scientists who didn't know him by sight. That thought in itself caught him by surprise. After so many years, he was still unknown by half the staff. He preferred to spend his time with the children, watching them mature into adults, loving them as though they were his own. Perhaps that was how he had so easily missed the change in authority.

*   *   *

Hawk and Rachel listened with concern as Yngve confided in them. It was unsettling to the young couple to find out that their gentle and loving leader was no longer their leader. It was even more unsettling to hear that his position had been filled with scientists chosen by the ruthless Lieutenant. Rachel shivered as she remembered her conversation on the rickety and weathered fishing vessel so many years back.

"He was SS, you know." It passed her lips as nothing more than a whisper but it was enough to silence both men.

"How do you know this thing?" Yngve's accent always thickened when he was distressed and Rachel looked at him with sympathy.

"He told me when he brought me to the island," she said. "He said he'd never been in favour of the death camps and hadn't killed Jews, but that he had been put there by *The Committee* to keep an eye on Hitler. He said that Hitler didn't commit suicide. He was commissioned by *The Committee* to murder him and make it look like a suicide."

"I see…" Yngve's voice trailed off as he remembered Hitler's perverted and cruel experiments on some of the concentration camp subjects for *The Project*'s sake. Yngve had never witnessed any of it, but the video footage and written documentation was overwhelming and he shuddered at the fleeting idea that the Lieutenant might have been involved. He threw a worried glance in the direction of the scientific complex, his mind churning at what he had allowed to occur without knowing it.

"So, my friends, what do we do? How do we find out what our illustrious leader is up to? We must know and stop anything that would cause suffering to another human being—no matter how small and underdeveloped that human being may be. I still believe in the idea of *The Project* but not at the cost of creating another Adolph Hitler."

Hawk had been silent for some time, concentrating on a spot on the ground before him. Lifting his normally expressionless face, he allowed a small smile.

"I have an idea, but we'll need to have a chat with Charlie Wong," he said. "I think he might like to be a part of this."

Rachel lifted a questioning gaze to her husband, allowing him space to explain.

"Charlie's wife Natasha just had a set of identical twins, right?" Rachel and Yngve nodded. "The strange thing about it is that the children don't really look like they belong to Charlie and Natasha. I was talking to Charlie yesterday and he made an unusual observation. He said they looked more like Eve's boy, Brandon, than either of them. I never thought anything about it until I saw Eve later carrying her son across the compound. I asked to see him and you know what? Charlie's right. The twins look almost exactly like Brandon."

Rachel frowned, pulling a mental picture into her mind of the three boys. Their faces were typically round and chubby like most babies, but yes, come to think of it, they did look quite a bit alike and quite different from both sets of parents.

The three friends walked the path that led to a similar cottage at the far end of the island near the cliffs that had claimed Asad. They chattered lightly, all trying to avoid the subject that was foremost on their minds. No one wanted to begin the pursuit of ideas until all were present, and so filled their conversation with lighter, happier talk of family and home. Yngve even endured lighthearted teasing about a match for him, and all would have shuddered had they known their talk ranged very closely to a parallel conversation amidst a gathering of wealthy men.

*   *   *

"I think our dear Dr. Yngve needs a wife. I also think *The Project* would benefit from his genetics. The man is a genius and should contribute."

The Lieutenant sat back and watched as his words were bounced around the table for discussion. He said nothing more and his granite features showed even less, allowing the other nine to come to their own conclusions. For several moments the positives and negatives were exchanged and inwardly the Lieutenant smirked. *These small-minded men don't even know what they're talking about. I could propose anything on the island and they would still debate it just to show each other—and me— that they can. How tiring.* And yet he never gave voice to his amused thoughts but waited patiently in silence until the discussion drew to a close.

"Do we have a consensus, my friends?"

A large-boned, white-haired man nodded and answered the question with one of his own.

"Who do you have in mind?"

"I was hoping you would ask," the Lieutenant said. "Our dear doctor has recently turned fifty—still young enough to father children. He has retained a youthful look so I don't think attraction will be a problem.

"The lady I have in mind is a missionary in India. She is a lovely woman from Italy who is twenty-nine years of age. Her father died years ago and her mother lives with one of her sisters. She's so entwined in her work that she seldom has time to communicate with them, and from my research I sense that they don't mind.

"The woman has an incredible mind when it comes to medicines and botanical science, remembering the smallest detail and property of any plant she comes across. This is a knowledge that should be incorporated into the human condition in order for mankind to stay ahead of any disease out there.

"She also has a basic grasp of many of the dialects in India, not to mention her native Italian. She taught herself English and French and shows the ability to absorb and retain just about anything pertaining to language and science—a handy thing to have on an island where so many languages are spoken.

"I propose we use our contacts within the government of India to have her taken to a meeting place where I will, from there, escort her to the island. I'm sure she will be fascinated with the medicinal potential that our small paradise has to offer."

The white-haired man continued with his questioning.

"Will this not alert the media? We can't afford another fiasco like the one raised with the death of the American President. How will you cover your tracks this time?"

The Lieutenant gritted his teeth at the subtle challenge. He had sensed competition for the position of chairman from this man before, but never quite so openly. Offering a cool smile, he continued to voice his plan, allowing the thoughts of murder to hover in a quiet corner of his mind.

"If it's reported that she was rushed to a hospital in India for one of the many hideous diseases that proliferate there, and that she died of it, it shouldn't be a problem. She will be 'quarantined' and her body will be 'cremated' for the safety of society. We will find some way to honour the young lady for her work, effectively and quietly closing the door to any inquiries as to her true whereabouts. You see, gentlemen. I *have* learned my lesson from the American assassination."

He sat back and relaxed as each head nodded its consent of the plan. Even his opponent had to admit that it was a good idea and one easily carried out. The vote was unanimous.

*   *   *

He read the diary several times, noting the steady decline in the man's sanity. The only correlation the Lieutenant could make was that it seemed to parallel his involvement in the cults. But Hitler had chosen the wrong path, according to any of the research he had done. Instead of enlightenment, the German leader had yearned for domination. After so much recent study in spiritualism the Lieutenant was convinced that there was a good side and an evil side to the acquisition of power. The many and diverse books he had read thus far made that quite plain. Hitler had simply chosen the wrong side.

The Lieutenant set the book aside and ran his fingers through his hair, arching his back to work out the kinks brought on from sitting at his desk for so long. It would take more research, more convincing, before he could ever take any step into something as seemingly insubstantial as the spiritual realm. And yet, if he hoped to influence the island's inhabitants, that was exactly what he must do. Having settled that much in his skeptical mind, he hunched over the small book one more time.

* 11 *

AN ELEGANT-LOOKING FIFTY-eight-year-old woman tapped a small wooden gavel on the podium in front of her, allowing the loud knocking to echo through the hall, drawing the attention of its occupants.

The room was crowded with people from all races and nations. The purpose of such a diverse gathering was unknown to the outside world. Those who couldn't afford to join the meeting had been brought in at the woman's expense. Those who could pay the price came willingly.

Beside the lovely elder sat a man of Native blood. He was close to her age and sat in stoic silence, waiting for the quiet that would eventually come.

"I would like to bring to order the first meeting of 'Lost Children.'" Mrs. Stillwater's voice rang clear and strong and was edged with an excited determination.

Andrew Gray Bear turned his piercing brown eyes to rest on her, silently admiring her strength and purpose. He had marveled at her ability to track him down and still, on occasion, shook his head at her resourcefulness.

"All of us are here for the same reason. We've endured the abduction of a loved one and desire to have that family member returned to us.

"Several years ago, a letter written in my daughter's hand was delivered to my husband and I. It was such a colossal shock to us that it caused my husband to have a stroke, leaving me with the burden of understanding its meaning and what I could do to bring our daughter home. At the time, I could do very little other than write letters and tend to my stricken husband. However, upon my husband's death, I became devoted to finding out what happened to my child. Many of you have read this letter and know its contents to be of a sinister nature.

"What many of you are unaware of is that our own President was murdered in an effort to verify the information Carolyn passed on to her father and I."

A large gasp whispered through the room, bouncing off the cement block walls and waving back over the gathered crowd. Mrs. Stillwater raised her manicured hands for silence and continued with her monologue.

"In the year that followed his reading her letter, our President started an investigation into the very things Carolyn suggested. Before his assassination, he uncovered a fair bit of information, including the details on something known as *The Project* and a list of the children who had been incorporated into that project. It was that list which brought me to all of you.

"Thanks to some influential friends of my own I was able to obtain your names and addresses based on this list, which I also have copies of. Unfortunately, those same friends have met their own mysterious ends, leaving me to emphasize the importance of utmost secrecy in all that we discuss here today.

"I have spent most of my own small fortune to bring you all to this place because I feel you all need to know what has become of your loved ones. After being kidnapped, they were placed on an island somewhere where the Caribbean and Atlantic Oceans meet, for the purpose of being crossbred like hybrid animals in order to recreate the human race in its broader form."

She paused, allowing the crowd to express their angry murmurings. Throwing a brief glance at the man beside her, she drew strength from his quiet demeanor and then pushed on.

"When our president was killed, I closed my mouth and played the innocent. I had plenty of people who 'casually' tried to fish information from me, but when they decided I knew nothing, they left me alone.

"People, you need to understand that there is a committee of extremely wealthy men behind this project who will stop at nothing to see their plans completed." She drew a breath to continue, but a Chinese man stood and called out.

"What would you have us do?" he said. "If these people are so powerful, how can we possibly help our children?" The question was punctuated by rumblings from across the hall.

"I think that my friend Andrew Gray Bear would be better able to tell you what must be done at this time to save our children." With that, the woman clamped her mouth shut and offered the podium with a gesture of her small hand.

Andrew had never spoken in public before, and the sheer size of the hall and the weight of many eyes focused on him intimidated him. He cleared a nervous throat and began his tale.

"My son was stolen from me as a boy in the 1940's. I have been without my only child for over twenty years. In that time, I have never stopped pleading before the God of all creation to protect my son and return him to me.

"At first, my faith wavered. I didn't think I could bear to lose my son after having lost his mother at his birth. But God was good to me. He surrounded me with people who encouraged me to pray and trust. For many years, I struggled; only hanging on by the knowledge that God had lost his Son for a time, too.

"One day, I could take no more, and I cried out to Jesus, asking him to show me whether my son was alive or dead. I challenged the God of the universe to prove his love to me by helping me let go. The next day, I was visited by this determined lady..." he motioned to Mrs. Stillwater, and smiled at her modest blush.

"She showed me the same letter she has shown to all of you, and it gave me hope. In return, I shared with her my plea to God to help me find answers. Together, we spoke to the leaders of my church, asking for guidance. Their words of wisdom tore the hope from my chest, and yet were profound. We were told to pray—to storm the gates of Heaven with our pleas. They understood the futility of fighting against such a powerful group of world leaders, but these spiritual men also understood what I had failed to see—that God is greater than any scheme or plan that man could invent.

"And so we prayed more fervently and with a renewed hope, and then a very unusual thing happened. The young man who had kidnapped her daughter—although he is no longer so young—managed to discretely contact Mrs. Stillwater. He had a brief meeting with her, in which he was able to relay that the children are alive and doing well, and that if there is ever a way for him to help return them, he will do all he can. He is one of the many pilots who fly in supplies, and although he can't smuggle anything in or out, he is willing to give us an idea of where the island is."

Another voice called out from the back of the room.

"Why don't we just alert the authorities? I'm certain they will help." This was accompanied by more mutterings and nods all around.

"Do you not think we would have done so if we could have? Do you not remember that the President of the United States tried that very thing and lost his life for it? If they can kill a president and abduct hundreds of people without the world knowing, don't you think they could kill us all?" The room stilled as each solemnly considered the questions thrown at them.

Andrew continued in a more controlled voice, hoping the group would listen to reason.

"We must find a way to contact the children without these leaders knowing. We need to pray that God will open a door that will help us bring our families home. I know you all have your different beliefs, and I can't do anything about that. But I will challenge you to study my beliefs and see why my prayers were answered. And then I will hope that all of you will do your part in praying to the God of the universe, through his Son Jesus, that he will bring our children home.

"If you can't do that, that is your choice, but please...please...say nothing to anyone outside of this room. I plead with you to listen to me for the sake of our own safety and that of our children."

With that, Andrew Gray Bear sat down and the meeting was adjourned, leaving the crowd to mingle and discuss the bizarre events that had brought them to that place.

*   *   *

"They look just like Eve's baby. What's going on, Hawk?" Rachel's voice was shaky as realization flooded into her mind. She glanced back at the twin boys nestled in their mother's arms. Natasha looked up at her, a mother's determined love deep in her eyes. But there was more there. Concern. Anger. Hurt. Shame.

The two babies had deep brown hair, coarse but not like their father's. Their eyes were changing from the blue of birth to a deep brown. Their skin was a golden shade as though someone had taken a palette of all the different hues of human skin tone and blended them until they became a single color that contained them all. They resembled neither parent in features, and that was the most surprising part. Natasha had the almond shaped eyes of the Mongolian tribes of the far reaches of the Soviet Union. Charlie was oriental, also bearing eyes of similar shape. These children had eyes with a more muted, subtler lift to them, rounder than they should have been.

"Well, I'll be..." Yngve's voice trailed off as he searched the boys' features.

Hawk looked at him sharply and waited, knowing the doctor would finish his thoughts.

"It appears that the Lieutenant has gone beyond the moral boundaries just as Sir Horace had feared he would," the older scientist said.

"What do you mean?" Natasha's voice quivered and Charlie stood behind her with his hand resting protectively on her shoulder.

"There was talk a few years back about a new process that could speed up *The Project*. One of the younger scientists had theorized that it could be possible to harvest the cells responsible for reproductive organs from an unborn child and manipulate them until he created that unborn child's child.

"The idea was to create babies in test tubes from all of the island's couples. From there, the DNA would be matched, creating pairs, if you will, from the test tube specimens. Once that process was complete, they would draw the needed reproductive cells from each and create yet more test tube babies. According to the young scientist, the process could go on indefinitely until there was a consistent genetic base.

"When that was established and all the desired genetics were there to make children of completely mixed race with the traits that all of you had been chosen for, those test tube babies would then be implanted into the mothers' wombs, and the children could continue to develop.

"It was a hideous plan, and we older ones thought it could never come to that. I think I now have an idea of what is happening in the sealed-off wing." The older man looked at each of them wearily and sighed.

"I think you might be holding your grand or even great-grandchildren."

*   *   *

"Eve hasn't eaten in a week and I'm worried about the child she carries." The Lieutenant presented himself as one truly concerned, and the other nine men paid close attention.

"What should we do?" the newest member from India asked.

"We must find another husband for her."

"That won't be easy," the American said, his ever-present cigar disrupting his flow of speech.

"Actually, I was thinking of a man I know who would love to have a wife," the Lieutenant said. "Because he was born sterile, most women are not interested in him. He is a gentle man and would treat the woman with kindness."

"Do you think he will agree?" the heavy-boned, white-haired member asked.

"Perhaps we won't give him a choice."

"You would do that?"

"I will do what is necessary to further *The Project*," the Lieutenant said.

"What is his name?"

The Lieutenant paused for dramatic effect, allowing an amused smile to hover on his lips. He looked down at the table, forcing the question to expand in the silence of the room. And then he lifted his gaze to the nine who shared his world of power.

"His name is Adam. Adam Denning. Fitting, don't you think?"

*   *   *

Two new people arrived on the island the same day, but at different times on different flights. A pretty dark-haired lady was brought in with the floatplane that carried medical supplies. Unconscious, the sturdy-framed woman was taken from the craft on a stretcher and hefted into the back of a truck to be delivered to a hospital bed in the medical center.

An hour later, a plain-looking gentleman with dark, cocoa-coloured skin, thick glasses, and a charming smile stepped off another floatplane that carried some new technological gadgets brought in to further the work in the genetics laboratory. The man was taken to a small but brightly-lit office to wait for introductions and accommodations.

*   *   *

The woman had been deposited in the health clinic so the drug could wear off. The nurse tending her, however, was not prepared for the volatile temper and commanding manner of the vitriolic missionary, and scurried from the room under a barrage of drug-slurred orders and accusations. The nurse found the woman slowly and feebly pacing the room in a fierce mood when she returned to timidly inform her that she had a guest.

"Welcome to our island, Miss Francesca. I'm happy to see you've recovered from your brief indisposition so quickly." The Lieutenant's tone was smooth with amusement, and the woman's nostrils flared in response.

"Where am I? I demand to be returned to the mission. You have no right to kidnap me. I am a citizen of Italy and will be missed soon enough." She crossed her arms imperiously and glared at the black-suited man. The Lieutenant merely smiled and settled a shoulder against the doorframe of the sterile room.

"I'm afraid that's impossible, Isabella, since you no longer exist anywhere off of this island. It seems you came down with a severe case of the plague or some such thing. It was such a pity that India had to lose one of her most devoted missionaries to such a horrible disease."

Pushing himself from his resting spot, the Lieutenant sauntered over to the bedside table to smell the gentle fragrance of the vase that was filled with an array of the island's flowers. With a small measure of fussiness, he pulled at the few dead blossoms, removing them from the arrangement, and then settled himself in the room's single chair.

"I assure you that the government of India will honour you with a beautiful memorial service, but they did regret the necessity of having you cremated. Your mother and sisters weren't very happy about that, but they understood when they realized the contagiousness of your disease."

Isabella's face went white with fear as the words soaked into a brain still recovering from the effects of a tranquilizer.

"I...I don't understand what you mean. I'm not dead. I don't have a plague. What are you saying?"

The Lieutenant tipped his head to one side, truly enjoying the play of emotions across the woman's face.

"We needed you for our project, Isabella. Your abilities in the area of medicinal herbs and your penchant toward dialects and languages make you a valuable asset to the restoration of mankind's genetics. We've found a perfect mate for you and I think you will complement each other quite nicely. He's one of our scientists. A little older than you, I have to admit, but I think you'll find him a pleasant mate once you get to know him."

"Mate? What do you mean 'mate'?" Isabella's temper was the one real nemesis to her Christian work and she struggled daily to hand it over to the Lord. But she hadn't been prepared for so outrageous a tale, and the shock of it pushed her beyond her own control. Her voice rose as she began to rattle off a string of sentences in her Italian tongue, and the Lieutenant's eyebrows rose as he recognized, if not the words, the jist of her tirade. He stood calmly and made his way to the open door, surprised by the fire in her tone and the rapidly rising colour in her olive-hued face.

"I can see that you aren't interested in discussing this calmly, so I'll leave you to absorb what I've told you. You'll be expected to join the community by the end of the day and you'll meet your future husband at that time. I would suggest you get over your anger quickly, as you don't have left as many child-bearing years as the younger ladies do. I suppose a few months should be enough time for the two of you to adapt to each other, and then we'll call for the Reverend so you can continue with the purpose you were chosen for—the bearing of children."

Isabella gasped at the callousness of the man and picked up the nearby vase, hurling it at the quickly closing door. She sank down onto the bed to mull over the bizarre information, and then the tears came. Great hot droplets of water dripped from her eyes onto tightly clutched hands as her heart cried out to the heavens above.

"Lord, I've followed your leading unquestioningly. I've gone into the world to minister to people you chose and I've never wavered in that calling. Why, then, did you pull me from that work and put me here?" She lifted her tear-stained face to the ceiling, hoping for some reply. No answer came, but Isabella was not surprised. God didn't always answer her right away.

Slowly, she pulled herself from the bed and pushed the tears from her face. Stooping to gather up the shattered remains of the vase, she caught the sweet fragrance of the scattered flowers and curiosity got the better of her. Gently, carefully, she lifted a single bloom and stroked it tenderly. And then the peace came, settling over her like a warm towel. God knew what he was doing. It wasn't the first time she didn't understand his ways and it wouldn't be the last. She would have to take each moment as it came and hope that her temper would not get in the way of the Almighty's work.

*   *   *

Yngve spluttered with nervousness and indignation as the Lieutenant repeated a similar conversation to the older scientist. His shock, although not nearly as dramatic as that of his bride-to-be, was nevertheless deep, and he plopped down in the chair opposite the officer's desk while he absorbed the information.

"I don't understand. I've done all that's been asked of me. Why are you doing this to me?"

The Lieutenant laughed—a foreign, hollow sound—and his surprise was evident in his tone.

"I thought you'd be overjoyed, Yngve. You've worked so hard for so many years that I thought you'd be pleased to be part of *The Project*." He approached his benumbed associated and clapped a hand on the man's shoulder in a stilted gesture of companionship.

"Believe me, Doctor. You'll enjoy getting to know this woman. She's...shall we say...interesting. You'll find her to be quite intelligent and I'm sure you'll appreciate all she knows about medicinal herbs." The Lieutenant noted the dazed look on Yngve's face and chuckled again.

"Come now, Doctor. It really won't be all that bad. You'll finally have the wife you've been denied for so many years. This is a good thing, Yngve. Enjoy it."

And then, after one last pat on the shoulder, the Lieutenant strode from the office, leaving Yngve to process this new twist in his formerly ordered and safe life. For the first time since he had been brought on to *The Project*, Yngve understood how wrong the whole thing truly was.

*   *   *

Eve sat by the small window, looking out onto the common area while her four-month-old son slumbered heavily in his small bed. So many young children laughed and scampered about with their friends and siblings, and she felt a twinge of jealousy. She had never had siblings. She had had few friends. Asad had seen to that. Rachel had stuck by her, though, always visiting when her husband was away from their small hut.

It had been Rachel who had led her to Jesus and she was grateful for that. She pushed her plate of food aside and massaged her belly, barely recovered from new birth and already holding her second child. She wasn't hungry. She hadn't been truly hungry since the funeral took place. She had tried to love her husband, but he had rejected every attempt she made. He had hated her. She had failed.

Two fat drops of salty water trickled down the smooth, dark cheeks of the beautiful face and Eve sighed at the sorry excuse that was her life. In her heart, she cried out to her God, begging him to be the love that she needed—craved.

All the hurt and anguish; all the defeat and worthlessness, she poured into the cupped and waiting hands of her Heavenly Father. And after a time, she let his peace and love fill her as it always did when she most needed it.

The children continued their games and laughter and she smiled sadly, glad that those children had loving parents and good friends. Suddenly the chatter stopped and all heads turned to look down the path that led from the sprawling complex.

Eve craned her neck to see what it was that the children were looking at and she shuddered as the Lieutenant's form came into view. She wanted to hate the man, and knew that if Jesus weren't controlling her world, she would have. She also knew she would have looked for a way to kill the one who had destroyed her life with his selfish ambition. As it was, she struggled constantly to be civil to him as she hadn't yet found a verse in her Bible that said she had to *like* him. Love and like were different, after all. Weren't they? She mentally shook the thought away and continued watching out the window.

Another man walked beside the Lieutenant and she squinted her eyes against the afternoon glare, startled by the rich darkness of his skin. There were others on the island who were dark-skinned, but not like Eve. This was the first time she had seen someone so black, and she involuntarily glanced at her own deep chocolate skin. His skin glistened with a beautiful sheen and his black hair curled in tight close-cropped knots. He had a plain face, nothing extraordinary, and his glasses were thick, reflecting the sunlight and preventing her from seeing his eyes. He spoke with animation and she could see a gentleness in his manner. Another guinea pig for *The Project*. She snorted in disgust and turned away from the window.

Settling herself at the small table, the lonely woman continued to cut the pieces of a dress from the batch of flowered material that was draped there. She hoped to have the garb made soon, since her waistline was still too large for her other clothes and she wanted something different than what she had worn during her last pregnancy. The knock at the door startled her and she rose wearily and padded her way across the room to open it. The Lieutenant stood there with a pleasant smile on his face and Eve struggled to mask her dislike and suspicion.

"Yes?"

The island's ruthless leader chuckled quietly at her poorly concealed emotions and glanced over his shoulder at the man who had been his tailor for the past several years.

"Eve, could we come in? I would like you to meet someone."

She nodded slowly and stepped aside, forcing a stiff smile onto her full mouth as she allowed the two men into her small home.

*   *   *

Hawk's laugh was infectious and Rachel couldn't help the giggles that slipped from her own mouth. Yngve stood in the cave entrance, a wild look on his face. He had just explained to the young couple what had happened and Hawk couldn't help but see the irony in it.

"So, Doctor, how does it feel to have your life mapped out for you?"

It might have come across sounding bitter, but Hawk really didn't feel he had anything to be bitter about. He had a lovely wife and eight delightful children. His only regret was that his father and uncle couldn't be part of it all. However, for the most part his life was good. It was pure impishness that drove him to push the good doctor a bit. He just couldn't help himself.

"This isn't funny, Hawk. I'm expected to fall in love with that woman and I can't even get her to stop yelling at me. *I* didn't do this. This is the Lieutenant's work. He thinks he's flattering me by adding my genetics to *The Project*, but I don't *want* to be married. I like being single. What am I to do?"

The middle-aged man raked his fingers through his thinning hair and plopped himself down on a chair without being asked. Rachel threw an amused glance at Hawk and stepped in.

"Yngve, listen to me. Did anyone consult us when we were added to the list of subjects?"

The flustered man looked up and guiltily shook his head.

"No. That's right. They didn't. Do you think we're happy here?"

Yngve dropped his hand and looked from one to the other, really looking, for the first time, at the contentment shining on their faces. He scanned the room, seeing the furniture that had been crafted with loving care and then tidied and cleaned with a parallel affection.

"Yes. I suppose you *are* happy, aren't you?"

Rachel nodded and knelt before their friend, taking his hand in hers.

"We're happy because we choose to be. In spite of our circumstances. That's what the Bible meant when it said in Hebrews 13:5 'Keep your lives free from the love of money and be content with what you have, because God has said, "Never will I leave you; never will I forsake you."' Perhaps God has decided that you aren't to be alone. This woman is a missionary, you say? I don't think that's much of a coincidence, do you, Yngve?"

The scientist had been fighting the stirrings in his heart for a long time. Many an hour had been spent in the quaint cavern home as he debated with the young couple over the validity of the scriptures. He had tried hard to dispute the Bible, but more and more he was seeing that some invisible Being was manipulating the world around him and that the Bible had not only spiritual validity, but historical accuracy and relevance as well.

He was smart enough to know that this Being was working hard to bring Yngve to a place where he must choose, and it was becoming increasingly difficult to ignore the invisible hand that was nudging him to that decision. He smiled a small, tight grin and shrugged.

"I suppose this God of yours has been dropping hints to me quite a bit lately. Perhaps Isabella won't want to be married to someone who doesn't yet believe." He sounded worried suddenly, and Hawk saw into the heart of his anxious friend with a clarity that made him work to control his amusement.

"Yngve, you need not worry about this woman's view. If they have matched her as well as you matched us, you'll be a happy man. As to your beliefs—don't make the mistake of taking on Christianity in order to please her. God is patient and wants your heart when the time is right for you to give it. He'll help Isabella understand this if she truly is a follower of Christ." Hawk turned to his wife and winked. "Maybe Rachel should drop in on our new community member. She'll put in a good word for you."

Yngve's head snapped up and his face reddened deeply. And then the small grin widened as he wrapped his extremely gifted mind around the possibilities.

*   *   *

Adam watched the beautiful black woman with awe. She was stunning and moved with an effortless grace. He swallowed hard and tried to focus on all that his friend was saying. The introduction had gone well. Both had smiled at the irony of their names and then he watched as the guarded look came into her eyes while the Lieutenant spoke.

"So you see, Eve, I've brought you someone who will treat you with the honour and respect you've deserved for so long. I know you don't like me much and I can live with that, but I feel that I've made a real mess of your life and must do something to make that right. We'll continue to produce children for you, however, because those genetics are needed. Adam understands all of that as much as he understands the pain of rejection."

Eve threw a stiff look at the stranger and noted with small satisfaction that he squirmed awkwardly. He dropped his gaze to the floor and she instantly felt sorry for him. Part of her was furious for the interference she must once again endure. Yet, another part of her was curious about this new man. From nowhere a question popped into her head, and with cynicism born of years of experience, she voiced it.

"What life were you torn from, Adam?" She couldn't resist the goad and lifted her chin at the Lieutenant's narrowed gaze. The stranger looked from his associate to Eve and back again. Confusion covered his features as he tried to understand her question.

"I...I was the Lieutenant's tailor. I make his suits for him. At least I did. Don't misunderstand, please. I haven't been torn from anything. The Lieutenant heard me remark about being alone. He's offered me a gift as I see it. Not many women want a man who can't give them children. I'd be happy here and I'd try to be a good father to your children."

Speechless, Eve looked from one man to the other while the silence grew. And then she voiced her convictions, throwing the words at the Lieutenant while her eyes returned to Adam's earnest face.

"I'm not ready for this, yet. Nor will I submit as easily as I have in the past." She turned to the Lieutenant to finish her thought. "I want the freedom to get to know this man, and if I like him and he's good to me, I'll marry him. But I will not live with him until then. I'm a Christian now and it would be wrong for me. I'm not asking, Lieutenant. I'm informing." She lifted her chin with a new stubbornness and the leader smiled thinly and nodded.

"As you wish, Eve. But know this. You *will* continue to mother children, happy or no, with a husband or no. I don't care how it happens, really. You can choose what you wish to do, but you need to understand that Adam can't leave the island now. He knows too much and *The Project* can't be jeopardized." With that, the Lieutenant rose stiffly and ushered himself out, leaving confusion and frustration in his wake.

The two strangers sat facing one another, uncomfortably looking everywhere but at each other. Finally Eve took a deep breath and offered Adam something to drink. Her voice was flat and he could tell she was trying to be polite. He shook his head and stood to leave.

"I'm sorry for how all of this has happened, Mrs. Mohammed. It wasn't my intention to make things difficult for you. I'll find where I am to stay and I'll be content with getting to know all these remarkable people who've given so much to be part of this project."

Eve's head snapped up and she gestured for him to wait.

"What did the Lieutenant tell you, Adam?" she asked.

The man looked more confused than before and his dark eyes peered at her through the thick lenses of his glasses.

"He told me that hundreds of people had volunteered to be part of an experiment in genetics. It's quite remarkable, really."

Eve smiled sadly and she shook her head as she asked further.

"How long have you known the Lieutenant?"

The man furrowed his brow in thought.

"Five years now. Why do you ask?"

"He lied to you, Adam. None of us volunteered. We were all stolen from our countries. I guess maybe I wasn't. Papa Yngve says I was found in the desert of Libya and I was half-dead and abandoned. He doesn't lie, so that must be true. But the rest of the people have been kidnapped and manipulated for the sake of a project to re-create the human race."

Adam blinked as his mind absorbed all she told him, and then he sat down hard. Absently, he pulled his glasses from his face. Reaching into a suit pocket, he pulled out a small square of linen and methodically began to polish the lenses. It was a mindless exercise, busying his hands while he thought through what she had said up to that point. Eve watched with fascination as each thought shifted and molded the expressions of his face to match his inner conflict, and then his eyes cleared and he returned the frames to their perch on his broad nose and shook his head slowly, embarrassment dominating his visage.

"You must think I'm pretty stupid?"

"No." Eve sighed, feeling an unwanted urge to pat his shoulder. "I think you've been skillfully manipulated by one of the best manipulators history has ever seen. Just like the rest of us." She turned then and poured him a small glass of fresh fruit juice.

"Here, drink this. It won't help any, but at least you'll know that I don't have any hard feelings against you."

Adam looked up at her again and smiled a sad smile.

"I should have known it was too good to be true. He told me that you were a widow looking for a man who would help you raise your children."

He looked over to the woven wicker cradle tucked into the tiny room's corner.

"May I?"

Eve nodded her head and followed him as he rose and quietly moved to stand over the sleeping child. The boy lay with his rump raised, knees tucked tightly beneath his belly, and a soft blanket pulled up under his cheek. Thick dark lashes fanned down over soft skin, hiding eyes that were a strange blue interspersed with heavy brown flecks. His mouth worked furiously, drawing on a tiny thumb, and he sighed his contentment. Adam smiled as he looked at the boy, feeding on each detail of the perfect face, wishing the child was his.

Some part of his thoughts—his regret at hoping for what now seemed impossible—showed in his wistful glance and Eve found herself feeling pity for this man who had been so easily duped. Her anger toward the Lieutenant was renewed as she was forced to introduce Adam to the darker side of the island's experiments.

"My children have been injected into me somehow by scientists who found a way to create them outside of my body. They formed them from my dead husband's seed and my eggs. Sounds romantic doesn't it? It gets even better, though, because everyone on the island knows that the Lieutenant murdered my husband but no one can do anything about it. I don't know whether to hate the man or thank him since my husband despised me and beat me regularly. You were brought here in a pathetic effort to make me happy so I would produce better. I'm sorry you've been deceived."

Adam barked a short cynical laugh and looked away through the open window much as Eve had done earlier.

"Well, aren't we a fine pair? Here I thought I'd finally find a woman who could love me for me and you thought you were finally free of the burdens of having a husband. And if that isn't enough of a twist, we have to share the names of the world's first parents. How bizarre is that?" He rose again, his shoulders drooping and he opened the hut's door.

"It was nice meeting you, Eve, but you don't need to feel any obligation to me. I'll have a few words with the Lieutenant and then I'll find my place in this community as best I can. I appreciate your kindness in view of the shock this whole thing must be to you."

Adam glanced over at the table and nodded in the direction of the partly made garment.

"If you'd like, I would take pleasure in helping you make that. I am a tailor, after all. It's the least I can do in the circumstances. Good day, Mrs. Mohammed." With that, he stepped through the portal and quietly closed the door.

Eve watched him cut across the compound toward the science buildings and she heaved a sigh. He was an interesting man. She would pray for him and hope that God would help him settle into the community with ease.

*   *   *

"Isabella, I can understand you're hurt and angry. But have you considered that maybe God has brought you here to help us in his work?"

Rachel watched the new woman to gauge her reaction to her words. Isabella stood at the wooden counter in her small hut, hands clenching the handle of the teakettle. Her mouth was pressed into a tight line and her eyes pierced the empty space of the compound through the open window. Rachel felt as though she was standing on uneven ground. She barely knew the woman and had no idea what her true beliefs were. Sure, she was a missionary, but that didn't mean that she was necessarily a believer in Christ.

"It's a lot to take in," Isabella said. "And I don't understand why God would take me from the mission. I don't want to be married. I have work to do in India. The people there have suffered so deeply and live in such terrific bondage. How can I show them Jesus' love when I've been dropped on an island in the middle of nowhere?"

Rachel stepped over to the distressed woman and gently placed a hand on the tense shoulder, relieved that she could appeal to her desire to show Jesus' love to mankind.

"I know. Believe me—we all know what it's like to have our worlds turned upside-down. It's frustrating and trying. There are days when all of us islanders feel like glorified cattle being bred for market. But we're where we are for God's purpose and he wouldn't have allowed us to be here without a very good reason. I wouldn't be a believer if I hadn't come to the island. I guess I could go so far as to say that if I had died in Israel, I would have gone to eternal torment. God used my kidnapping to bring me his salvation. I've been blessed beyond measure because of what I could have seen as trials."

At that, Isabella turned and allowed a small flicker of curiosity to register in her expressive face, and then Rachel continued.

"My husband was torn from a loving father who believed in Jesus and taught his son well. Hawk has brought the gospel to people who were raised with religions that kept them in the same type of bondage you spoke of—or they had no religion at all. I've seen Christ move among these people who had no hope. Imagine what'll happen if this project succeeds and we're all sent into the world as believers. It'll be a new chance for Christianity, too.

"In the meantime, we can hope and pray that God will rescue us and stop *The Project* and its hideous experiments. I can't help but think that he's brought you to us to reach the many who still despair. If they can see hope in you, as one who has had so much taken away, they might believe that Christ is real."

Isabella dropped her gaze to her clenched hands and sighed.

"You are right, Rachel. I'm sometimes not very good at the faith. I think you are going be a good friend to me." She lifted her large dark eyes to her new acquaintance and smiled.

"Now tell me about this man—England—English— what's his name?"

"Yngve." Rachel returned the smile with her own brighter one.

12

THE LIEUTENANT LOWERED THE BOOK on Eastern Mysticism and leaned back in the leather armchair that graced his spacious office in the east wing of the medical complex. Hitler's diary had been useful as a brief introduction to the spiritual realm, whetting his appetite to the unseen world around him. But it wasn't enough. And so, the Lieutenant had begun the search that would bring him knowledge of the occult world and how it could be mastered.

He allowed his mind to linger briefly on some of the other things he had learned from the diary. A smirk flickered across his stiff features. The small book held some very condemning information on *The Committee*—information that he could possibly use in the future. No wonder they had refused to let it slip into the hands of the public.

Glancing down at the ancient and heavy text on his lap, he brought his thoughts back to the present and felt a brief spark of excitement. He had learned much since returning the diary to its home in *The Committee*'s secure warehouses. At present a different kind of book rested solidly on his crossed knees. Books on the New Age, finding a spirit guide, and drawing upon the powers of angels littered the desk before him.

He had studied them all, tossing the pro's and con's around in his complex mind. It wasn't a decision he took lightly. Like any of the religions, it still required a giving up of a small portion of self-control and, not being a man who liked to give up control, he had struggled hard with that. But a spiritual element was needed on the island to counteract the silly Christianity that was sweeping through the ranks of the isolated citizens, and he was willing to do what must be done to stop its weakening effects and further *The Project*.

Again, the feeling of excitement surged in his breast and he set the book aside, resolve toward this difficult decision clicking firmly into place in his intellect. It didn't matter how he analyzed it, there was a certain amount of faith involved and he knew he must be convinced of the reality of spiritism before he could continue. Digging through his emotions, he searched for that elusive substance named "belief," hoping there was enough to complete the process. There was promise of wisdom, power, a different kind of control—if only he could believe enough.

Moving from his comfortable chair, the Lieutenant settled himself on the floor and crossed his legs, as was the fashion of some of the Eastern religions. Looking from side to side, he self-consciously began the chant recommended to empty his mind of thought. It was difficult and he felt more than a bit silly. He had never emptied his mind before and wasn't sure he could. Thoughts and schemes that constantly kept his mind working struggled against the iron will power that fought to dominate them all.

His back muscles cramped slightly and he shifted to ease the distraction. The room stilled, disturbed only by the quiet single-noted hum of his own voice. One by one, each cluttered room in his mind emptied of the abstract and noisy images until he saw nothing and his whole being grew stagnant with the strange absence of awareness. The chant faded into a distant hallway and for the first time the Lieutenant experienced total nothingness.

In the office itself nothing changed. No thunderbolts struck. No furniture shifted or creaked. But there was an altering in the spiritual realm. A voice drifted from a distant dimension across the fabric of the universe and gently coaxed, whispering his name, calling to him as he drove his mind deeper into the mental vacuum. The Lieutenant heard the voice and felt a cold shock as it thundered into his barren and hollow brain. Eagerly and with desperation, he grasped at the call, relieved that the disturbing, alien emptiness of his mind had been filled.

It was a sweet, haunting voice and yet, although there was a liquid warmth to it, its center hid a coldness that could not be described. Involuntarily, the Lieutenant shivered, the action carried out by his still and senseless body like a dried cornhusk would tremble in an oncoming winter breeze.

"You are Friedrick Austerlitz, servant of my work." The voice caressed him, wrapping around him, pulling him deeper into its hypnotic timbre.

"I have chosen you to do my work. These children are mine. This race of people is for me. I have designed them through you and your scientists to fulfill my purpose. Come to me, Friedrick, and I will give you a place in the new order. Give yourself to me and I will give you the power to lead my children into their place in the world. I am preparing to enter this world and I seek a vessel into which I must pour myself. Are you to be that vessel or shall I seek another?"

The Lieutenant floated in the warm embrace of the soothing voice, feeling the tug of its enticement. He allowed his mind to believe the deception of warmth as the ethereal fingers of another being stroked his other, immaterial self, whispering layers of lies over layers of falsehoods.

"But won't I go mad like Hitler did?" He felt the concerned question leave his thoughts in a desperate desire to be convinced by the overwhelming presence. He sensed the fatherly chuckle more than he heard it, and the voice continued in its crooning.

"Hitler was foolish. He chose the path of violence. He wished to dominate and devour, as was his nature before he met me. You must choose correctly. You must desire leadership and nurturing. You must trust and follow without question. Hitler was not willing to do so. He was not able to look beyond his own selfish desires to see what I wished to accomplish in this world."

The Lieutenant paused, uncertain of his path for the first time in his life. He wavered, afraid to give up control of his own destiny. The voice waited, patiently, sending its warm waves of beguiling kindness and false peace into the Lieutenant's psyche. Visions of the new race swam before his mind's eye and in those visions he stood at the forefront of a multitude of perfect beings as the commander of a great and awesome army.

His mind stumbled back to the meetings he had endured with *The Committee,* and a sudden resentfulness rose to the surface, aided by an unseen hand. Unknown to him, the spiritual entity manipulated memories of slights and offenses until they became huge, ugly, living words of hate. The helpful advice of a companion was twisted into the criticisms of a spiteful enemy as the pathetic and lost soul within the human shell was fingered and twisted into a gnarled mass of confusion and contradiction.

In the distance, another greater, truer voice called to him. A sad voice. A voice filled with pain and longing. A voice that he didn't want to hear. It called him by name as it had done throughout his childhood. It pleaded to him to reject the lies and deceptions. It begged him to return to his younger days when God's word was read in the lichen-encrusted stone chapel in the small town in Germany. It waited then in silence as the man welcomed the cacophony of the first lie, allowing it to reverberate through his essence, drowning out the Creator's voice for all eternity.

And then his will collapsed upon itself. Nodding his head hypnotically, unaware of his physical surroundings, the Lieutenant surrendered to the Deceiver of mankind, wallowing in the newer voice as it crowed its wicked approval. He felt his very core shift as though making room for another to occupy the glove that was his own human flesh. The voice was suddenly clearer, no longer coming from outside of him, and a face of incredible beauty swam before his mind's vision.

"Well done, my friend. Well done. You chose well. It is time for you to change, Friedrick. No longer will you carry the title of Lieutenant when you interact with my children. You must befriend them. Teach them of my peace and love through your actions. They must learn to trust you and together we will eliminate the foul religion that they are clinging to."

"I will try. But who do I tell them has come to me? They hate me. What do I do to convince them?"

"Show them my love. Be gentle with them. Laugh with them. Offer them words of understanding and hope. I will come to you from time to time in your dreams. I will guide you and teach you what to say to them. When you need me, I will answer. I am god. And as I am your god, so I will be theirs. Once you have won their affections you must tell them this."

The Lieutenant felt the sudden shift once more as the being left him. The room spun into focus and he looked around, blinking, to see that all was the same. And yet all was different. As though he had walked through a door into another existence, he no longer saw the world around him through human eyes, and he inhaled the surge of energy that came with his first moment of possession as one inhales an overpowering and intoxicating fragrance. A new thought jumped into his mind and he smiled as it was accompanied by the vision of him standing before the crowd. It was time to win some hearts—and a throne.

*   *   *

"Eve! What a beautiful dress. It fits you so well. Where did you get it?" Natasha walked across the lush and verdant common area to greet her friend, a twin toddler on each hip.

"Adam made it for me." Her ebony skin hid the blush that rose to her cheeks but Natasha understood the look and grinned.

"He did a lovely job. You look beautiful."

"I feel like a cow. I don't remember being so big with Brandon."

The little boy sat on her knee enjoying the slow bouncing. Natasha tilted her head and looked at the forlorn woman shrewdly.

"Eve, there is nothing more beautiful to a man than a woman carrying a child. Believe me, I know. Charlie told me many times, and you remember how big I was." She jostled the twins as a reminder. Eve glanced down at the lovely dress and eyed the bulge that was to be her second child. She looked away, seeing nothing.

"He seems like a very nice man."

Natasha nodded, setting her boys down to play in a small sand pit nearby, and took a seat on the bench. She waited while Eve lowered her son onto a blanket spread on the ground in front of her before she answered.

"Charlie really likes him. So do half the women on the island."

Eve looked at her sharply and Natasha chuckled at the jealousy that suddenly flitted across her friend's features.

"They like him for his tailoring skills. Don't worry. He seems to only sew for the married women and never measures or tends to them alone. You're the only exception and I notice he's very careful that others are nearby. He's a man of integrity, Charlie says. We both noticed that he likes to visit you often." She grinned again and Eve dropped her gaze to the boys as they busily wrestled in the sand.

"Yes. More and more often. I'm afraid, Natasha. I'm afraid he will change. He's so nice to me, but is that really him? Will I ever be certain?" Her voice quivered with insecurity and her friend reached over and squeezed her hand.

"You are a child of God, Eve. You trust him, don't you?" Eve nodded as a tear slipped from her eye and tracked down her cheek.

"So let him guide you. Have you had many conversations with Adam?" Natasha asked. Eve just shook her head and looked down at her hands splayed across her large belly.

"No. We always sit outside. He's so nervous he doesn't say much, and I'm so cautious I don't say much. It's been months since he arrived and I don't know any more about him than I did then."

Natasha nodded sagely and rubbed Eve's shoulder.

"Doctor Natasha has just the remedy. Why don't you come for dinner next week? I'll ask Charlie to invite Adam. We'll invite some of the others and have a bonfire. This way, you'll see him in a group. It's time he was welcomed to the island officially, anyway. He's so quiet and he keeps so busy that we've never really taken the time to get to know him. In the meantime, you sit down and write out all the things you want to know about him. Pray over the list and ask God to show you those traits if he wants you to be with Adam. You'll know soon enough. God doesn't play games with our minds and hearts."

Natasha winked then, a mischievous grin plastered across her generous mouth.

"Maybe God wasn't being so subtle when he put an Adam and an Eve together on the island. Maybe you needed such a big hint, my friend. At any rate, hand it over to God and he'll tell you if you're to be the second Adam and Eve."

Eve nodded and smiled, grateful for her good friend's advice.

*   *   *

"I don't know what's happened to the Lieutenant. He's just—different."

"You don't think that he's become a Christian like the rest of them have, do you?"

"No, this is something...different. I don't understand it. He still has that creepy feeling about him. But he's become lighter—friendlier. I don't trust him. Gentlemen, we would do well to watch him."

"That goes without saying, my friend. That goes without saying."

* * *

The dinner began as an awkward affair. Both Eve and Adam sat quietly while the children dominated the adults' attention. Eve watched the three boys with a soft smile on her face as they squealed and giggled their way through the meal. Charlie and Natasha worked hard to set their two guests at ease, all the while trying to keep the boys' food in their mouths and on their plates.

On occasion, Eve would shift her eyes across the table to find Adam watching her, and then both would drop their gazes to their plates. Charlie looked at Natasha in those moments and rolled his eyes impishly. It was all his wife could do not to giggle.

The meal finally ended and Eve lifted her bulk with the intentions of helping with the clean up.

"Oh no, you don't." Charlie took her by the elbow and turned her to the front porch. "Adam, would you do me the favour of making certain this lovely young lady settles herself down out front. Natasha and I will tend to the dishes—" he glanced at the mess smeared across one end of the table,"—and the boys—and then we'll join you on the porch for some juice while we wait for the others to show up. I hope you brought your singing voice for the bonfire."

"It would be my pleasure to escort Mrs. Mohammed to the porch." The quiet rumble of Adam's voice in no way hid the intensity it held as he slipped in to take Charlie's place at her side. Eve refused to look up at him as he towered beside her, assisting her through the door and into one of the porch chairs. She felt huge.

154

They sat for some time, listening to the night sounds and trying to find something to say. Finally, Adam coughed a bit and asked his standard opening question.

"How've you been today, Eve?"

"Fine. Fine…thank you for asking. And you?" Eve wanted to groan at the lameness of her reply.

"Oh, fine. Beautiful night."

"Yes it is. God couldn't have made a prettier one." That was better, she thought. She flickered her nervous gaze in the general direction of where he sat, unsettled by the shadows which hid his face. It was frustrating that she couldn't watch him without being noticed. How else could she know what he thought?

She turned away, searching the darkness for something to focus on. She'd never been nervous with a man before. Only afraid or indifferent. The feeling was strange. She analyzed it, seeking the source of her restlessness. Adam had been a perfect gentleman all evening and she enjoyed the softness of his manner and movements. Would it be such a terrible thing to befriend such a man? A thought tugged at the corners of her mind as she contemplated the person beside her.

"What was your old life like, Adam?"

He was surprised by her sudden interest and shifted slightly in the shelter of the overhanging grasses that made up the porch roof. Eve could feel his dark eyes watching her and could sense his caution. Drawing in a breath, he began to describe his small apartment in London, England, enjoying the memories of the close-knit community he had been part of.

"I grew up in the Bahamas." He paused as he scanned the abandoned clearing, muted and eerie in the warm darkness of the tropical night. A small trace of that other life lingered in the pronunciation of his words, mixing with the stronger and more precise British tones, and Eve enjoyed the musical lilt of his speech.

"It wasn't much different than this. It feels strange to be here—like I've come home. We—my family and I—moved to England not long after the war. The place was a mess. I've never seen so much devastation. I thought we were poor in the Bahamas, but we really struggled in our new home in London. It wasn't much of a home at the time, but my mother worked hard to keep it respectable.

"I so enjoyed the street music as more and more people emigrated from the Caribbean islands to London. It wasn't easy being black in a white community and we sometimes had to face ridicule and cruelty, but my parents were hard workers and they loved the music. Once in awhile, we would sit on the balcony of our apartment in Notting Hill and the seven of us would sing hymns. We couldn't afford instruments, but God gave us voices, so we used them. People would stop on the street and listen and sometimes they would toss a coin or two.

"My mother worked as a seamstress for a wealthy family and my father worked as a street sweeper. All of us struggled hard to earn money in some way. I shone shoes, and when I didn't do that, I accompanied my mother at her work. That's how I learned to sew. My father wasn't really happy about it, but as I became good at it, he resigned himself to the fact that his youngest son would follow in his *mother's* footsteps."

Adam leaned forward in his hand-crafted chair, pulling himself from the shadows. The moon bathed his features in its pale blue light and Eve could finally see the distant gaze that accompanied the wistful words. His mind slipped back into that earlier world and she felt jealous for the memories of family and home, no matter how impoverished it had been.

"The family we worked for had three sons. One of them didn't like the idea of his clothes being made by a woman, so he hired me to do it. In exchange, he paid me a small sum of money and taught me to read. I became known around the wealthier circles as a proficient tailor for young boys and my earnings grew. In spite of our landlord, we managed to save enough to buy our small building where I opened a tailor's shop. I still had to pay for 'insurance' against the hoodlums of Notting Hill and it wasn't always easy to make ends meet. In spite of that, I continued to prosper, drawing more and more of the wealthier British clients."

Adam shifted his bulk deeper into the seat of the chair, the creaking legs breaking the brief silence. Tipping his head back he feasted his eyes on the beauty of the haunting and pervasive crescent moon surrounded by its vast collection of stars in the blackened night sky.

"One day, a few years ago, a man showed up in the shop. He was a frightening man in some ways, cold and silent, but he was drawn to my work so I tended to him without question. He said very little and always paid in cash. Who was I to complain? Once, when I was serving him, one of the neighbourhood bullies came to collect their 'rent.' The man was obnoxious and demanded I immediately tend to his affairs. When he left, my customer asked me if this sort of thing happened often. I told him it did and he simply nodded and left his purchases to follow the man."

He stopped then and a muscle twitched in his jaw as his mind brushed against thoughts and questions better left untouched.

"It was the last time I ever received a visit of that kind or a 'request' to pay for 'safety insurance.' And that is how I know the Lieutenant. I'm afraid I've never really experienced his more diabolical side before this—although I had an idea that it was there—but I can't say that I'm suffering too badly for the deception he has played on me."

There was an extended silence then and Eve tried to see into the shadows where he had retreated. After a pause, his voice reached her again with its gentle and soothing cadence.

"You must find all of this boring. I'm sorry. I didn't intend to ramble on like that."

Eve shook her head, her smile widening.

"I enjoyed it, Adam. I've never really had the opportunity to converse with a man like this and it was interesting to hear you talk of something you love so well. Tell me about England. This island is all I've ever known—with the exception of a vague memory of a hot, dusty place. Papa tells me that was Libya."

Adam looked at her questioningly.

"Your father is here?"

Eve chuckled then, the first in a long time, and it was a deep musical sound.

"Doctor Yngve Sigverd is the only father I've ever known and I've always called him Papa. He's been good to me and I love him. I was happy to see Isabella come onto the island because I've often thought he must be lonely."

"And you're not?"

The question caught Eve off guard and she looked away into the darkness, trying to hide her embarrassment as she formed her answer.

"Yes, Adam. I'm very lonely. In some ways. But God has filled my heart with so much love that I'm content with whatever he chooses for my life."

"What if he chose me, Eve?"

She looked at him sharply then, searching for duplicity and deceit and strangely hoping there was none. A small panic edged into her thoughts as she remembered the many times she had longed for her husband's love and had been cruelly rejected. Her heart suddenly began an anxious drum roll against the confines of her ribcage and the many overlapping thoughts would have overwhelmed her had she not remembered the promise that God had revealed to her in the small Bible study she attended. He had vowed to "never leave her or forsake her." That meant that he was present at that moment, waiting for her to trust him—to surrender that moment of alarm into his care. She released a tightly held breath and her face relaxed into a small smile as she offered a silent prayer of thanksgiving for God's faithful reminder.

"Then he will have to reveal that to me, Adam. And he will have to help me learn to trust. I had known Asad since I was three. I tried to love him all of my life and was scorned with every attempt. It makes one's heart hard and cautious. I have to learn to trust you and to take chances with you bit by bit if you are chosen by God. Only time will show that."

Adam rose to his feet, his six-foot frame towering over Eve as she remained seated in her chair. And then he knelt beside her, bringing his face close to hers.

"I'll be patient then, Eve. But know this. I don't believe in coincidences."

He leaned forward and placed a gentle kiss on her full lips, his finger tracing the high cheekbones of her ebony face. She closed her eyes, her heart crying for the love and attention just as the cracked and barren desert cries for rain. When she opened her eyes again, he was sitting in his chair looking up into the night sky and, as the other guests began to filter into the clearing, she wondered if she had dreamed the kiss.

13

1975 CAME IN A FLURRY OF CHAOS. Many changes overtook the varied civilizations scattered across the planet. In Spain, Francisco Franco died. His successor, Prince Juan Carlos, tried to nudge his country in the direction of democracy and moderation. France inched toward socialism while Italy went in the opposite direction. China tried to forget its bloodbath known as the Cultural Revolution and focused its attention on replacing Mao Tse-tung, author and enforcer, with another strong leader, leaving the infamous Gang of Four, led by Mao's widow, tenaciously grasping for that same power.

Communism was sweeping across not only Cuba, but Africa and Latin America, with the aid of the Soviet Union— of course. Argentina had elected a woman to head their government and Isabel Peron became the first woman in the Western Hemisphere to do so. Saigon and South Vietnam fell to North Vietnam, sounding the death knell of the Vietnam War.

And Yngve sat in his rocking chair, reading it all while his wife tended to their second son. The newspapers were scattered around the base of the handcrafted chair, a wedding gift by Hawk and Rachel. They had presented the treasure the day before the ceremony, teasing that it would serve two purposes at the same time. At his age, he could enjoy the chair himself or rock his future children to sleep in it. Yngve had loved it and the humour behind it.

He yawned, relaxed as he scanned the different articles and columns. He was shocked at how many things the island took for granted that the free world claimed had been newly invented. Chuckling, he examined the bulky and awkward computers displayed in the grainy newsprint photographs as his mind pictured the sleek and fast-moving machinery used in the offices of their own complex, supported by their own communication system.

He flipped page after page, bored with some things, surprised by others, but mostly saddened by the corruption, disease, and disasters that were sweeping the world. How fortunate they were, indeed, to be sheltered from it all, he decided as he glanced up from the American newspaper to admire his small family. Who would have thought he would have been blessed with a wife, children and a safe island to enjoy them on? He mused happily and turned his attention to the classified advertisements in the Los Angeles paper.

He enjoyed reading the messages of humanity. Some were silly. Others were naughty. But most were simply interesting. For the past year, the Lieutenant—Friedrick— had been supplying the island community with newspapers from all over the world. He had said that it was his way of showing them how horrible the societies of the planet had become and it was his reminder of their purpose on the island.

Yngve looked up again, noting the sameness of his boys' appearances. They looked like all the other children, he noted sadly. Oh, maybe not entirely. There certainly were differences in facial feature and personality, and each child was still very much an individual, but they all shared the same hair colour, eye pigment and skin tone. Gone was the beauty of diversity. Yet he knew that would change some day, too, as tribes formed and intermarried.

His mind wandered to the change in Friedrick. He was a very different man of late. There had been a spiritual experience somewhere in that man's soul, but for the life of him, Yngve didn't know what to think of it. Friedrick talked about God's will and peace and joy, but the words rang hollow. When anyone brought up Christianity or the teachings of Jesus, Friedrick's eyes glazed over and he just smiled. Sometimes he would change the subject. Other times he would listen patiently, a glassy emptiness filling the blue eyes.

Hawk had expressed concern to Yngve and the others who formed the council of Christian elders. It was rumored that Friedrick had begun to hold secret meetings with some of the islanders and that a small group of people were beginning to practice strange rituals. When Friedrick had brought the newspapers with the added comment that "it was time to broaden the community's view on religion and the world in general," Hawk grew worried and mentioned it to Yngve. But what could they do? They were, after all, still captives.

Yngve's eye wandered aimlessly across the columns of chatter, refusing to focus in on any one notation. And it was that very absentmindedness that caused him to connect two words, one beginning a note, one ending it. He stared in disbelief as a name jumped from the page to sear itself into his instantly alert brain—Carolyn Stillwater.

*   *   *

Carolyn cried for a long time, reading the classified ad over and over, believing, and yet not believing what she read. Yngve stood patiently, concern for her weighing heavily on his mind. Isabella sat beside the weeping woman, her boys playing by their feet with simple wooden blocks, and she rubbed her friend's shoulders sympathetically.

"It has to be real. But what can I do about it?"

Isabella shushed the distressed woman and tried to comfort her.

"We've sent for the others. Let's not be premature about this. We will let everyone read it and then we will all decide what can be done, *ci*?"

*   *   *

"You must contact him, Friedrick. He is not an enemy as the others have told you. The others are corrupting my world. It is time for them to be dealt with. It is time to rid the world of those who would destroy beauty and decency. You must contact him."

The Lieutenant sat in the accursedly uncomfortable position as he listened to the voice floating around the room and through his mind. With each contact, he was losing more of the detachment that had settled over him initially, and he felt each muscle pull in rebellion as he worked to keep himself still.

"But is it safe to set such an action into motion?"

"Did I not ask for your trust, Friedrick? How long have I guided you faithfully, and still you question? But I will continue to be patient with you, for I desire that my will be done. I will answer your questions to that end," the voice said. Friedrick could almost hear the impatient sigh and he cringed in embarrassment over his lack of faith. And then the voice whispered on.

"He has created the ultimate illness. It will destroy all who come in contact with it. It will pass from mankind to mankind, killing all in its path. What he does not know is that it will kill him, too. And all the evil that has corrupted the planet since the beginning will end.

"Disease will cease. Murder will end. My children will wait until the end has come, and when the animals have devoured the remains of the weak and perverted populations, you will lead the new race back into the world where you will reign over them. They will worship me through your teachings and all other religions will be dead.

"Does this not justify what must be done? Your *Committee* knows nothing. My children are pure and must not mix with the rest of the world. It is time to cleanse the world of all that would corrupt what has been made."

Friedrick's eyes glinted with the addictive and consuming narcotic called 'power.' He would be a god in this promised new world. The voice continued breathing out its evil designs, molding his thoughts and dusting away the small specks of conscience. Again, as always, he nodded his agreement, failing to acknowledge the soft chuckle that drifted through the atmosphere as the spiritual predator lusted after the millions of souls he longed to devour.

*   *   *

Carolyn,

I miss you and, through prayer, have been led to this last measure to make contact. You have been gone for so long, I despair ever seeing you again, but I continue to have faith that God will somehow lead you home from your long journey. I hope this message reaches you with its full importance. You need to talk to your dennTisT. He will help you. In the meantime, I, your mother, send you my love and remind you to trust in the God of STILLWATER.

Charlie read the note with intermingling shock and doubt and then darted his eyes around the room.

"This is really reaching, guys. I'm not sure how you're so certain after all these years that our parents are still looking for us."

"Would you give up looking for our children?" Natasha snapped at her husband and immediately regretted her harsh words. "I'm sorry, Charlie. It's a mother's heart speaking here. And mothers don't give up that easily."

Eric sat holding Carolyn while Hawk and Rachel shooed the children out into the common area to play. The small crowd of tots scampered away, squealing with pent-up energy and eager to be far from the somber atmosphere in the small hut.

"I'm certain it's Carolyn's mother. Let's look at the obvious. This is the biggest newspaper in California and Carolyn's from California," Eric said. "How many Carolyn Stillwaters could there be out there? It isn't exactly a common name, is it? This writer talks of not having seen her for a long time and mentions a journey. She sounds desperate. I think the line about the dentist is significant, although I can't really make a connection, yet."

Yngve dropped his chin into his hand and thought hard. The room was still, disturbed only by the chattering and laughter of the children as they played and the distant hum of the ever-present floatplanes.

Suddenly he lifted his head and shot a look out the window. Snatching the paper, he strode out the open door and gazed off into the distance, ignoring his friends as they gathered around him, eager to know what had grabbed his attention. He lifted the notice to scan it once more and then looked at the sky again.

"I think I have the answer." And he stalked toward the landing docks, a small crowd of adults scurrying to keep up with him.

By the time the group reached the beach, a figure was hunched over a stack of goods, straining hard as he worked to unload supplies onto the dock. He ignored the noisy approach of the group of islanders, eager to finish his job so he could grab a bite to eat in the complex's well-stocked kitchen. It was a ritual that he partook in before enduring another long flight back to wherever the next batch of supplies was to be picked up from. A guard stepped forward, rifle at hand, ready to block what he perceived as a possible escape attempt.

Yngve stopped, his forehead knotted with concentration, and he turned and marched back up the beach in distraction. The others shook their heads and followed again, hoping the scientist hadn't lost his marbles.

Finally, he sat down some distance from the plane and opened the paper again, drawing his friends around him so he could explain his agitation. The guard watched from a distance, curious about the odd gathering while the pilot continued to ignore them and finished his work.

"Carolyn, you see this strange line about the dentist?" She nodded and the others crowded in closer. "Notice the spelling of the word. The author used two 'n's and emphasized the 't's. Don't you find that strange?" Again they all nodded.

"What word do you have if you remove the 't's, Carolyn?"

Her eyes grew wide and she whipped her head around to look, once more, at the floatplane pilot. Yngve read the message again, this time without the 't's.

Carolyn,

I miss you and, through prayer, have been led to this last measure to make contact. You have been gone for so long, I despair ever seeing you again, but I continue to have faith that God will somehow lead you home from your long journey. I hope this message reaches you with its full importance. You need to talk to your dennis. He will help you. In the meantime, I, your mother, send you my love and remind you to trust in the God of STILLWATER.

"Don't you get it, people? She has somehow found Dennis and is telling us he's our contact to the free world." Yngve nearly choked on the whispered words and all of them turned to stare at the kidnapper as he began an easy saunter in their direction, his hat pulled low and his face expressionless.

14

THE LIEUTENANT WAITED CALMLY in the heat of the Middle Eastern day. It had been a long and tiring flight—one he'd had to make in the utmost secrecy—but the man was energized with the mission his spirit guide had given him. He scanned the dry and cracked desert floor, filling the vast emptiness with visions of mankind wasting away from the effects of the promised disease. He smiled, enjoying the faint echoes of that other voice as it shared in his mind's images.

A small dust storm swirled in a single spot on the horizon and he knew his ride was approaching. The military jeep could barely be seen in the obscurity of the tan cloud and the haze of the extreme temperatures warped and contorted the bit that he could see. Friedrick licked his dry lips and stepped away from the shade of the plane, knowing that this meeting would be brief and he would soon be flying back to the tropical paradise where he could continue to enjoy the bestowed blessing of godhood.

A briefcase bulging with money rested on the dusty ground by his feet and his mind was pulled back in time to another case of money that had started the chain of events that had led to this very moment. It was in times of reminiscence such as this that he missed the killing, and he savoured the memory of Hawk's kidnapper's death, tasting each detail, slowing the shifting and morphing of the man's expressions and movements as mortality sunk its bony fingers into him.

The jeep skidded to a halt, interrupting the Lieutenant's bloodlust, and a smallish man with dark skin and hair stepped from the rumbling vehicle. His military beret sat at a jaunty angle on his round dome and his eyes glittered with demented excitement. Few words were spoken between the two as the briefcase exchanged hands, and Friedrick could taste the same impatient hunger for murder in his new associate.

And then it was finished. The Lieutenant had given up much money and had only one small piece of paper to show for it. He waited for the man to climb back into the jeep and fishtail his way across the barren and thirsty terrain before he glanced down at the words that brought a chilling smile to his lips and made his mouth strangely water.

> *My Dear Lieutenant Friedrick Austerlitz,*
>
> *I was rather surprised by your call and your request. This is a very large sum of money for you to offer, however, leaving me no choice but to say yes. I must say this will definitely speed up the work of removing the world of the stench of the unfaithful so our kind will rule once again.*
>
> *The Ebola saturation shall begin with the continent of Africa. We have created a new virulent strain and it will be administered through human contact there on the continent. It should overwhelm the population within three months, rendering the continent empty. North America and Europe will be more difficult, but we have agents willing to die for the cause. They will be injected before boarding aircraft scheduled to fly to the various destinations. Once the contamination process has begun, I will await your arrival to take my people and myself to your mysterious island. No one will know until it is too late. I will wait patiently for you to tell me when the contamination is to begin.*
>
> *Your willing servant,*
> *Abrahim Sahir*

*　　　*　　　*

Dennis smiled uncertainly, his shame and guilt evident in his inability to meet their eyes. They stood under the shade of a group of palm trees, leaning or sitting with a careless ease for the guard's sake. It was fortunate for them that he had chosen to stay with the plane, leaving the pilot the freedom to join the small gathering of islanders. Dennis was the first to speak, surprising them all with his abrupt announcement.

"Let me guess. You found the message in the newspaper." He glanced uneasily at the guard. "Look, I can't talk long and we can never meet so openly again. I can smuggle similar messages out and I'll put them into the New York newspaper's classifieds. There's been a sudden increase in subscribers worldwide and I'm sure they'd be interested in anything you've got to say. But be careful. It's the best I can do."

Carolyn stepped forward and looked at Dennis strangely.

"Why are you doing this?"

Again he looked cautiously at the guard who began to crane his neck, hoping to hear the conversation. And then Dennis dropped his eyes to the sand.

"Call it an act of atonement. Look, the guard is getting antsy. What do I tell him to keep him from asking questions?"

Without warning, Isabella stepped forward and slapped Dennis across the face, following her sudden action with a long stream of rapid Italian. Shocked faces gaped at her and Dennis brought his hand to his stinging face. And then she raised her voice and switched to English, turning a little toward the guard.

"If you ever come sniffing around my hut again when I am bathing, I'll take the fire iron to you, you filthy pig! I don't know who you think you are but don't think we will forget this. I demand an apology and then I want you to get your foul stench away from us."

She crossed her arms and stood tapping an impatient toe while the silence settled around them. Yngve immediately put his arm around her and tried to look the part of the offended husband. Hawk looked away for fear his face would reveal his amusement. And Dennis dropped his head, mumbling quietly, a grin tugging at the corners of his mouth.

"Leave your message under the rock there by the tree stump. I'll get it before I fly out tomorrow." Louder, he added an apology that would soften the heart of any.

And then he turned and sauntered back to the dock, a smirk riding his lips as he flipped his gaze over to the chuckling guard.

*   *   *

They were an odd-looking couple. She was red-haired and slim, with a dimpled face that had a perpetually merry look about it. He was massive, heavy-boned and dark haired with the coffee cream skin tone of the Polynesian peoples.

Pamela was the only daughter of a traditional Scottish family who had emigrated to a sheep ranch near Mildura, Australia, before she was born. Michael was a child of the volcanic paradise of Kona, Hawaii. He disappeared during a family vacation. She was taken from her grade one school playground.

Where her genius was chemistry, his was technology. He had once managed to send a radio signal of sorts to Florida where a truck driver in Miami picked it up. It took him nearly twenty minutes just to convince the driver that he wasn't some spoiled brat playing a practical joke on him. He had stayed on the airwaves while the trucker stopped at a public pay telephone to call the police.

That phone call had triggered a series of events that Michael would never forget. According to the trucker, a police officer was on his way to meet up with the truck where he would talk with Michael. The next thing Michael knew, the police officer was on the CB radio informing the lad that he was to sign off because the driver had been arrested. And then the radio went dead. Fifteen minutes later, a security guard entered the technology wing and forcibly removed Michael from his cubical, confiscating the makeshift radio at the same time. Michael was never allowed into the building again without an escort.

Everyone who knew him also knew that he had continued to try to make contact with the outside world. He and his family were watched constantly for fear they would some day succeed and the anonymity of *The Project* would be jeopardized. But Michael and Pamela were a resourceful couple.

*   *   *

The small band of islanders sat there, saying little, anxious about the note they had left under the stone by the tree. They had watched from a hidden vantage point above the beach to see if Dennis would check. He had. That had been in the morning and now they sat quietly, draped with a casual nonchalance around the front entrance of Michael and Pamela's small dwelling while they listened to the evening sounds that were familiar and common in the jungles of the island. After a long stretch of silence a whisper carried on the warm air currents, disturbing their inner musings.

"Do you think he'll really do it?" Charlie sounded skeptical and Natasha rubbed his shoulder to reassure him.

"I think he will," Carolyn said. She seemed certain, and Eric nodded his agreement.

"I agree with Carolyn on this. As much as I don't like what the man did, I have to say he's certainly tried over the years to make up for it. I don't know how many times I've seen him sneak candy to the children. He's brought Adam and Eve sewing stuff." Turning to Hawk, he queried, "Didn't he get you a new hunting knife?"

The native man nodded.

"I think we need to trust him on this. What's the worst-case scenario? He reveals the note and we're still stuck on the island. So what's new? It's worth the risk."

Heads nodded sagely in the concealing darkness and the silence settled around the group once more as they all fought to contain their concern and hesitant anticipation. But Yngve's mind dwelt on other things. He watched through the single open window of the hut as some of the older children talked quietly among themselves. They had offered to tend to the younger ones who slept on pallets on the floor.

Even *they* noticed the sameness of the newborn children and had commented to their parents, questioning why they all looked alike. It was time that the adults did something about it. The abomination of genetic manipulation could not continue.

Yngve cleared his throat, drawing the others' attention.

"I think it is time for us to intervene on behalf of the unborn children in the complex." He squinted through the night at the faces of those gathered and waited for their softly mumbled replies of agreement before he continued.

"As you all know, my access to the east wing is now nonexistent, but Michael has agreed that, if he can get the proper materials, he could make me a security key that would allow me to slip in at night. Hawk and Rachel, would you be willing to do some shopping—undercover, of course?"

The two looked at each other, a silent question tossed back and forth, and then nodded as he continued.

"Charlie, could you and Michael come up with a list of the things I would need to gain access to that wing?"

Charles Wong had waited patiently for the conversation to turn in his direction and he smiled knowingly.

"We could, but it might be simpler than you think. In the office where they have me working there's a supply cabinet. I happen to know a way into that cabinet, and it holds the unprogrammed plastic keys for the new computerized locks. It would take some time, but if Michael could find me a computer, I could probably figure out the access codes for the east wing and duplicate one."

He then turned to his host and asked, "Mike, could you do it? I know you're watched and all, but is there any way you could get me to a computer with the right programs?"

Michael smiled and squeezed his wife's hand.

"I can do one better. Since my little run-in with the radio years ago, I've gone underground—so to speak. What the meatheads don't know is that I've created a full system right here in my own little home. Over the years, as the new technology came in or as I created it for them, I always made sure there was a backup. No one questioned it because I always told them the parts were to be stored in case they were needed as replacements." He then looked at the floor and grinned.

"No one ever suspects a woman when things disappear, do they Pamela?"

All eyes turned to Michael's impish wife.

"You got that right, love. They always think I'm being such a good wife when I come in to bring Mike lollies. And I always make such a show of affection that it makes the other workers nervous. They turn away. I've gotten pretty good at slight of hand, haven't I, love?" She planted a mushy kiss on Michael's lips while all present turned to look elsewhere. After a full minute of intense kissing, she sat back and scanned the room with satisfaction.

"See? You all looked away. I rest my case."

Michael rose and entered the hut, holding a finger to his lips to indicate silence to the older children. Dismissing the small pack of babysitters, the adults waited until the group sauntered out into the night before following the large Hawaiian into his home.

He waited patiently and then closed the door behind them, motioning for them to stand by one wall. He then removed a chair from its resting place, pushing back the heavy woven matt to reveal a three-foot by three-foot square of wood. This he wiggled loose to reveal the black and gaping maw of a tunnel. Taking a coal oil lamp, he motioned for the others to follow him as he squirmed through the entrance and lowered himself down the ladder.

*   *   *

> *Mom,*
>
> *I read your notice with great joy and wanted you to know that all is well with us.*
>
> *Thirty-five years is a long time to wait, but the years will seem like a blink when I come to visit you. Keep praying for us and hopefully we will find the right path home.*
>
> *Love STILLWATER*

Janet Stillwater-Gray Bear's old heart fluttered with excitement as she read the response to the notice she had placed in the newspaper. It had been the pilot's idea and she couldn't help but feel cautious. What if it was a trap to find out how much she knew? She dropped her chin and muttered a short prayer for God's divine protection, and then rose from her lounge chair.

"Andrew...Andrew come here! We have an answer!" And while her new husband scanned the small reply, Janet bustled to the phone and placed her first call in what had become a worldwide telephone chain.

*   *   *

"I still don't know how you can say this is authentic." The voice was strained and angry. Janet Stillwater-Gray Bear and her husband, Andrew, understood the emotion and doubt behind it. Once again, the gathering of parents had been orchestrated, this time without Janet's financial backing. It hadn't been necessary. Upon hearing that Carolyn had made contact, most of the parents were more than willing to scrape together the necessary funds in order to purchase their own passage.

Andrew stood and waited patiently for the agitated murmurings to die down.

"I can understand your doubts," he said. "It's an amazing answer to our prayers."

"How can you say that?" another cut in, "We've prayed, too, and gotten nothing!"

Andrew smiled and begged the indulgence of those who had assembled. He opened his worn and battered Bible and cleared his throat again.

"Please people, bear with me while I read for a moment. 1 Kings 18: 16-40 says:

> *'So Obadiah went to meet Ahab and told him, and Ahab went to meet Elijah. When he saw Elijah, he said to him, "Is that you, you troubler of Israel?"*
>
> *"I have not made trouble for Israel," Elijah replied. "But you and your father's family have. You have abandoned the Lord's commands and have followed the Baals. Now summon the people from all over Israel to meet me on Mount Carmel. And bring the four hundred and fifty prophets of Baal and the four hundred prophets of Asherah, who eat at Jezebel's table."*
>
> *So Ahab sent word throughout all Israel and assembled the prophets on Mount Carmel. Elijah went before the people and said, "How long will you waver between two opinions? If the Lord is God, follow him; but if Baal is God, follow him."*
>
> *But the people said nothing.*
>
> *Then Elijah said to them, "I am the only one of the Lord's prophets left, but Baal has four hundred and fifty prophets. Get two bulls for us. Let them choose one for themselves, and let them cut it into pieces and put it on the wood but not set fire to it. I will prepare the other bull and put it on the wood but not set fire to it. Then you call on the name of your god, and I will call on the name of the Lord. The god who answers by fire—he is God."*
>
> *Then all the people said, "What you say is good."*
>
> *Elijah said to the prophets of Baal, "Choose one of the bulls and prepare it first, since there are so many of you. Call on the name of your god, but do not light the fire." So they took the bull given them and prepared it.*
>
> *Then they called on the name of Baal from morning till noon. "O Baal, answer us!" they shouted. But there was no*

response; no one answered. And they danced around the altar they had made.

At noon Elijah began to taunt them. "Shout louder!" he said. "Surely he is a god! Perhaps he is deep in thought, or busy, or traveling. Maybe he is sleeping and must be awakened." So they shouted louder and slashed themselves with swords and spears, as was their custom, until their blood flowed. Midday passed, and they continued their frantic prophesying until the time for the evening sacrifice. But there was no response, no one answered, no one paid attention.

Then Elijah said to all the people, "Come here to me." They came to him and he repaired the altar of the Lord, which was in ruins. Elijah took twelve stones, one for each of the tribes descended from Jacob, to whom the word of the Lord had come, saying, "Your name shall be Israel." With the stones he built an altar in the name of the Lord, and he dug a trench around it large enough to hold two seahs of seed. He arranged the wood, cut the bull into pieces and laid it on the wood. Then he said to them, "Fill four large jars with water and pour it on the offering and on the wood."

"Do it again," he said, and they did it again.

"Do it a third time," he ordered, and they did it the third time. The water ran down around the altar and even filled the trench.

At the time of sacrifice, the prophet Elijah stepped forward and prayed: "O Lord, God of Abraham, Isaac and Israel, let it be known today that you are God in Israel and that I am your servant and have done all these things at your command. Answer me, O lord, answer me, so these people will know that you, O lord, are God, and that you are turning their hearts back again."

Then the fire of the Lord fell and burned up the sacrifice, the wood, the stones and the soil, and also licked up the water in the trench.

When all the people saw this, they fell prostrate and cried, "The Lord—he is God! The Lord—he is God!"

Andrew closed the Bible and threw his piercing gaze across the room, meeting as many eyes as possible.

"Do you not remember our last meeting? Did I not tell you to challenge your gods? Well, I challenged mine. And Janet challenged him, too. Did your gods answer you?" His voice thundered the question. "Did they?" Eyes dropped to the floor and people shifted in their chairs.

"My God answered my challenge, not because I dared him to, but because he loves all of you—and your children. He knows your hearts. He knows your doubts. He answered my prayer for your sakes. Will you now throw it back in his face? Will you reject his help and his love?" The silence stretched on. And then from the side of the room came a thick Australian voice.

"Mr. Gray Bear, maybe if you tell us a bit more about your God, it will help. I don't personally believe there is a God, but if there's a way of finding out and if it brings my daughter back to me, I'm willing to try." Andrew dropped his head momentarily, giving himself time to organize his thoughts.

"I will be as brief as possible. I'm sure you all have stories of how the world came to be. Most of those stories are likely similar to my beliefs, but some of you either have no god, as has been mentioned, or follow another. So, let's, for the moment, assume that some greater being created the world. I will call that greater being Jehovah as the nation of Israel was instructed to do thousands of years ago. According to the Bible, he made the world perfect and mankind disobeyed, bringing evil upon himself and bringing a wedge between himself and Jehovah.

"All through the Old Testament, he tried to mend the separation but our wickedness was so great that we could do nothing to gain his favour. Jehovah decided to commit the ultimate sacrifice and take on the punishment for our evil. And so he poured himself into a human form and came to earth as a baby.

"He lived thirty-some years in this world, experiencing the temptation of sin without ever giving in to it. He allowed himself to see man's predicament from the ground level and then he chose to die a cruel death, carrying the punishment of all our evil to the grave with him. It didn't end there. Jesus Christ rose from the dead three days later, proving that he was Jehovah and that he had conquered death for us.

"In his days on earth, he made many promises. He promised that if we trusted him, he would guide us and then take us to Heaven when we died. He also promised that it wouldn't be an easy path—in spite of what some of the so-called Christian teachers say. He even used the term 'take up your cross,' meaning that we would suffer as he did. But he gave us hope when he said, 'I will never leave you or forsake you.'

"This world is filled with the plague of evil, but Jehovah God is still in control. Although it was not likely his plan for us to be separated from our children, he allowed it to happen. Does he have a purpose for it? You can believe he does. We may have to wait to see that purpose fulfilled, but he does promise to be with us through the pain of it all.

"I propose one last test of faith. Do you still doubt that my God intervened when your gods didn't?" Only a few hands rose. Most sat mesmerized by the native man's boldness, determination, and confidence in his faith.

"I propose we send four notices in next week's newspaper. We will choose the four now, as a group. Then we will pray, as a group. And we will let God do the rest. Who do you propose should be the first chosen?" Andrew stepped back to allow the discussion among the hundred or so gathered there.

"I shall be!" The small man stood, his ancient frame pulled ramrod straight as he lifted his chin. "You have challenged your God, so I will challenge him too! I have prayed to Buddha these many years and he has been silent. Now I will see if your God will speak." The wealthy oriental man scanned the room with his imperious gaze, daring anyone to refute him. A quiet applause rippled across the gathered crowd and Andrew nodded.

A Russian woman stood and her anger could be felt as she threw her own challenge forward.

"I think Mr. Gray Bear should be on the list. He talks much about challenging his God but I have yet to see him send a notice." Voices muttered in agreement and again the clapping verified the decision. Andrew stepped back up to the microphone.

"I will agree to the challenge. I have one condition. My wife must also be on that list. It is her daughter who will expect the next message. Is that agreed?" The response was unanimous.

The Australian rose again.

"I think I'd like to be on that list, too, mate. I think I need a bit more proof from this God of yours, so what can it hurt?"

The choosing was complete and the voices of the great collection of diverse people were lifted to the throne of Heaven, daring God to respond, hoping he would be found by those who cautiously sought him.

In the dimensions beyond mankind's perception there was a mighty stirring and shifting of power and might, and all of the winged servants bowed low in awe before the great and awesome Creator of love as he stirred himself in response to the cry of his children.

15

HAWK SCOOPED UP THE UNOPENED bundle of newspapers shortly after they had arrived at the compound with the rest of the supplies. No one thought it unusual as he easily slung the package over his shoulder and disappeared up the trail to his home. Later, when his energetic twin sons came charging down the path, again, no one thought much of it. And one by one, as the day wore on, various adults dropped what they were doing and strolled off into the woods for a walk.

*   *   *

"Oh my gosh! There are four of them! Someone has outlined them in ink!" Carolyn's voice whispered excitedly as the group huddled around the newspaper classifieds.

"Let me see. Where did you see that? Do you think maybe Dennis did that?" Eric leaned over his wife's shoulder as he skipped past her mother's message to three others following. Yngve sat back and cleared his throat as he always did before he spoke.

"Why don't we all sit back and let Carolyn read the articles?" Reluctantly, the small group found places to settle and waited with unconcealed impatience.

> *My dear Carolyn,*
> *I was reminiscing yesterday and remembered your childhood. You were so prim and quiet and obedient. Do you remember?*
> *STILLWATER*

Carolyn looked up, perplexed, her brow wrinkled with uncertainty.

"I wasn't like that at all. Just the opposite."

Again she dropped her head and continued.

> *To the noble bird who soars across the great white north...*

"I guess that would be you, Hawk"

> *...I long to share the hunt with you when you return from your long journey. This time you must be careful not to get cut again. You roared like a GRAY BEAR when you saw the scar it left.*

Rachel giggled and everyone turned to her curiously.

"I get it, Carolyn. They are testing us to see if it's really us. If you write back that you weren't prim, she'll know it's you. Hawk has a scar in an...um...interesting place. Only his father—and his wife—would know that. What do the other two say?"

> *Venerable son,*

Carolyn continued,

> *I hope your business is running well. I always knew you would be successful in the technological world. Our temple has never been the same since your most memorable visit. I have been asked to inform you that MRS. CHANG sends her regards.*

Charlie Chang threw his head back and roared with laughter.

"Yep, that's my dad. When I was five, I stole a battery from an American diplomat's car in Beijing. We lived there near the Buddhist temple. I fed some wire—also stolen— from the battery to the temple fountain. The priest got one huge shock when he put his hand in the water. I got caned thoroughly and couldn't sit for a week. I still think it was worth it to see the old man's face when he got zapped. My father wasn't amused, though. Fortunately, the priest told no one. He was probably too embarrassed."

Chuckles circulated the room and then Carolyn read the final notice.

> *Pammy. Your sisters are fine. Your father still works with the camel rancher.*
>
> *We miss seeing you at the races. Didn't you just love the animals? Love from down under.*

"Camels?" Carolyn raised her query to the tiny Australian woman.

"Don't ask. Disgusting things." She crossed her arms and her face tightened at some distant memory.

Natasha looked around the room and scooped up a note pad and pen.

"Well people, I suggest we answer these immediately. We must word them so not to be identified by anyone but those who've written them. Who wants to go first?"

*   *   *   *

"He's up to something. He can't account for the huge sum of money pulled from *The Committee*'s accounts. He told me it was something to do with more equipment for the stem cell research but I don't buy it."

"He's changed. Perhaps someone should monitor him a little closer. Perhaps it's time to find a replacement. We can't risk the work now that it's nearing the completion stages."

A third voice broke into the conversation.

"Allow me to tend to this small interruption, gentlemen. I can keep an eye on him without risking exposure to *The Committee*."

"As you wish. Agreed by all?"

"Agreed."

*   *   *

"You have done much good for the cause, my chosen one. Your reward will be great. History will remember you as the one who saved mankind." The voice owned Friedrick and he basked in its magnetism and charm. He sent his thoughts back through the echoing channels of his mind to the voice, praising it and thanking it for the chance at greatness. And then he allowed the visions to consume him—visions of a world without corruption—visions of a world at his feet.

*   *   *

The room was packed with the same people—and yet they were changed. Gone was the doubt and anxiety as each listened to five notices being read aloud through the P.A. system at the front of the hall. Andrew and Janet sat to the side, tears streaming down their cheeks, while the woman from Russia read the responses, and they praised the God of Heaven who was showing his love and mercy to them.

Carolyn had written her terse reply and Janet had no doubt that this was her daughter writing to her.

I don't think the STILLWATERS have the right 'C.' I was a firebrand and all who knew me will attest to that. If you remember, you couldn't even keep a single pin in my hair.

Hawk's note brought a smile to Andrew's face.

To the Canadian BEAR. I enjoyed your notice a lot more than the memory it stirred. Although the scar is shaped like a smile, I wasn't happy about its proximity to a certain piece of anatomy.

Laughter reverberated around the room as the meaning was understood and all eyes turned to Andrew, who joined in, wiping at the few tears and nodding at the memory of his son slicing the skin near his groin during one of his earliest hunts. Mr. Chang stood when he heard his son's greeting.

> *To the honourable MR CHANG:*
> *I am filled with gratitude that you have written. I hope the temple master is not still angry at me for electrifying the fountain waters. I still say it was worth the caning to see the shocked—definitely no pun there—look on his face. The stealing, I very much regret, though, and the shame it brought you. Give MRS CHANG my love.*

The old man continued to stand as the tears of release beat tracks through the folds and wrinkles of his timeless face. He raised his hands to the sky and shouted in a strong voice.

"There is no God but the God of Israel and of Andrew and Janet Gray Bear!" A murmur rippled through the room at the change in the old man. And then the Russian woman wiped at her own tears and resumed the task of reading the final response.

> *Hello all. I hate camels! They smell and I'll never forget the best racer spitting on me the year before I went on my long journey. I could smell the stench of the animal's breath for days. PAM.*

Bedlam broke loose then, as all realized the truth of what had happened. People began to cry. Others dropped to their knees, lifting fearful and repentant voices to the Heavens. The gavel pounded on the podium in a vain effort to quiet the crowd.

"I have one last reading that you might find interesting. The only reason I am reading it is because it makes reference to the four children. Here goes:

> *The doctor recommends that you all be patient. CAROLYN, PAM, CHARLIE, and the bird are fine and look forward to the day when they can be reunited. We will let you know when there is news of our return. Until then, we leave it in God's hands.*"

*   *   *

"I don't know what you're talking about." Dennis' voice was strained with the fear that caused him to break out in a cold sweat.

"Come on, Mr. Gueterman, you can't hide from me. I've done my homework. I found Mrs. Stillwater."

The woman stood there, arms crossed and hip cocked, her curly red hair whipping madly in the rising coastal winds. She had been pestering him for days with little hints and probes, but this was the first time she had come right out and thrown her ferreted information at him so bluntly. He stilled, his hands freezing in the act of loading one more box into the makeshift cargo hold of the one time eight-seater float plane moored to the dock. He said it again, quieter this time, with less conviction.

"I don't know what you're talking about."

"Really? How's this for a try," she said. "I've been here for the past six months sniffing around. This particular plane, according to my research, has unlimited clearance— something bestowed upon it and its pilot from really high government levels. Somehow this thing manages to land and take-off without any notice from the local authorities and without a flight plan or any other kind of official documentation. Now, how does that work?"

She tossed her fiery hair and leaned in closer, hoping to intimidate the pilot.

"I don't dare mention what I know to anyone because I don't really feel like ending up in the looney bin like that trucker who made contact with some mysterious kid claiming he was being held captive on some island off the coast of America a few years ago—yes, I do know about that strange little incident. It was that story that led me to you, believe it or not, and I don't plan on letting it all go easily.

"So you've got yourself a war surplus airplane stripped down to the bare essentials so you can stockpile the same things month after month to deliver to who-knows-where without any interference whatsoever by every existing law enforcement and military authority in the country to the same neck of the woods as a reported island full of kidnapped kids, and I have to ask myself why."

Dennis lowered the box and whipped around to face her, clearly distressed.

"Look. What do you want from me? I can't tell you anything and I can't help you." He looked around the dock area, gauging the reaction of the nearby people, and then lowered his voice. "I wish I could help. But I can't. Just leave me alone."

He resumed his loading while she stood and watched, disapproval written across her face. She waited, shifting her weight from side to side, until he loaded the last box. And then she played her last card.

"I know you've been helping them make contact and I want to help too. Mrs. Stillwater-Gray Bear believed me when I told her that there is a way to help them get free." Dennis let out a slow sigh and allowed his gaze to wander across the leaden and shifting waves as they slapped at the overcast horizon.

"Ok. Let's pretend this whole thing is true," he said. "If—and I stress if—it were, by what you say, there's no way to get to these people without alerting the authorities. If you alert the authorities—according to your own research—they'll just bury it and you with it. So how is that going to help them? And what's in it for you?"

His penetrating eyes turned on her, cutting through the layers of professional distance to glean out the essence of the true person. She lifted her chin stubbornly, refusing to feel his intimidation.

"If I can get access to the people, I can document everything on film."

Dennis shook his head in exasperation as what she proposed registered. He turned back to his clipboard, trying to ignore the rush of words as she pushed on with her plan.

"I won't go to the authorities, but I do have a friend in the editorial offices of a pretty influential newspaper in New York who would just love a story like this. With film footage and interviews we could bypass all the security and hush-hush nonsense and get the truth to the world. As to what's in it for me—I'm a freelancer. This could be the biggest story I've ever had. What more does a writer want?"

Dennis lowered the clipboard cautiously, eyeing the eager pixyish face with suspicion.

"So you're just going to waltz onto the island, trot up to the nearest victim, shove a tape recorder in their face, ask a few questions, snap a few photos, and waltz back off the island?"

"So there is an island?" She smiled then, ignoring the sarcasm.

Dennis snapped his mouth shut into a thin, angry line. He took one last look at her, his eyes flickering over the wild, red hair, brown eyes, and freckled nose, and then he turned and began to muscle the plane's door shut.

"Look," she said, the desperation evident in her words. "I'm offering to help. I know it's a risk, but I'm willing to take it. These parents are hurting. They've never been able to give up. They know their kids have spent the last thirty years in some glorified research lab and no one should have to live with that. All I want from you is to be smuggled on and off the island. I'll even fix it so that if I get caught, they'll think you didn't know about it. What do you say?"

She threw her best puppy-dog look at him, her large, pleading eyes tugging at the soft core of his heart. Dennis stood still, his hand resting on the cargo door as he stared at the water that lapped greedily at the plane's half-submerged thirty-nine foot hull.

"I'll think about what you said."

And then he checked one last time to make certain the plane was secure and walked away, carrying the weight of one small world on his tired and sagging shoulders.

*   *   *

Jackie Fuentes had watched the plane and its pilot for a long time before she'd even considered approaching the man. All that silent vigilance was going to pay off, she reminded herself with determination. He'd been in port for almost two weeks gathering supplies from all manner of places, and she knew he would fly out soon. But not before one last load, from a cleaning supply company, was delivered to the aging algae-soaked docks.

She stalked away from the flying cargo carrier as though intending to leave the area, but instead slipped into an abandoned warehouse to wait. Jackie knew that the day before Dennis flew out Gator Cleaning Company always delivered several crates of product ranging from laundry soaps to disinfectants.

They arrived on the dock in the early afternoon—or at least they had for the past five months—and left their product to be loaded later that evening while the older pilot found a place to treat himself to the local cuisine. If she were able to slip her diminutive frame into one of those crates, no one would notice her until they were airborne. She had a hunch that once committed, this man Dennis would see her plan through.

She glanced at her watch. 11:30 a.m. Surely she had time to slip out for a bite to eat. Jackie's stomach growled an answer that she couldn't ignore. Quietly, she stepped into the open doorway, threw a furtive look toward the bobbing twin-engined Goose, its fifty feet of wing waving a silent goodbye, and made her way back to her waiting mini. She poured herself into the reliable, if tiny, vehicle and roared off down the street in hot pursuit of a sandwich.

*   *   *

Dennis watched the small woman slip from the warehouse, sneak down the far side of the abandoned street, and hop into a rusted and abused car. He stood still, blending with the shadows of the decrepit fishing trolley several berths down. He knew she was planning something, but what it was, he wasn't sure. Maybe he should speed the process up for the last load and then he could be off and away from the journalist's prying questions and determined suggestions.

The knot in his stomach tightened as he thought of the consequences if anyone found out what she knew. With only minimal hesitation, he slipped down the street to a small restaurant that hosted a public phone booth and dialed some numbers, keeping his eye on the spot where her little automobile had last been spotted.

*   *   *

Dennis worried a fingernail with his tobacco-stained teeth and mentally tried to rush the two men who were loading the last of the supplies. He scanned the silent evening shadows, searching the alley openings and empty warehouse doorways for that one slight movement of deeper darkness that indicated they were not alone. The final crate was secured and he stepped back, throwing one last glance around the decaying collection of buildings and ramps, and then slammed the cargo door shut with a metallic thud.

Pulling himself into the pilot's seat, he checked the rows of switches and buttons, confident that the trusty Goose was primed and ready for the long flight ahead. His tired body relaxed more as he revved the engines of the floating transport and directed it out into the coastal waters. And when the reliable aircraft picked up speed and began its ascent into the heavy clouds, he even smiled.

"You can come out of the box now." His voice must have sounded muffled through the layers of packing material and wood, but it carried sufficiently that he soon heard a rustling of sound coming from the tightly packed warehouse behind him. Within moments, a red mop of hair popped above the rim of an open crate hardly large enough to hold a small adult let alone the remaining bottles of disinfectant the reporter had buried herself in. It had been a precaution she had chosen to take in the off-chance that the wooden box was opened.

"How did you know?" She sounded disgusted with herself as she plopped her small frame in the seat beside him and proceeded to pick the strands of shredded paper from her hair.

"I watched you do it. You aren't very good at sneaking around, you know. How you got this far without getting caught is beyond me."

"It worked, didn't it?" She leaned back and stuffed a small wad of packing paper behind the seat.

"Only because I didn't report you to the guys loading the stuff." Dennis focused his gaze on the instruments as they guided him higher into the clouds that had settled in the sky like wads of thick wool. The cabin area was quiet for a moment and then Jackie turned her brown eyes on him.

"Why *didn't* you?"

He shrugged and settled into his seat.

"Maybe this is a better way to get rid of you. Maybe you'll end up stuck on the island, too, and no one'll ever know." For the first time, Jackie felt a quiver of fear. Who *would* know? Her brow furrowed and she dropped her eyes to the hands that held the plane's throttle steady.

"I can't believe you'd do that," she said. When silence answered her, she turned her anxious face back to the pilot's remote expression. And then the timid question followed. "Would you?"

Dennis chuckled and shook his head with a quiet "No."

Jackie sat back and waited while the older man collected his thoughts. It gave her a chance to study him more deeply, and she liked what she saw. He was tall. That was the first thing that had caught her attention when she laid eyes on him so many months ago, but she'd never had the opportunity to watch him so closely. Sitting beside him, she felt dwarfed by his size. His eyes carried a soft weariness and his hair curled into gray wisps. His face bore the lines of his fifty-nine years, but he looked fit in spite of his increasing age. And then he sighed and began relaying his decades-old tale.

*   *   *

"So telling Mrs. Stillwater-Gray Bear was an act of penance?" Jackie watched his guilt ease as he finished pouring out the years of oppression that he had been a part of.

"I guess," he said. "You need to understand that I never meant it to go so far. Once I realized who these people were—are, I knew that I couldn't help the children by trying to break it all open. I figured they'd just find a way to shut me up—like your truck driver. So..." he turned to look at her questioningly, "what now?"

"I guess I'll just climb back into the crate and hope I don't get discovered." She shrugged her dainty shoulders and fiddled with the lens on the camera she wore around her neck. "If I can get some good shots and get back into civilization again, I'll make sure the whole world knows about these people."

Dennis nodded, determination suddenly shadowing his weathered face.

"It's probably time for you to get into your hiding place, anyway," he said. "Look. You pack the stuff around you again and I'll make sure the lid is secured once we land. I'll get the guys to load the truck and I'll take the load up to the compound myself. If luck is with us and everything goes well, maybe we can get you out of the crate and into Yngve's house before anyone sees you.

"I'll warn you now. Once this plane lands and you're off-loaded, you're on your own. If you're caught, I didn't know a thing. It's the best I can do. You've got one shot at this. I'll spend the rest of the night with the plane. I'm scheduled to fly out tomorrow anyhow, but if you can get back to me earlier, we'll leave right away."

An abrupt and sober nod was Jackie's answer. She wriggled her way back into the cramped confines of the crate and pulled the packing material and the bottles of strong-smelling disinfectant around her. And then the plane dropped from the sky, skipping across the smooth surface of the ocean until it came to a gliding stop.

Jackie chewed her lip nervously as the lid was secured onto the crate, absently counting each thump of Dennis' palm as he tightened it into place. She held her breath and waited to hear the final knock of knuckles meant to let her know that she needed to be still.

From a distance, she heard the shouts of other voices, and then closed her eyes against the queasy feeling that accompanied the crate's journey to land. She was loaded, with a loud thud, into a slightly battered Deuce and a Half Cargo Transport and winced as her head cracked against the rough oak surrounding her. The container bumped and bounced for what seemed an eternity as the truck jostled its way up a rutted track. And then air—beautiful, sweet air—wafted into her little hideaway as Dennis parted the camouflage, offering a hand to hoist the battered and bruised reporter from her nest.

Night had fallen hours prior and the sky was speckled with large stars seldom seen through the haze of city life. Jackie glanced briefly around the darkened compound, wishing for her eyes to hurry the task of adjusting to the absence of artificial light. A firm hand clamped onto her arm and she was stuffed unceremoniously into the bushes beside a quaint hut, leaving the relative safety of the covered twenty-one foot idling behemoth behind her. She heard the whispered voices of Dennis, another man, and a woman, and then she was ushered quickly into the homiest little cottage she had ever seen. Her reporter's eyes consumed each detail of the simple dwelling, pleased with the meticulous work of the frame structure roofed with a thatching made of dry fern fronds and grasses.

She watched silently from the shadows of the open doorway as Dennis climbed back into the truck and pointed the vehicle toward a large collection of modern steel-sided buildings. The man was intent on delivering the rest of the Deuce's contents to their destination and, not for the first time, she felt a twinge of fear as the realization hit that she was on her own.

16

"I'VE BEEN HEARING RUMOURS."

"Oh?"

"There is talk of biological weaponry filtering through some of my contacts."

Nine men looked uneasily around the table, fear stirring them. One of the ten was missing from the gathering.

"Who has told you this thing?"

The large-boned man walked around the table, taking his time to assess the mood.

"I have my contacts."

"How do we know this isn't just a power struggle on your behalf? Any fool can see that you and the Lieutenant aren't exactly—close. Rumors are a dangerous thing for a man's career. Especially if they are wrong. We can't risk military action—or disciplinary action, either—on hearsay, my friend."

The huge man nodded, willing his facial muscles into a mask of humility.

"As you wish. My sources tell me that our old friend Abrahim Sahir has discovered a new biological weapon—as we have instructed him to do. Unfortunately, he has gone a little farther than we had hoped. The people I have been in contact with are filled with fear because Sahir is bragging about a rich backer who wants him to wipe out the earth so he can start again under the banner of religious purity. His boasts have been on a very low-key scale. After all, he is not a foolish man in that sense.

"Of course, my friends felt the need to inquire a little deeper—using a lovely narcotic that has a tendency to make a person become quite verbal. What I found most disturbing was his reference to an island full of genetically perfect people who will bring 'the faithful' to their rightful place in this new world religion of his."

The man stopped and allowed the parallels of the information to grip the handful of men encircling the boardroom table.

"Do I have this august group's permission to pursue my inquiries in a more in-depth manner?"

The show of hands left him with no doubt as to the direction he must follow.

*   *   *

The sound of a camera shutter barked its cough, rattling the stillness of the night air. Yngve gritted his teeth at the alien sound, hoping no one would hear its echo throughout the compound. He hoped this woman had enough common sense to put the thing away and duck into the bushes if any security personnel happened to pass by.

The three of them scrambled from shadow to shadow, drawing closer to another cottage that nearly backed onto the scientific complex. As the huge structure loomed closer, backlit with its own modest security lights, Jackie pulsed with excitement at the significance of what she was seeing. With each step closer, she hurriedly snapped photo after photo of the building. And then they ducked into the darkened home that was their destination.

No one kept their doors locked on the island. Had they been permitted to have locks to do so, no one would have, anyway. There was no need. So it was a shock when three shadows rattled around in the still cabin, muttering quietly under their breaths as they barked shins and various other parts of anatomy on furniture pieces hidden in the room's shadows.

Michael rose with stealth from his bed and grabbed a small chair as a weapon while his frightened wife struggled to light the lamp on the nightstand. For a moment, all activity ceased as five sets of eyes blinked against the glare of the single flame. And then Michael lowered the chair again and stared unbelievingly at the three intruders.

"What are you doing, Yngve? And who is this woman?"

The old scientist shushed his friend and whispered for him to extinguish the light. He waited until the small crowd was plunged back into the darkness, and then he answered his friend.

"Michael. Pamela. It's time." The single terse sentence, spoken in a whisper, shouted at them from the blackness, and they felt a tingle of excitement.

"This is Jackie Fuentes. She's a newspaper reporter freelancing for some newspaper in New York City. She's got a camera, Michael. We've got to get her inside."

Michael felt his way through the room, glancing uneasily toward the loft where their small crowd of offspring snored and mumbled softly in their sleep. He looked back at his wife, still huddled under the covers but recovering from the fright.

"Pammy, you've got to stay with the kids. I'll go get Hawk, and I might need Charlie's help, too." He squinted through the muted room at the three standing awkwardly. "Please, everyone, find a chair if you can. I'll be gone for a bit. Make yourselves comfortable."

Isabella coughed delicately. "Perhaps we should all turn around and allow the two of you to change first." The other two accommodated and Pamela chuckled quietly as she slipped from her bed while her husband donned some clothes. And then, after changing from her own nightclothes, she maneuvered through the room, stirring the coals in the small fireplace. Placing the kettle on to boil, she graciously turned.

"Please, have a seat. Jackie…is it? I would suggest you sit under the back window there. If a curious neighbour sees the firelight and, in spite of the late hour, feels the urge to investigate, you can slip out the window if need be." And then they watched as Michael slipped through the opened door, leaving a silent group behind him.

*   *   *

"Isabella and Pamela aren't going to be happy about being left behind."

Hawk nodded in the darkness as he and Michael slipped from cover to cover.

"They'll understand why we need Rachel to go. She understands terrain better than anyone."

"I know that and you know that—nuts! Even they know that—it doesn't mean they're going to be happy about it." They heard Rachel's soft chuckle drift back from in front of them.

"You boys let me look after Isabella and Pamela. They're reasonable woman and they *will* understand."

The three of them slipped into Michael's cozy home under the cover of the inky night. Charlie had arrived earlier after being aroused from his own deep slumber. He had left Natasha to wait and pray in their little cottage. Gone was the drowsiness and all were fully awake and ready for action, the adrenaline pumping through their veins.

Hawk would have been the natural leader for the expedition, but he, in his wisdom, deferred to Michael. In the time that had lapsed since the Hawaiian had first revealed the computer, the team had worked diligently at extending his tunnel to its conclusion behind a large clump of ferns near one of the least-used exits of the east wing. A pile of rocks gradually and conveniently grew around the small board that covered the narrow opening. It would be difficult to see it without deliberately looking, and the security personnel had better things to do than scour the shrubbery looking for tunnels.

They had used the burrow often enough in their experiments to create a passkey that would allow them to slip into the east wing unseen. Success had been a long time in coming before they were all allowed a brief peek into the forbidden hall, but then they had abandoned the entrance and the tunnel until a plan could be formed. And that was as far as the small band of rebels had been able to go. They had been unable to think of anything that would stop the genetic work or help them reach the outside world. And so the tunnel and the key had sat for weeks, patiently waiting for someone to use them. Jackie had brought with her a purpose for both.

*   *   *

Again the camera shutter whirred busily as the group spread out to explore every nook and cranny in the large laboratory. It was a stroke of luck that their key accessed that room, as well, but none of them were prepared for the horrors they found behind the innocent-looking door.

Steel tables were scattered throughout the long and narrow laboratory, filled to overflowing with an organized chaos of papers, test tubes, medical doodads and other things at home to a scientific environment. This they glanced over without so much as a second thought. It was the shelf on the far wall that immediately drew their attention and the camera lens of the red-haired journalist.

Row upon row of jars lined the sterile metal shelves. Each jar was filled with a clear solution. Each batch of solution supported and surrounded the floating corpses of children in various stages of fetal development. Yngve dry heaved at the realization of what he saw. In smaller jars, floating in the same fluid, were organs and tissue samples, dissected for the sake of *The Project* and its perverted cause.

The group abandoned all pretense of stealth as they wandered, shell-shocked and horrified, through row upon row of the lost and forgotten children. Rachel began to cry softly.

"Hawk. Some of these could be our children."

Her husband nodded, his expression grim and angry as he began to read the labels. They were numbered. Charlie grabbed a loose piece of paper and a pen and jotted down some of the numbers. Michael shook his head, clamped a hand over his mouth, and left the room. Jackie dropped her lens down, her eyes too clouded with tears to focus through her camera.

"Look here, guys." Charlie had taken the slip of paper to a massive collection of filing cabinets, matching the corresponding numbers the best he could. Grabbing a nearby instrument from off of a lab table, he pried the cabinet open and began leafing through the files until he found the right one. He pulled the file and laid it out on the table.

"Jackie, you better photo this. This child was taken from an illegal abortion in the slums of the Bahamas. They used it for stem cell research and duplication experiments—whatever that means. They call it 'cloning.' Look here. It says that, using stem cells, they were able to manipulate cells from a host specimen—the number is written down—to alleviate a potential chromosomal flaw that could lead to a neurological disease.

"Further down, it says something about duplicating the purer cells and re-introducing them into a specimen with the desired traits. Look at the bottom of the page."

Charlie stepped back and allowed the others to read the bottom paragraph on the summary report. Yngve's voice was a mere whisper, barely heard over the renewed clicking of Jackie's camera.

"Success attained. Trial fetus implanted into Mary Africa. Number 3728490 fetus has developed attachment to uterus lining and shows no signs of absorption. Extraction of uterine fluid to determine genetic stability will take place at third, fifth and seventh months. Twelfth generation mutation is complete upon birth."

"Twelfth generation?!" Hawk whispered his shock, and then the lights flickered on in the laboratory.

"That's correct. Aren't you impressed, Dr. Sigverd? What you were so unwilling to do, we have accomplished." They all swung around to stare into the cold and unfeeling face of Lieutenant Friedrick Austerlitz.

17

THE GENTLE AND ACCOMMODATING FRIEDRICK was gone, replaced by the more familiar Lieutenant they had all known for so long. In his hand was a gun, and Hawk immediately maneuvered Rachel behind himself. Jackie snapped a few more pictures, making certain to get a clear photo of the Lieutenant as he slowly advanced, a smirk riding on his aging face.

"I'm sorry, my dear, but you won't need that camera." He cocked his head to one side and looked at her closer.

"I know your face, but I'll be curious to find out how you managed to get onto the island." He looked around the vast room and smiled. "Rather impressive, isn't it?"

"What have you done with Michael?" Hawk spoke with outrage as he realized their friend was missing.

"Oh, don't worry, Hawk. He'll have a headache tomorrow but nothing more. Now, you all have a choice. You can leave the complex and return to your homes, with the exception of this young lady..." he nodded toward Jackie. "...or you can die. Personally, I would choose to go home. Stay silent. We wouldn't want the other residents to worry. Ms....Fuentes, isn't it? You can hand the camera to me and we will have a little chat about how you got here. After that, we will find you a nice place to stay, because you won't be leaving the island again."

He waved the gun toward the door, indicating the direction they should take. Yngve never moved from his spot near a large refrigeration unit. His face was white with a combination of sorrow, fear and fury. Slowly, he leaned his hip back against the bulky appliance, crossed his arms and shook his head stubbornly.

"No, Lieutenant. I don't think so. Not this time. I will die here, but not before I stop this house of horrors from continuing in its butchery."

Yngve kept his eyes steadily focused on the evil man, trying hard not to show what he had briefly witnessed seconds earlier. It had only taken a slight move of the hand for Charlie to slip the pair of long, thin-bladed tweezers into Rachel's hand. From there the woman nudged her husband, allowing him to feel the cold steel against his bare arm, but retaining her grip on it. The doctor's hope was to take the Lieutenant's focus off of the others, and it appeared to be working.

The middle-aged ex-Nazi swung the gun toward the doctor, taking several steps closer to the man as a sudden rage clouded his eyes. It was what Yngve had hoped for as the Lieutenant drew close to the collection of intruders. In that moment of inattention Rachel stumbled, dropping to her knees and thrusting upward with the improvised weapon. It plunged deep into the Lieutenant's thigh, and he yelped as he clutched at the shiny metal instrument protruding from his leg while the crafty Israeli fighter rolled clear. Hawk lunged, wrapping a meaty hand around the man's wrist, and the gun fired off a shot.

"Run, Jackie! Get that film to the free world! Go!"

Jackie didn't need Rachel's screeched commands to prod her into action. She had noticed that in the brief scuffle a small slip of folded paper had dropped from the Lieutenant's pocket, and she scooped up the small scrap from the sterilized tile floor. Wrapping her small fist around the unnoticed treasure, she took off like a rabbit, zigzagging through the tables to the open door. Behind her, she heard the crashing of metal and glass and heavy grunts as bodies locked in a fierce struggle. Her reporter's curiosity told her to look back, but her common sense and fear drove her on. The only hope she had was in reaching the safety of the darkness and the waiting airplane.

Just beyond the laboratory doorway laid the crumpled form that she recognized as Michael, and she hurdled him like a professional athlete in her scramble to the exit door. The darkness wrapped itself around her and for a brief moment she felt relief. And then a gunshot reverberated again through the night and her fear drove her faster.

The rocky path worked to impede her progress, leaving her to stumble often, but after what seemed like hours, Jackie found herself on the soft sand, her breath bellowing from her in loud gasps. Down the beach she could hear the floatplane's two Pratt & Whitneys roar to life and figured that Dennis had heard the gunshots too. The adrenaline pushed her on and she pounded onto the dock, flopping into the open cargo door with relief as another shot rang through the air and pinged off of the metallic body of the deep-hulled Goose. One final round accompanied the plane as it crept from its berth, and Jackie cringed in fear, waiting for the bullet to find its mark in her.

"Get that door shut, woman!" Dennis screamed at her as he turned the plane toward the open ocean and revved the engine. They were airborne in a heartbeat and Jackie lay there, allowing her pounding pulse to slow its rhythm, one hand cradling her precious camera, the other wrapped around the crumpled piece of paper. And then the plane lurched and she raised her head in alarm to look into the cockpit. She could hear Dennis' laboured breathing and scrambled to her feet, staggering her way toward him.

"I've been hit." He said it in such a matter-of-fact way that she wasn't sure he was serious, but when he pulled his hand from his shoulder she saw the blood.

Jackie was a woman of action, having seen much in her twenty years as a freelance journalist. She scurried back to the cargo area and pulled the first aid kit from its bracket on the ribbed interior.

"Just hold on, Dennis. Let's get the bleeding slowed down. I'm afraid you are going to be stuck with the job of flying this thing because I'm mechanically inept." He looked at her incredulously as she pressed wad after wad against the wound, holding it there with a steady hand.

Time crawled by and the man sat silently, struggling to stay alert, watching the instruments through pain-hazed eyes. Fearing he would pass out, she shoved a canteen of water at him, forcing him to sip it.

"Trust me, Dennis. You don't want me flying this thing. I had to try three times just to get my driver's license." Slowly, she eased the pressure on the wound and, reaching from behind him, lifted his shirt collar to check the blood flow.

"It doesn't look too bad."

Dennis grunted and pulled himself a little straighter, sweat beading his forehead and trickling into his jacket.

"No. I think you're right. But it hurts like you-know-what." He scanned the instruments once more and pushed the graceful bird to its full twenty-five-hundred feet.

"We can't land in Florida." He gritted his teeth as Jackie pressed more gauze into the wound and tried to secure it tightly to keep it all in place. "They'll be waiting for us. I wouldn't be surprised if there's a search plane out already. We can't stay out here. Got any ideas?"

Jackie smiled and nodded.

"Yah. Actually I do. How far are we from the Bahamas?"

"Not really that far. Why?"

"I've got a friend. Head that way if you can."

"How are we going to land? I don't have clearance. I probably won't get any, either. It wouldn't surprise me if these guys have someone waiting for us there, too."

"Don't worry about clearance. This friend has a bit of an unsavoury reputation. I went to high school with him when his family moved to America from the Bahamas. When we were done school, he moved back. He's got a private landing strip. Is there any way you can come in quietly?" She threw him an embarrassed look as she realized how silly it was to suggest that a two-engine floating tank could do anything quietly. Dennis returned the glance with a smirk.

"Your friend is a drug lord, isn't he?"

Jackie chuckled and nodded her head.

"Yah, he is...or rather, he was. He turned over a new leaf and retired. The law there leaves him alone because he has tried hard to bring money and jobs into the economy—in an honest way. What used to be a marijuana operation is now a plantation for different fruits and vegetables. He employs locals and pays them well. Most of his stuff is exported and he's finding that he enjoys the upright life. If you can keep the plane low enough to get in under any radar out there, you could probably land without too much notice."

Dennis nodded and eased the plane slowly out of the clouds until it was mere meters from the waves. He would have to keep a close eye to avoid any ships, but he could probably keep out of sight.

Time ceased as the plane droned on, and a few times Jackie had to grab the controls and ease them up. Dennis was soaked with sweat and allowed her to guide his hands while he rested his head against the seat for a few moments. And then the island came into view just as dawn eased its spidery fingers over the eastern horizon. Again, he shifted in his seat, allowing the pain in his shoulder to jolt him back to his senses.

Jackie pointed out various landmarks that would lead them to her friend's estate, hoping her guiding would keep him conscious for the few miles left. They slipped over a tree-covered hilly range, and there, like a white pencil on deep green paper, stood the runway. With some effort, Dennis activated the landing gears—and cursed as a loud rattle told him that something was wrong.

"What's the matter?" Jackie looked at the pale man with concern.

"I don't think the landing gear opened. I don't understand it. I used it not that long ago. It should have dropped, but it didn't."

"So what do we do?"

He looked at the fuel gauge and grimaced.

"We land anyway. You'd better strap yourself in, dearie, because this is about to get bumpy." Dennis slowed the plane, gritting his teeth as a steady crosswind buffeted the craft. He eased the throttle as they plunged toward earth at an unnerving rate and only felt a temporary relief as the plane bumped and jostled along the track. He worked the flaps, trying hard to slow the torpedo as it careened through the dirt at a steady angle. They plowed along the runway and he struggled to keep it steady. Smoke trailed the craft as the sand and friction combined to burn the paint from its belly, heating the undercarriage to dangerous temperatures. The pull of the sandy soil finally slowed the craft, and the injured pilot gripped the controls for one final jounce. And then the plane stopped and settled itself on one wing's stabilizing float, the dust and smoke drifting to stillness around the injured bird. Dennis killed the engine. And promptly passed out.

*   *   *

"It's foolish for you to think this is over." The Lieutenant held a cloth to his bleeding leg. The gun was back in his hand and several other security personnel stood scattered throughout the room, their own weapons drawn. Hawk nursed a bullet wound in his side—a superficial thing, but painful nonetheless—and allowed his wife to tend to it, applying pressure to stem the flow of blood. Her furious gaze cutting into them, Rachel stared at the intruders. Had they not arrived, Hawk might have killed the Lieutenant, so great was his rage over the abuse of the children, and Rachel, against her own conscience, almost wished he had, as memories of the Nazi camps with their brutality flooded her mind.

Yngve sat next to the large refrigeration unit, his head in his hands. The poor doctor was shaking with reaction and adrenaline and he pulled in breath after ragged breath to calm himself. Charlie worked hard to pull the drowsy and disoriented Michael to his feet when the Lieutenant waved his pistol once more.

"I think you all should leave the building immediately. Your reporter will soon be dead and my pilot won't be far behind her. I'll have a word with the beach sentries in the morning about their inability to shoot straight. I never thought Dennis would betray me like that, but...oh well. You never know who you can truly trust, do you?" He sighed somewhat dramatically and then smiled cruelly.

"They won't get far. Her photos will never be published. You might as well let that hope die." With one last jerk of his head, he and his thugs ushered the beaten group from the room, locking the door behind them. Five figures limped their way through the east exit, the door slamming shut after them, and they ignored the tunnel as they headed for Michael's home.

"What happened?" Pamela anxiously slipped her arm around her husband's waist and helped lower him onto the bed, staring worriedly at the clump of blood drying at the edge of his hairline. Hawk settled onto a chair and allowed his wife to wash and wrap the wound. The bullet had passed right through the flesh just below his bottom rib and they were both grateful that it hadn't connected with anything of importance.

"Let's just say we lost this round—I think." Rachel patiently explained to the two women what had happened while they fussed over their invalids. A foul-smelling brew was soon bubbling in a small pot by the fire as Yngve and Isabella prepared a poultice to fight potential infection, and then the stillness of shock settled over the group. The images of the carnage came forward in their minds and quiet whispers drifted around the room as they shared in the sorrow of such a violent and evil project.

*   *   *

"You heard about the reporter?" Eve's voice carried a hint of excitement for the first time since Adam had arrived on the island, and he nodded encouragingly.

"Yes, Hawk told me about it. I'm just glad they're all right. Do you think this woman will make it back safely?" He didn't really care to go back to the known world unless Eve went with him, but he showed interest for her sake.

"I don't know. The Lieutenant is pretty resourceful." She thought on it, frowning. "But I guess the reporter must be, too. After all, she did get here, get a bunch of pictures, and get off the island. I guess we can only hope."

"Would it be a terrible thing to stay on the island, Eve?" She looked at him oddly then, surprised by the question and yet somehow expecting it or something like it. She sighed, deciding it was time to face some of her own fears.

"It's the only thing I've ever really known, Adam. I don't think I would mind staying here." She paused for effect. "But it would be nice to see London, England, sometime. And to see where a certain tailor used to work." Adam brightened, allowing hope to worm its way into his heart.

"Would it be something you would want to see alone?" His voice was quiet—probing.

"No. I don't think so." She looked through the man's thick lenses into deep brown eyes filled with longing and loneliness. "I think I would want my husband to be with me. After all, don't you think he'd make the best tour guide of his own city?" And with that, she gently reached up, slipped his glasses from off his nose, wrapped her arms around his neck, and kissed him fully.

Three children tittered mischievously as they stopped their play and watched the couple on the porch in their embrace. A mother sitting nearby glanced up from her weaving, looked in the direction of the children's pointed fingers and chuckled quietly before turning back to her work.

*   *   *

"Hey, man! How's my favourite journalist?" The thin black man pulled himself from the jeep and swaggered across the open field to the airplane. He glanced with amusement at the shredded wing float and the scored underbelly of the aircraft as the plane smoked and steamed in the humid Bahamian sun.

He couldn't believe what he'd heard over the two-way radio when his security guy reported a floatplane coming in on the airstrip. It was amazing they hadn't crashed. He was doubly amazed when he discovered the pilot had landed with a gunshot wound in his shoulder and the single passenger was none other than an old and trusted friend. He smiled warmly as she pulled herself wearily from the pile of metal, a saucy greeting already on her lips.

"You really need to do something with that landing strip, Davy." And then she wrapped the lanky man in a bear hug, relieved to be where she knew they'd be safe, and planted an affectionate kiss on the dark, bristled cheek. He smiled a crooked grin and then held her at arm's length for a moment and threw back a retort in his rich, thick accent.

"It helps if you've got wheels on the plane, girl. So tell me, what're you doing dropping from the sky into my little paradise? And with company?" His eyes flickered over to the still form being gently lowered onto a makeshift stretcher. "I'm assuming you won't be wanting a hospital visit?"

Jackie took a moment to calm herself before shaking her head.

"Davy, we need to talk. We tried to come in under the radars but I don't know if we did. If we were detected, we're cooked. It was an illegal entry." Her friend frowned and guided her to the jeep.

"I'll have my own doctor look at your friend's wound. We'll make sure he keeps it quiet. I have some pretty influential friends I can be calling on, but I think we'll be talking about this back at the house, if you don't mind."

Jackie nodded, relieved, and allowed her friend to settle her into the jeep's front passenger seat. The air was cooler than she had expected, and she leaned back and closed her eyes, allowing the breeze to play with her red curls. She could smell the sweet fragrances of growing bananas, papaya, and pineapple all mixed in with the spicy jungle scents, and she breathed deeply as her exhausted mind drifted away from her present dangers.

Following a rough and bumpy ride, they pulled up to a surprisingly small bungalow surrounded by greenhouses, gardens and patios. Behind the conglomeration of buildings was a fenced-in swimming pool, and a cluster of palm trees provided an idyllic backdrop to the overall picture.

"Come into the study, my friend. Can I get you a drink?" He poured a glass of some fruity concoction, offering it to her as she settled into a wicker chair. She shook her head and watched as he sipped from the glass and smacked his lips appreciatively.

"Lots of fruit and just a touch of bite. Now, how can I help you?"

Jackie sighed with exhaustion and looked around absently.

"You've already done more than you know just by letting us land here without alerting the authorities."

"Aw. That's nothing, Jackie. What they don't know won't hurt them, hey?" He chuckled the same throaty laugh she'd always remembered, and she smiled warmly at him. And then he grew serious.

"Jack. You know I'll always be indebted to you. If it hadn't been for you I'd be rotting in the jail now. You were the only one who believed me when I told them I didn't kill that kid. No one wanted to be bothered with a druggie." He chuckled then. "I'd probably still be dealing, too, so I'd likely have ended up in the can anyhow. I guess you can pretty much take the credit for making me an honest man all around."

He settled his long frame onto a plush chair and set his drink aside. He was so good at looking casual that many took him for a slow man. Beneath that nonchalant surface, however, lay a bright mind and an alert and shrewd character. While the rest of his body exuded a relaxed and easygoing aura, his eyes settled on Jackie's face with an intensity that would unnerve a lesser person.

"So tell me what's happening."

Jackie pulled herself straighter and returned his attention with her own weary look.

"Have you ever heard of a secret society of ten men who maneuver behind the scenes of most of the world's political leaders?"

Davy tipped his head back as though to search the ceiling for the answer.

"I've heard rumours, but nothing I ever really believed. Why?"

"It's true. They exist. And you won't believe what they've done."

Jackie poured her story out to him, starting with the truck driver, moving on to her investigations, her secret meeting with Carolyn's mother, her plane trip to the island and the discoveries there. Halfway through her monologue, her friend pulled himself into a more compact sitting position, tucking his gangly legs closer, and turning all of his concentration on her tired words. She ended her story with Dennis' mad takeoff and their low skimming flight across the ocean.

"And the rest, you know."

He unfolded himself again, slouched back against the cushions of the chair and wrapped himself in the mental processing of her information.

"Getting you off the island won't be a problem. My yacht comes and goes without too much notice. They used to search it regular times, but not any more now that they know I don't circulate in the drug world no more. This committee of yours will be expecting you to head to New York with your film, so we won't disappoint them with that. We'll wait until your friend can fly his plane again and he can be your decoy. I'll slip you into a nice little dock just south of the big apple and the rest is up to you."

"Is this going to get you into trouble? Won't they recognize your yacht?"

"You let me worry about that one, my friend. I like a challenge. You just work on getting your friend healthy again."

*　　*　　*

Three days came and went and no one heard, one way or the other, what had become of the wayward pilot and his tenacious reporter friend. The small group avoided the Lieutenant's smug glances and would have given up hope had it not been for the fiery but faith-filled Isabella.

Charlie, Natasha, Michael and Pamela had joined Yngve and his younger wife for a relaxing picnic along the freshwater pond near Hawk's and Rachel's caves. Their children splashed and frolicked in the icy cold of the spring-fed water, their riotous laughter working to penetrate the cloud of doubt and despair that had followed the small crowd for the past thirty-six hours. The adults picked at the banquet spread out on a blanket thrown across the pebble-strewn ground, and little was said.

Isabella had planned the picnic for the purpose of lifting their flagging spirits and she was growing more and more disgusted at the despondency in her friends. They weren't even trying to move on. Finally, she could take no more and, plopping a half-eaten chunk of fruit onto her wooden plate, she turned on the group with a small temper.

"You people surprise me. You talk about faith in God, but when he places a test before you, what do you do? You begin to doubt and whine because the answer isn't instant. You must not give up hope.

"In my time in India, I saw much poverty, sickness, and hopelessness. Those who grasped onto the mercy of Christ finally understood what life was really meant to be. Do you think their situation improved right away? No! For some of those young believers, it worsened. But they knew what you all don't seem to realize—that God is still in charge. And he can help us to continue to be content right where he has put us." She stopped, her arms crossed and her eyes snapping with anger, silently challenging them to contradict her.

"You are right, my dear," Yngve sighed and rose to put his arm around his wife's shoulders. "I think we need to begin to pray continuously for these two people. Why don't we each choose a time every day and pray for their souls, their safety, and their mission. We'll also, as my wife has alluded to, pray for our own contentment and submission to God's will. Do you all agree?"

Sheepish nods accompanied the idea and they dropped their heads to begin a continuous plea for the safety of the courageous pilot and journalist. As their voices gained confidence and their repentance was released, squeals of childish laughter, intermingled by the burbling of nature's happy fountain, accompanied their words to the throne of God.

*   *   *

"It appears the Lieutenant is losing his touch."

"So it would seem."

"I don't understand how the woman got on and off of the island so easily."

"I have heard that the Lieutenant's own trusted pilot is now an accomplice. His plane has completely disappeared. I don't know how, but they have managed to elude our search and rescue attempts."

"Perhaps it crashed and sank."

"We've thought of that, but there would have been debris of some sort and we've found nothing. Let's hope it's that simple and we can relax. If they have managed to escape, however, we could very well be in trouble."

"I suppose we must wait and see, then."

"I suppose so."

18

"STOP MOTHERING ME!" Dennis swatted away the proffered pillow and pulled himself upright, wincing as he did so.

"I'm not mothering you," Jackie said, as an injured expression peppered across her pixy features.

"I just asked if you'd like an extra pillow. It was a gesture of kindness to a grouchy, ungrateful..."

"Ungrateful!" Dennis could feel his temperature rising. "You've got nerve. I never asked to be part of this and I certainly had no desire to get shot at by some raving lunatic."

"Oh nonsense. You know you're glad you helped and that wound is all but healed up." She plumped the pillow and offered it patiently, ignoring his grumpy expression. "And I *wasn't* mothering you, I was just being nice."

Dennis reclined on the sofa, frustrated with his weakened state. He had awakened to a lot of bandaging, stitches, and much bruising around the wounded shoulder. His arm was stiff and tender when he tried to move it, but he worked the joints anyway, ignoring the pain as much as possible. Jackie had given him a play-by-play of the events that had taken place after the landing, enjoying his reaction to the suggestion that he fly decoy while she found a way to contact the newspaper editor she knew so well.

It was actually a very good idea, but there was no way he'd admit it this soon. He was still angry with himself for not being ready when she'd hopped onto the plane, and angry with her for putting him in this position in the first place. He threw a cross look her way and saw that she had replaced the hurt with amusement at his childish behaviour.

"Ok. I'll take the dumb pillow." She tossed it at him then, smiling at his grunt when it connected with his face. "And thanks."

*　　*　　*

"It was a frayed cable that stopped the landing gear from dropping. I think that's been a long time needing repairs. There's not much we can do with the wing float and I didn't think the paint job would matter. Other than that, she's good as new." Davy wiped his greased hands with a rag. He could have asked one of his mechanics to repair the plane, but Davy was a man of action and had enjoyed the work while his new friend had recuperated.

"Is there any way you can make the plane look like you had engine trouble? If they think you been all this time on the water, they won't be looking in New York for Jack."

Dennis rubbed the bristles of his rough beard, a by-product of his forced confinement, and he nodded.

"Yah, I'll think of something. Maybe I can mix a bit of extra oil with the engine fuel just before I come in. It ought to smoke things up a bit. I'll give a mayday call an hour or so before and that'll send anyone in New York my way." He paused, a somber expression crossing his haggard features.

"Davy, I got to say I'm a little unnerved about the whole thing, though. These guys are more likely to try to make me disappear—permanently, if you know what I mean."

The black man smiled and turned his eyes on Jackie before answering.

"I don't think so, man. Show him, Jack."

Jackie pulled out a rumpled piece of paper, smoothed it open, and handed it to Dennis. He read the small paragraph, letting out a low whistle before handing the sheet back.

"Where'd you get this?"

"It fell out of the pocket of the guy with the gun. I'm assuming he's the one referred to in the letter." Dennis nodded then and turned back to Davy. Waving the paper before him he shook his head in concern.

"This doesn't surprise me. I've known the man forever and I can believe he's capable of this. So how can we use it?"

"I suggested to Jack that we copy it and send a copy of it to whoever you normally deal with," Davy said. "We'll tack on a note saying that unless you are freed, copies of these letters will go to every major newspaper and then this committee will have their hands full. We'll also make it plain that we have no desire to reveal *The Committee*'s identity, but only wish the islanders, you, and Jack to be free to live your lives without interference. What do you think of that?"

"Is there any other choice?" Jackie directed her question to her old friend, too practical for her own good. "If we stay here, you are put in jeopardy and the islanders are still prisoners. If we try it on our own, we'll disappear." She looked from one man to the other, a spark of excitement lighting her eyes. "So when do we leave?"

*   *   *

Three things happened almost simultaneously. While a floatplane was making its way across the ocean, riding low to avoid detection, a yacht of some sizable proportions was stealthily cutting through the night waters off the northeastern coast of America. Across the continent, a letter chugged its way westward, via courier, to its final destination—that being the home of a very influential man.

Somewhere in the wee hours of the New York darkness a curious editor waited on a dock for a small life raft to drift to its berth. A car was parked not far away, waiting for its driver and an unknown passenger. No one saw the motorized raft putter toward the dock, drop one of its two passengers, turn around, and continue its puttering back to the yacht. When morning came, chaos broke loose in three different states.

In California, a man of substantial proportions, both physically and financially, peeled open the courier's envelope, revealing a photocopy of a letter that immediately caused him to swear and dash for his telephone.

In Florida, an injured floatplane limped its way into the waters near Miami, announced an hour earlier by a distress call that sent the authorities—and other interested parties—scrambling to the rescue.

New York's reaction was equivalent to a declaration of war. The headlines blared a caption that no one could miss:

> ## CHILDREN WORLDWIDE KIDNAPPED
> ## FOR GENETIC EXPERIMENTS
> *See accompanying story page A2...*

The city awoke to the revelation that there was an island full of people that the world knew nothing about. The pictures were more proof than anyone would ever need. A photo of the Lieutenant holding his gun in a laboratory filled with jars holding what could be plainly seen as preserved babies filled the first page of the newspaper, and the city's citizens clamoured to buy every last paper available in order to read the rest of the earthshaking story.

Jackie's article was a masterpiece of documented research and eloquent word play. Davy sat chuckling quietly as he sipped his orange juice. His yacht cut through the water on its graceful journey back to its Caribbean home while he sat in the sun on the deck and read a hastily purchased copy of the newspaper, which had bumped another front pager in favour of Jackie's work. He was enjoying his friend's bold writing immensely and returned to the top of the article to read it through for the third time.

"One assumes that we live in a secure world where we have the right to believe what we want, live where we want, and love who we want. Not so on a small tropical island in

the mid-Atlantic Ocean. For there, amidst the beauty of the jungle paradise, is a settlement of adults, stolen from each of our planet's continents during their childhoods and raised to be guinea pigs for some perverted project to create the perfect human race.

"It was a mere coincidence that allowed me to stumble onto this heinous project, and I have one very co-operative truck driver to thank for that. A few years ago, this truck driver, who shall remain nameless, received a distress call on his radio. At first, he thought it was a practical joke, but eventually realized the caller was truthfully telling him about their situation as victims in this terrible experiment.

"The driver contacted the authorities with the hopes of helping the distressed caller, only to find himself forcefully admitted into a psychiatric hospital. Fortunately, this reporter got wind of it and made enough noise about the injustices of the justice system that, after deeper investigation, the man was quietly released.

"The whole process left me wondering what had really happened. No one should be labeled mentally unstable and committed to an asylum without intense and accurate medical assessment to back that decision. But this poor man was. Something was definitely fishy about the whole thing. And so, I began my search.

"I was appalled at what I turned up. Parents who had been searching for their children for thirty years had finally received contact through the courage of one of the island's supply pilots. The man who flew me, just three weeks ago, to that very island, was the same one who smuggled messages from the victims to their families during supply runs. When I arrived on the island, I was overwhelmed by the kindness and resourcefulness of these people who have had their lives brutally stripped from them.

"Just when we thought the world had had enough of human atrocities, I was ushered into a laboratory of unbelievable size. In that scientific playground, children were

taken and experimented on, their genetic code manipulated as their life was sucked from them. All stages of pregnancy were represented in the macabre collection of bottles lining row upon row of shelves. And just when I thought I'd heard and seen it all—horror upon horrors—it was explained to me that once the perfect human being is created, it is then implanted into the wombs of the unsuspecting wives. They aren't birthing their children, they are birthing children that shouldn't be born for a few hundred years from now, and it is an abomination to them.

"Through the courage of that same pilot, I was able to escape, my camera filled with the evidence of their sorry plight, and soon enough, he and I will fight for our own survival against a group of people who would try to decide the fate of mankind. Meanwhile, hundreds of human beings are waiting, hoping for someone to act on their behalf as they live in the tropical paradise that has, for years, been to them a prison of invasive experimentation—a place where they have been bred like so many cattle beasts. Will you help them?"

*   *   *

"This is an outrage! How could he let this happen!"

The portly man spat the words as eight other men shifted anxiously in their plush leather chairs. The large oak table shone with mirror-clarity beneath multiple layers of newsprint that lay scattered haphazardly upon the buffed surface. The article had been picked up and carried around the world within hours, and the nine men glanced at the bold captions that screamed at them in several different languages.

"It gets worse, gentlemen. Do you remember the concern about the biological warfare?" Heads nodded around the table as another gentleman rose and began to pass out a single sheet of paper to each of his associates.

"This arrived at the home of one of my contacts the same day the pilot was captured and the article was released. I think we have some serious work ahead of us, my friends. We could clean things up much like the American President fiasco back in the sixties, but I don't think that would pose well in view of the article having gone worldwide."

The men took a few moments to scan the letter and a shocked silence settled over the room. It was short and to the point, leaving them with little alternative but to meet the demands.

My Dear Lieutenant Friedrick Austerlitz,

I was rather surprised by your call and your request. This is a very large sum of money for you to offer, however, leaving me no choice but to say yes. I must say this will definitely speed up the work of removing the world of the stench of the unfaithful soour kind will rule once again.

The Ebola saturation shall begin with the continent of Africa. We have created a new virulent strain and it will be administered through human contact there on the continent. It should overwhelm the population within three months, rendering the continent empty. North America and Europe will be more difficult, but we have agents willing to die for the cause. They will be injected before boarding aircraft scheduled to fly to the various destinations. Once the contamination process has begun, I will await your arrival to take my people and myself to your mysterious island. No one will know until it is too late. I will wait patiently for you to tell me when the contamination is to begin.

Your willing servant,
Abrahim Sahir

P.S. I don't know who you are, nor do I care. I only wish for a meeting to discuss options for Dennis, myself, and the people of the island. I'm sure you can contact me at your whim so I won't bother with addresses, etc. Jackie Fuentes.

The man dropped the sheet of paper, leaving it to settle on top of the newspapers, and he dropped his head, suddenly weary with the huge task ahead.

"As you can see, we are in a bit of trouble. Does anyone offer any suggestions?"

The Chinese representative stood and searched the faces around the table.

"The people of China are not so foolish to say much to the leadership. They are too afraid, but this has affected them, deeply. They have become suspicious of their neighbours and unsettled in their work. It could lead to an uprising and we are not prepared for that."

The American stood.

"Our government officials are being bombarded with letters and phone calls to set the people free. It has rattled Congress' cage and they want to act. The President has promised to investigate the allegations made by this Fuentes woman and has pledged to prosecute those behind the experiment. She's opened a can of worms bigger than anything I've ever seen."

"Yes, I know." The man who introduced the letter to the others began to pace. "Perhaps this could end better than we might think, though. I mean, really, the woman has done us a favour in revealing the Lieutenant's interesting course of action."

The large-boned man jumped to his feet, eager to carry on the direction of the conversation.

"She has proof, as anyone with a newspaper can see, that Austerlitz was the kingpin, if we want to lean that way. It would cover our tracks. We could allow the military to rescue the people, after we cleanse the island of certain valuable specimens. The work could continue elsewhere. It could all end very nicely. As to Sahir's stockpile of nasty viruses, please allow me to handle that."

The men seated themselves again—all but the letter bearer, who continued his pacing.

"I suggest we meet with Ms. Fuentes. She will not be permitted to see us, but we'll see if this can all come out for the good. Yes?"

All heads nodded in agreement.

* * *

"You have not failed yet, my faithful one. I understand the deceit of those we should be able to trust. But my designs can still be completed. Make contact with our associate and instruct him to release the pestilence that will cleanse the world."

Friedrick sat with his eyes closed and his face still. His mind answered with an adoration of empty thought. *Yes, my lord.* And then he reveled in the exquisite feelings that always accompanied a visit from his spirit guide. Warm ethereal fingers stroked the sterile and paralyzed grey matter and his skin tingled in response. All phrenic ability ceased as creatures of diverse shapes and sizes wormed their way in and through numbed and torpid neurons. An hour passed as he communed with the overwhelming presence and then the voice whispered again.

"Enough, my friend. You must go now. Begin the destruction so we may begin the rebirth."

He awoke then from his trance, the narcotic of euphoria trailing him as he arose and dialed the phone number he had committed to memory so long ago.

"Tell Sahir that the time for the new world has come." His voice sounded distant, as though muted by the tremendous power that surged through every cell of his body. The phone clicked and a dial tone buzzed its answer. Friedrick smiled.

* * *

The prayers of the gathered rose and fell in waves of raw feeling, punctuated by an occasional tear-choked "Amen" or "Halleluiah." A woman's voice rode high above the thick emotion, carrying a single corporate petition across the crowded space of the cinderblock hall. It was a prayer uncontained by the restrictions of the building and it rose beyond the rust-spattered steel roof, through the drizzle and the mist and the low-lying clouds, through the outer atmosphere, past the stars and their velvety backdrop. This plea rose to the very feet of Jehovah and he inhaled it—embraced it in hands that had formed the first man—and smiled at its fragrance.

"Thank you, Lord, for this woman's courageous act. We lift our governments to you and ask you to stir them to action. Bring our children home. Protect them and guard them from any harm that the evil one is planning against them. We ask you to bind up the powers of Satan. We ask you to loose your angels to cover our children, our leaders, and our world with your protection. We pray that your words may be spread from one end of this globe to the other until all nations have heard of all you have done—until all peoples have been told of your sacrifice and your salvation. In the name of Jesus Christ."

A thunderous "Amen" shook the walls of the hall where the families of the victims were gathered yet again. And then someone began to sing a song of praise to God and the song picked up momentum as others joined in. Soon the hall was filled with the rich sounds of voices from across the world raised in worship, the different tongues intermingling into a single new language that only God understood.

In the spirit world, a battle erupted and darkness screamed in agony as the chains of Christ's power encased it in a mighty grip. Angels of vast numbers drew their swords and lifted them high, their perfect voices joining in song, and the celestial realms shook with the thunder of the permeating hymn of adoration. The one known to Friedrick as "the voice" covered his ears at the cacophony of sounds which burst through the multitudes of elemental layers. The small and unknowing group of believers continued in their sincere and hearty rejoicing, and he cringed as he watched the Almighty rise from the great throne and move across the face of the earth.

*   *   *

Jackie never saw the van as it drew to the curb beside her. She was enjoying a hotdog from a nearby vendor stand and nearly choked as she was dragged from the sidewalk along Time Square. Quickly, a man chuffed her unceremoniously into the vehicle's dark interior. A hood was pulled over her head and she felt two very solid bodies settle in on either side of her.

"If you kill me, those letters will be published worldwide. You'll have opened a Pandora's Box." She said it matter-of-factly, but inside, she trembled at the thought of it possibly being her last day alive.

"We wouldn't consider harming you, Ms. Fuentes. You requested a meeting. We're taking you there. The hood must stay in place or you'll die. We apologize for the inconvenience, but you must understand that the nine men—you already know the tenth—are not to be identified. Just settle back and enjoy the ride."

* 19 *

HER MIND SCREAMED at the cloying blackness. A part of her was reassured by the words of the rich voice beside her, and yet a deeper, baser instinct heightened her remaining senses, keeping her alert against duplicity. The sounds that came to her were muted through the cloth hood, and Jackie felt claustrophobic as it pushed and pulled against her face with each drawn breath.

Her journey could have been hours—or minutes. It was hard to tell based on the confused and warped sensations she experienced within the cocoon of thick, black material. She knew there was a car ride, a helicopter ride, another car ride. During all of it, the two large guards remained packed tightly against her, keeping her sheltered within a cloistering wall of muscle and bone.

She kept her hands at her sides when she wasn't clinging to the solid arms that assisted her from transport to transport. And when she thought she could take no more of the darkness, she felt herself lowered into a cold hard chair and a voice announced a new command.

"You may remove your hood."

Jackie did so, eager to breathe in fresh air and soak up the daylight. Her curious mind was disappointed upon seeing the bland cement walls that surrounded her. But her visual senses were grateful to be in use again and she blinked her deprived eyes to help them adjust to the brightness of the artificial light bulb hanging from the bland, dirty ceiling. A mirror covered the opposite wall and she knew instinctively that it was one of those two-way contraptions. *Fair enough*, she thought as she ran her fingers through her hair and straightened her jacket.

The metal folding chair that she sat upon was the only furniture in the room, its bare grey skeleton matching the peeling paint which occasionally flaked from the walls onto the rough cement floor. Rising from her rigid perch, she walked with purpose to the mirror, feeling only a bit foolish for addressing her own reflection.

"Ok. So how do we fix this mess?"

A soft chuckle echoed through the room and she looked up to the ceiling speaker above the mirror.

"I like a woman who gets down to business quickly." The Oriental accent identified the man's home continent but nothing more.

"Enough small talk," Jackie cut in. "I'm assuming this Lieutenant guy is one of your elite members and the world knows him now. How do I get what I want while you keep your identity quiet?"

"We could just kill her now, couldn't we?" Another voice floated through the speaker as though coming from a distance, and she knew he hadn't intended her to hear. There was a moment's silence, then, as Jackie stood, anger started to swirl in her chest. She said nothing, but her glare through the mirror spoke her thoughts eloquently.

"Yes, we could kill her," the first voice said. "What do you think of that, Ms. Fuentes?"

Jackie smiled a tight smile.

"You could. But if I die or disappear, that nice little letter would be opened by friends all across the globe so you would have worldwide panic on your hands and I wouldn't be around to care. Don't you think it would be easier to let the world assume that this was an isolated experiment?"

A gravelly and ancient-sounding voice answered her.

"Why didn't you release the letter to the press with your article, Ms. Fuentes?"

Jackie barked a short laugh and then turned to sit in the chair again, ignoring the grating of metal on cement.

"I'm not so cruel as to turn that onto the unsuspecting masses unless I absolutely have to. I realize that you people are going to continue manipulating the world governments long after I'm dead and gone. I can't change that. But I can, perhaps, protect Dennis and myself and hopefully allow prisoners a taste of freedom for the first time in thirty years. Is that too much to ask?"

Another silence followed and a younger voice picked up the conversation.

"This is the way it will happen, Ms. Fuentes. We will deal with the Ebola situation in our own way and the world will never know it ever existed. You'll find a way to destroy that letter and any copies of it floating around out there and you'll forget *The Committee* ever existed.

"You and your pilot will be set free to live your lives quietly. We don't care if you continue in your reporting. You are, after all, very good at it. We might even help you, from time to time, by dropping you a few tidbits of information." The voice paused. "You'll assist the various governments in finding the island and can even make a big public show of rescuing the victims.

"We'll cleanse the complex of certain necessary specimens and any condemning information that might raise questions in our direction. We'll leave anything pertaining to the families on the island for you and the pilot to sort out. Any blame will rest squarely on the shoulders of the Lieutenant, and you, the pilot, and all the others will never mention otherwise. Those who do will disappear. Are we clear?"

Jackie dropped her chin momentarily, running the directives through her mind several times before looking at the mirror again, her head tilted to one side.

"I think I won't destroy all the copies of the letter. I think that maybe that's my insurance. I'll add to any directives concerning the letters that they are to be burned upon my death—of old age, of course. You gentlemen had better work very hard at keeping me from having an accident.

"As to the silence of your existence, I think that can be arranged, but I'm going to need to get to the island before anyone else does in order to put that into action. Dennis can fly me there. There's one problem you seem to have overlooked. The Lieutenant has no reason to cooperate. He may just spoil everything."

A cold chuckle drifted through the hollow sound system.

"We'll tend to the Lieutenant, my dear. If all goes well, this time next year the families will all be reunited and we'll have disappeared from your minds. The world will be safe again and you'll be famous."

Jackie shook her head, surprised at her own response.

"No. I think I'll retire from journalism. There are some things I'm better not to know about and I'm getting too old for this kind of stuff. You people seem to get a kick out of manipulating other's lives, but I don't. I'll keep quiet for the good of the islanders and my own health, but I won't be your puppet."

"Have it your way, Ms. Fuentes. Please put the hood back on and we'll return you to your home."

Jackie slipped the hood on and waited. She heard the door open and the approach of heavy footsteps. She was half-standing when the hand clamped over her mouth and the strong-smelling fumes overwhelmed her. There was no time for struggle before the blackness swallowed her and she went limp.

*   *   *

"She's ruined everything!" The man screeched maniacally at everything and nothing. His hair stood out in all directions and his shirt was torn open and dirty, its buttons long since gone. All semblance of controlled reserve had evaporated and the Lieutenant ran through the compound, his pistol waving madly through the air around his head.

"The bloody reporter has destroyed my life's work! But she'll pay! They'll all pay! And I'll be a god at the end of it all!"

Mothers and fathers scooped their young children into their arms to shield them from the wild terror as he dashed from building to building along the compound. Small clusters of people began to gather on the outskirts of the clearing. They watched the madman with fearful curiosity as he ranted and raved through his tirade.

"I'll be your god. You will worship *me*. Just wait and see."

Friedrick stopped suddenly and looked around him with wild eyes. A small part of him acknowledged the frightened and awkward stares of the island's inhabitants and he smiled his chilling grin as the last portion of his brain attempted to regain sanity.

"Listen to me! All of you!" He turned, glaring at the small clusters of islanders spread here and there throughout the compound.

"I've released a pestilence on the world such as never before has been seen!"

He threw his head back and drew in a deep breath through flared nostrils as though scenting out the fragrance of the cruel death that would soon sweep the globe in its smothering embrace.

"In a year, you will be free to populate the world again. It will be ours. And I'll be your god. I will lead you in the new world and you won't have to rely on that pathetic and weak God of the Christian religion."

He laughed then—a shrill and nervous cackle as he watched the horror of his words seep through the crowds.

In the distance, the faint droning of turbofan engines drifted across the ocean waves and Friedrick snapped his mouth closed, cocking an ear to verify the sound. Panic

washed over his face then, and he dropped the pistol and ran
to a small lookout point that gave him a view of the recently
added airstrip needed to aid in the increasing demand for
supplies.

A Starlifter skimmed over the water toward the white
sand beach, ignoring the small dock where just weeks earlier
Dennis' smaller craft had bobbed. Friedrick watched as the
landing gear dropped from its hiding place in the cargo
plane's underbelly, allowing the one-hundred-seventy-foot
craft to glide to its resting place at the end of the asphalt strip.
The cargo door popped open like the mouth of a great
yawning beast and disgorged its camouflaged contents. Even
at a distance, the Lieutenant could see the weapons and he
patted himself down, forgetting where his pistol had gone.

This isn't good, he thought to himself. He'd been a soldier
far too long not to recognize what was happening, and he
knew he wouldn't last long if he were caught by this well-
trained crew. *The Committee* would have little tolerance for the
grasping and conniving decisions the Lieutenant had made
behind their backs. The voice whispered to him again,
reassuring him, directing him, draining every last ounce of
sanity from his battered and twisted mind. He turned and ran
back to the village, thoughts of escape driving away all others.
The pestilence would be spreading by now. He had only one
place to disappear to.

*   *   *

Yngve pulled his aging body up onto a large rock at the
edge of the clearing and made a feeble attempt to assemble
the growing crowd of his fellow islanders. His timid and
gentle voice was no match for the murmurings and rumblings
that spread like a rising tide through the compound and a
look of defeat covered his face.

He would have given up completely but a shrill whistle
pierced the afternoon air, drawing all eyes to the twenty-year-
old lad standing firmly planted in front of Yngve's perch.

Isaac, Hawk and Rachel's oldest son, pulled his fingers from his mouth, looked up expectantly at the grateful older man, and waited as a silence settled over the crowd.

"Most of you are unaware of the recent events that have caused our leader—of sorts—some distress." A nervous chuckle whispered across the gathering as Yngve's glance drifted momentarily to where the Lieutenant was last seen in his tirade.

"Some weeks ago, unknown to most of you, a newspaper reporter was smuggled onto the island in the middle of the night." He raised his hands to quiet the exclamations brought on by the revelation.

"With some help, she was able to gain access to the east wing. There, she took pictures of..." he paused and dropped his eyes to his feet "...horrible things that were done to children we didn't even know existed..." Yngve's voice drifted off as the enormity of the horrors gripped him once again and the rumblings of the crowd returned to their angry timbre, punctuating his words. And then he raised his hand to call for silence once again.

"We didn't tell you all about the incident because we didn't want to raise hopes of a rescue only to have so many people disappointed if her escape failed." He raised his eyes again and drilled into the expanding group, drawing himself to his full height with a dignity and authority which made them wait impatiently for the rest of his words.

"This reporter has succeeded in not only escaping, but she has also told the world of our existence and our need for help," he said. As one man, the crowd stilled, unsure if they had heard the doctor correctly. And then he continued on and smiles began to spread across face after face. "This is the cause of the good Lieutenant's distress. I'm not certain I understood everything he said, but I'm sure we all heard enough to realize our crazy leader has loosed something horrible upon the earth." The smiles faded again, replaced with concern and fear. The group huddled closer to the scientist's reassuring voice, hoping for direction.

"There are those among us who have been fooled by Lieutenant Austerlitz's false teachings. If you are interested in hearing the truth, feel welcomed to stay and listen. Many here will be willing to share their faith in the one true God of creation with you after I am finished. At this moment, however, I feel it wise for us to pray—and pray fervently—for the people across the world that are now in great danger. We must plead for the Creator to stop this wicked plan, whatever it may be. In so doing, we may, in the end, be reunited with our loved ones. Eric, would you lead us all in a call to Jesus?"

Yngve stepped down and allowed the German nobleman to take his place. The man stood tall, his brilliant blue eyes cutting into the heavens as though he were looking face to face with Jehovah, and his voice rang strong throughout the clearing.

"Gracious Father, we come before you to beg for help. For so long, we have asked you to bring us home to our families and have waited for these thirty years. Now you offer us a chance at freedom, and still the enemy wishes to work his evil. Lord, Almighty, we lift our voices to you now and ask for your hand of protection. You created this world and all that is in it. Will you now permit the workings of an evil and twisted mind to destroy all you have done? Will you allow your enemies to mock you? Let it never be so, oh Lord! Stand in the gap between this pestilence and your children, we beg you. In the name of your risen son, Jesus. Amen."

A chorus of "Amen's" rippled over the common and then a single child's voice lifted in a song, its purity matched by the love contained in the small heart. All who knew Jesus praised their Lord in the silence of their hearts, listening to that small musical utterance of what they all felt and knew to be true. And then, as one voice, they all joined in, the harmonies and baritones and vibratos swirling and dancing through the air around that one innocent youthful articulation.

*   *   *

"I hear singing." Dennis whispered to Jackie as they skulked behind the soldiers.

"I do, too," Jackie said and allowed Dennis to move ahead, somewhat obscuring her view of the dark figures before them. These weren't ordinary soldiers. They shifted from shadow to shadow, unseen but for the two who followed. They carried with them no military orders. No branch of any government knew they existed and the pilot and journalist nervously allowed them an ample head start.

They watched the special warriors meld into the foliage at the beach's edge, knowing that their goal was the eastern wing of the mammoth complex. Jackie and Dennis had a different mission.

"It's coming from up there." Jackie nodded in the general direction of the small community and shifted her course.

Dennis threw one last look at the plane before jogging toward the rough road that led up to the clearing, and the reporter scrambled to keep up with him. With each step along the dirt and sand track, past the many-stranded banyan trees, palms and clusters of pungent ferns, the rich sound increased. It drew the two on as though the sound had woven an invisible chord and fastened itself to them both, reeling them in upon itself.

As they approached the crest of the hill, they became aware of the large gathering of people singing their hearts out to God, and Dennis stared in awe at the size of the population. He hadn't realized it was so big, and he felt a twinge of remorse for disrupting so many lives for such a superficial cause. He cleared his throat to shift the lump that had formed, and a few people nearest them turned to look.

Mouths opened in surprise and they gaped at Dennis and a woman they had never seen before.

*　　　*　　　*

Yngve couldn't see the cause for the interruption. He only knew that the singing had slowly trickled to a stop. Eric, his face suddenly pale and stiff, leaned down and offered a hand to the doctor, sharing the rough granite podium with him, pointing his finger across the crowd. And then Yngve turned carefully on the boulder, following Eric's gesture, looked across the compound, and whooped for joy at the big smiles plastered on two familiar faces as they worked their way closer to him. With a toss of his hand, he offered an introduction to the islanders.

"Here are our rescuers now!"

The crowd cheered and clapped and Dennis felt the guilt ease away as individuals shook his hand and slapped his back. It took a good half hour to work their way through the milling people, stopping often to receive a hug or to be presented to a new face. But after some time, Jackie found herself standing beside Yngve with hundreds of expectant faces looking up at her. Tears filled her eyes at the joy she felt in seeing the hope and happiness glowing on each face, knowing she had helped put it there. At the same time, a knot twisted in her stomach at what she knew she must tell these victims, and she took a deep breath to help calm her nerves.

"Within the next twenty-four hours the island will have quite a few guests," she said. A cheer rose and more backslapping and hugging circulated around the large gathering.

"Ships will be dropping anchor off the shores of this island and soldiers will be bringing small boats ashore to load you all aboard. You will be taken to a medical facility for examination to make certain you don't carry any dangerous illnesses, and then you will be returned to your families—or what may be left of them." She paused, waiting for the ruckus to play out.

"I don't have much time to explain all of this, so I'm asking you to be quiet and patient until I'm finished. I'll then answer as many questions as I can," she said.

"I'm assuming you know this whole project was organized by a group of power brokers. Part of the conditions of your release is that you never mention it to anyone—ever. If you are ever asked, you are to reassure anyone that Lieutenant Friedrick Austerlitz was the one behind the whole project."

Jackie could almost feel the anger growing and she held her hands up in supplication and rushed on.

"We have no choice, people. If you and your children wish to live, you *must* forget there ever was a committee." She dropped her voice and scanned as many faces as her eyes could, hoping that each individual would feel the intensity of her words. "They will kill us all." The angry muttering faded to silence.

"As we speak, representatives from *The Committee* are cleansing the complex. I would recommend that you gather whatever belongings you wish to take with you and meet on the beach."

Rachel interrupted the reporter, her own voice filled with anxiety.

"Jackie, the Lieutenant just ran through here like a maniac not an hour ago screaming something about a pestilence being loosed on the earth. He's planned some way of killing everyone so our children can repopulate the world. You've got to get the word out somehow." Voices joined in worried agreement and the reporter again gestured for them to remain calm.

"I'm happy to relieve you of that burden my friends. *The Committee* reassured me that they would tend to the Lieutenant and his perverted plans. They know all about his intentions to wage biological warfare and have no desire to die themselves. In view of all they've done here..." her sweeping gesture indicated the massive buildings and the crowd before her "...I think they'll be able to keep their word."

Jackie looked up as the droning of a second Starlifter interrupted her monologue. The graceful contraption circled the island and glided in to settle itself near its twin. The crowd made room as she and Dennis quickly headed back in the direction of the beach, curiosity pulling them to the commotion on the runway below.

From the same lookout the Lieutenant had used just a brief while earlier, they watched as nurses, scientists, and technicians scrambled down the track from the complex toward the slant-winged craft which had already performed a tight turn and sat in preparation for take-off. One by one, the instigators and manipulators of the human genetic research facility were loaded into the hundred-foot-long cargo hold, each carrying their own evidence of the heinous work they had convinced themselves for years was merely a form of science. And then the four Pratt & Whitney turbofans lunged toward their five-hundred-mile-per-hour cruising speed, pulled the seventy-five ton bird back into the cerulean sky, and quickly disappeared into the higher atmospheres.

The crowd stood silently by, a strange emptiness holding each person captive while they all watched their "enemy" being spirited away. And then the silence was broken by a single voice.

"What did you mean by 'cleanse' when you were talking about the complex?"

Jackie continued to gaze over the shore as she answered.

"They will continue *The Project* elsewhere with samples they retrieved from each of you. They had them stored in a cooling unit of sorts. We haven't stopped them. We've only slowed them down."

A quiet laugh cut through the silence and Jackie turned her angry eyes on Yngve, wondering how the man could be so insensitive at such a time as this.

"How can you laugh at this atrocity?" She waved her arm again to indicate the island and all it represented. The old scientist motioned for her to calm down.

"Let me explain," he said. "Do you remember where I stood during the fight in the east wing that night? Did you notice the big unit that I was propped against? Did you not think it odd that I never once moved from that spot?"

Jackie frowned, forcing her mind back to that night.

"I seem to remember that big thing, yes." she said. "Why?"

"While you were all busy taking pictures, reading documents and distracting a certain lunatic, I activated the sterilization process in the refrigeration unit in the lab. I had a pretty good idea of what was in it, since it looked like a standard specimen storage unit." His face took on that certain stern authority that a professor adopts with a classroom of attentive students. Yngve actually clasped his hands behind his back and began to rock back and forth on his heels.

"The sterilization process heats the interior of the unit up to boiling point and keeps it there for a half hour. It then cools it automatically, leaving it sterile and ready for a new batch of samples. This sterilization process works through the use of two different chambers. The unit is cooled with liquid nitrogen, but that coolant is channeled from a secure chamber. The liquid nitrogen itself is not affected. Only the small compartment that holds the samples is sealed and heated. Once the sterilization process is completed, the compartment is reopened, allowing the liquid nitrogen to cool the chamber again." His eyes twinkled with mischief as he pulled a hand from behind him and began to examine the backs of his fingernails.

"Of course, when I say it's standard equipment, I am referring to the technology of this island, most of which the world has never seen before, so your soldiers will have no clue what it is or what it's for. They won't know that it's been tampered with unless they try to draw samples from the specimen chamber, and I can't see the soldiers trying to do that, can you?" Yngve resumed his teacher's stance and a frown wrinkled his brow.

"What I do find a bit odd is that those scientists and doctors who just left probably have hundreds of vials of useless samples. They would *have* to know that the unit has been cleansed. I must assume they haven't said anything or we'd all be subject to one more night's stay at the complex in order for them to retrieve new samples. I'm certain they must know that the test tubes they've taken with them are empty and sterilized. And they also must know that it won't make any difference what laboratory they're moved to. Except for miraculous intervention, this project is officially dead and not one of those scientists is doing anything about it."

Yngve chuckled once more, pleased with his dramatic revelation, turned his back on the speechless reporter and scampered off to find his family, leaving his friends to sort through all he had told them.

*   *   *

There used to be a secret military compound in Egypt's Western Desert. Had the government known it was there it might have been gone years before. But they didn't know. And so, for a long time, a small collection of slightly neurotic and dangerous resistance fighters had trained their extremist soldiers, made their bombs, and created their killer viruses, all under the protective covering of what looked, from the air, like a pile of rock formations, but which was, from the ground, a very secure rebel stronghold.

No one would ever know how the bombs were planted throughout the caves that sheltered these determined men and women. No one would ever discover exactly what viruses had been created or how extensive their soldiers' training had been. The world would only hear that an extremist group had blown themselves and their complex to pieces in an attempt to create a bomb of some sort. There would never be evidence to say otherwise. And the world would never know how close it came to annihilation.

20

THE SLEEK BOAT DRIFTED with the drowsy current. The man was only a few miles from shore, but far enough, he hoped, to keep out of sight. Friedrick watched the second Starlifter pick up speed as it skimmed across the asphalt, the smooth lines of the plane warped and blurred by the heat waves running parallel to the lapping salt water. Two planes had landed. Two planes had left. It should be safe for him to return to the island. They could all wait together and the people there would, some day, thank him for ridding the world of its perversions and corruptions. He would be a benevolent god to them and they would be grateful.

He smiled, his eyes glazed with the euphoria of his growing power—and something more. That which marks the presence of a human soul had become frail and feeble—almost nonexistent—and in its place was a wild and demonic look. It was as though a more intelligent and malevolent being lurked there, refusing to make itself known as it fed on the ethereal essence of spirit, and yet not quite succeeding in its effort to hide its presence completely.

The Lieutenant sat back in the small motorboat. He wouldn't admit to himself that the high-powered craft was nothing more than a toy brought to the island for his own pleasure. That would be vanity and he could not be vain if he were to be a god.

It was a fast and trim vehicle, but hardly big enough to do more than enjoy a speedy circuit of the island on a bright sunny day when the water was in one of its calmer moods. It was serving its purpose now when he needed it, however. He allowed it to drift with the ocean currents, biding his time until the activity on the island slowed and he could return to pick up the pieces of this new society.

He watched the plane until it was a mere speck in the clouds, and his mood darkened. They all thought they had won. He smiled again, reveling in his murky thoughts as they swirled through his mind. It would only be a matter of months before he could begin preparing the islanders for the adjustment of living on a much broader continent. He tipped his face to the sun, soaking in its warmth. Clasping his hands behind his head, he relaxed, allowing visions of power to wash over him.

He would take them to America first. Oh, there might be a few survivors after the plagues, but it wouldn't do any harm to allow those genetics to slip in. It didn't matter. He would be lord over them all. A thrill of excitement shot through him, and he breathed deeply.

Suddenly, thunder rumbled across the water, carried quickly on the gently lapping waves, and the Lieutenant sat upright, craning his neck around to follow the sound. A large black cloud mushroomed up from the island and he immediately knew that the complex had exploded.

Another rumble followed the first, and he watched with growing anger as orange tongues flickered into the air, consuming the east wing and spreading quickly. Even from this distance, Friedrick could see the sheet metal twisting in the intense heat as the fire tunneled through the collection of buildings, devouring all that was dry enough to ignite.

He sat, motionless, debating what he ought to do. Should he stay and let the buildings burn, or should he join the quickly growing collection of ants on the beach? He remained indecisive as he watched the ants form into a line that led from the water to the burning structure and the trees and huts surrounding it. They had formed a water brigade.

He sighed again and started the motor, angling the boat in a half-arc to return to the beach. If he didn't assist now, they would never follow him later, he reasoned, and he gunned the throttle, cutting through the deep sapphire waters toward the crescent of sand.

*   *   *

"I told you the samples were useless." The voice was a harsh whisper of anxiety.

"Shhhh! Do you want them to find out that we knew before we left the island?"

"They'd kill us."

"They may kill us anyway."

"Not if they think the samples were damaged en route."

"Can we pull that off?"

"I think so."

A pause shouted its silence in the hidden corner of the military cargo plane. And then a relieved sigh broke that silence.

"It was wrong, you know."

"Yes, I know. But did we really have any other choice?"

"There's always a choice, my friend."

"Yes, I suppose so. I think we made the right one this time, don't you?"

"Yes…yes I do."

*   *   *

The islanders were unrecognizable in their soot-blackened clothes and faces. Every move they made screamed of exhaustion, and all around the compound wisps of steam and smoke swirled into the clear and empty skies. Most of the huts were burnt to the ground, but no one was hurt, and that was all that mattered.

Yngve looked at the charred and twisted metal that had been his place of work for nearly thirty-five years, and he was surprised at the mixed feelings he experienced. The bomb had caught them all off guard and it had been a good thing the complex was empty.

The men who had set the charges had done so with expertise. The building should have contained most of the blast and the fire, but their reconnaissance had been faulty, and the soldiers weren't aware of the extra stores of fuel and solvents that were kept in a separate storage room near the laboratory. To compound it all, the island had recently endured a drier season, and at any time sparks are fickle and unpredictable things. The old scientist shook his head. It was amazing the whole island hadn't gone up in flames.

He looked around at his friends, people he'd known and raised for three decades, and his heart twisted with compassion and love. They would require so much help in order to adjust to the world again. He looked at the burnt mark on the ground where his hut had been, and then he smiled. Perhaps this was a fitting way to end this chapter of his life. He wouldn't look back.

People began to trickle up from the beach, shocked and exhausted, but proud of their part in the water brigade. One by one, they plopped themselves onto spare patches of unmarred ground and chatted quietly with those around them. Yngve suddenly realized how much he would miss all of these people, and a single tear smudged its way through the gray dust on his cheek.

"What is it, my dear?" Isabella's voice was gentle as she placed a hand tenderly on her husband's arm. He smiled at her through his tears and pulled her into a tight hug.

"We will be gone tomorrow, my dear Isabella. Who knows when we will see all these people again? I'll miss them all."

From out of the smoke and steam another familiar figure stumbled toward them and the smile faded from Yngve's face.

"I don't think I'll miss that one, though." He nodded toward the Lieutenant who had already begun to toss orders about to a few of the more rested islanders. For the most part, he was ignored, and Yngve and Isabella watched him with cautious disgust.

*   *   *

Not much rattled the Lieutenant. He was a man who was born to handle complex and difficult situations. But he had one vain weakness—he detested being ignored—and after barking the same order twice to a reclining youth, he finally reached down and grabbed the teen by his shirt collar, hauling him to his feet. The lad gagged and sputtered as the rough neckline pressed against his throat, and then the Lieutenant released him and stood waiting for him to catch his breath. He repeated his command again and the boy laughed at him and took a step away.

"You think you're in charge now, but you won't be tomorrow. They're coming to get us tomorrow. And they blame you for all of this." The boy waved his gangly arm to encompass the smoldering compound.

Friedrick's eyes flickered with uncertainty for the first time and he swiftly gripped the boy's arm.

"What do you mean? I let loose a pestilence that will kill them all. They can't come to the island. They'll kill us."

The boy laughed again and wrenched his arm free.

"They stopped your sick little plan. You're finished and we're all going home."

The teen had begun to walk away, but then he stopped and turned to face the shocked Lieutenant, anger simmering in the young eyes.

"I have grandparents and cousins that I've never even met, and you would've killed them all. I'm glad they stopped you. And I hope they make you pay." He turned again and stalked down the hill in search of his parents, leaving the Lieutenant to stand in furious silence.

*   *   *

The twins huddled in the damp cave, working hard to subdue the fear that they could almost taste. They were identical twins, but not because of the genetic manipulation. They were the last to be conceived outside the test tube and had been born exactly one minute apart. They were the perfect combination of Hawk and Rachel, and many had told them so.

Jesse was the firstborn of the two and had appropriated the dominant features of a single personality. Her lusty birth cry had all but drowned out the quieter delivery of her sister. Jilly was more introspective—a mostly subdued child, but certainly not passive by any means. Between them, the eleven-year-old girls made the personality complete. Not that they weren't individuals. But they had that connection that some twins have, and it was seldom that they were separated.

Such was the case now as they shivered together in the dim cavern beneath the island's cliffs. They were afraid—yes—but their fear was muted, subdued by each other's calming presence. These twins had that rarity of communication that only a handful could boast of. When one was sick, the other was sick. When one was angry, the other was angry. When one had an idea, it need not be voiced, for the other shared it. It was this ability to share thoughts, feelings and emotions that comforted the two.

Being Hawk's and Rachel's children didn't hurt, either. Both knew and had mastered every weapon fashioned by bare hands. Both read terrain like their mother had done at a similar age. And both knew how to use those skills to the greatest advantage. They just needed the right opportunity.

Jilly threw a disgusted look at her sister as the thought flickered through her mind that they had been tricked. She knew her sister had shared the thought with her as well as the next that followed closely behind it. *He said he was hurt and needed your help. I would have done the same thing.* Jilly threw her feelings of chagrin and embarrassment at her sister and felt the gentle and soothing touch of mental fingers as Jesse worked to reassure her. They both cautiously turned their gazes to the man hoarding the heat of the meager fire, and sensed each other's instant anger and impatience. Their parents would find them.

Again, their thoughts shifted, scanning the walls of the cave they had been forbidden to ever enter. For a brief moment, Jesse wished she had disobeyed them just once, because maybe then she would know how to escape. They sighed in unison and the Lieutenant's head snapped around to watch them. Their faces grew bland instantly, as their father had taught them. Expressions couldn't be read and interpreted if they didn't exist. Friedrick turned his face back to the fire, speaking to the flames as though it were they that needed to hear his words and not the girls sitting tied together against the stone wall.

"I wish I could say I was sorry for deceiving you girls, but I'm not. I don't really like twins to begin with. You have Dr. Sigverd to thank that you're even alive. Twins are an aberration as far as I'm concerned, and I would have drowned you both at birth if he hadn't stopped me. As far as I was concerned, you didn't benefit *The Project* with your genetics at all. But I guess you'll benefit me now, won't you?"

The twins just stared at him, struggling to conceal the horror and fear as it twisted its sharp claws into their hearts. Jesse would have eventually begun to cry, but a quiet, strong and steady prayer began to drift through her mind, and she relaxed into her sister's reassuring words. *Jesus, we're here, needing your help. This man's crazy but you're stronger than he is. Help us to trust you to rescue us. Help us to think clearly and take whatever opportunities you give us. In your name. Amen.*

*   *   *

Rachel sat on a fallen log, defeat evident in the slump of her shoulders. She had searched everywhere for the twins—thought through every possible scenario—and knew somehow that her daughters were in trouble.

253

Her oldest boys were just returning with their father from their own search and she knew by the looks on their faces that they, too, had come up empty. Where could the girls have gone? It wasn't like them to wander off without her knowledge. They had tracked the footprints through the bushes to a larger set of prints. All three trails led through the jungle to a shallow indent further down the beach where the tracks then disappeared into the water.

Isabella settled beside her and placed a comforting arm about Rachel's shoulders. She said nothing. What could be said? But the Italian missionary didn't hesitate to do what she did best. Bowing her head, she offered a silent petition for the safety of the two girls.

Salty tears clouded Rachel's vision as she fought against worst-case possibilities, and Hawk squatted before her to quiz her one more time.

"Tell me again where you last saw them."

She lifted her teary eyes to his and blinked to clear them.

"They were on the beach brigade. I wanted the four girls there so they could help without getting hurt. When the fire was out, the two were gone. I've searched everywhere, Hawk," she said, and a tremor caught her voice. "Where could they be?"

Hawk shook his head, unsettled by his wife's helplessness. He glanced over his shoulder at his four sons—all strapping young men—and called them over. Isaac and Jacob were the oldest and they shared the same kind of twin-bond as their youngest sisters. Joseph, at eighteen years, and Andrew, one year younger, dwarfed the older two. Hawk ordered them to spread through the community and inform their friends of the girls' disappearances, and the four quickly obeyed, heading off in opposite directions.

Gathering his wife into his arms, he held her tight and stroked her hair, grateful that Isabella was there to stay with her. His eyes connected with the missionary, and she shivered at the violence that brewed there. And so they waited in silence as the four boys gathered help from the citzenry of the island.

*　　　*　　　*

Joseph saw his younger sisters from a distance and jogged to catch up to them. At thirteen and fourteen years of age, Maria and Kathy were quickly budding into beautiful young ladies, and he felt an older brother's protectiveness surge up inside of him. They turned as he approached and smiled questioningly at his adornment of hunting gear. Maria was just about to tease him for caring more about hunting then the other teenage girls who flirted with him, when she noticed his somber expression. Her smile faded and her mouth snapped shut on the light comment.

Kathy was not so astute, and danced around her older brother, tugging playfully at the quiver slung carelessly over one shoulder.

"Haven't you grown out of this thing, yet?" Maria scowled at her sister, the concern deepening when Joseph didn't join in on the banter as he usually did.

"Jesse and Jilly are still missing and Dad wants to talk to you about it," he said. Kathy stilled, her eyes settled on the tall lad, and then she offered her full attention. "You'd better come with me. Mom and Dad have searched everywhere." The girls nodded then and the three headed back to the cave at a steady trot.

By the time they returned to the only home they had known since birth a sizeable crowd had gathered. Friends and fellow believers had left their own devastation, abandoning the charred patches of ground to lend aid to the family who had spiritually guided them for so long.

A small collection of men and women squatted, hand-in-hand, around the distressed mother, and the cries to a loving and caring God for help drifted on the tropical breezes. Intermingled with their heavenly conversation were male voices deep in the discussions of possibilities and strategies.

And then Hawk saw his older two daughters and son, and he went to meet them.

"I assume Joseph has told you what's happened?" His dark eyes looked fierce as he took his two girls' hands, and they shivered at this side of their father they had never before seen. "I need you to tell me when you last saw the twins. Every little detail matters. Let's go sit inside and find a quiet spot and we'll go over your morning."

The two nodded and allowed their father to lead them into the cave.

*   *   *

Jesse woke to the sound of harsh muttering, and she blinked against the dim light of the fire. Her kidnapper still squatted opposite the gyrating flames and the orange tongues flickered their eerie dance in his glazed and dilated eyes. She wasn't sure when she had drifted off to sleep, but she felt her twin shifting beside her and knew that she, too, had slumbered and was now awakening.

Scanning the cave, she took note of the receding water that gushed and crashed along a channel that ran the length of the far wall. The fire crackled near the edge of the rock shelf where they all huddled, and the Lieutenant sat between that and the water. He waited patiently, throwing a distracted glance at the churning water.

With a violent and magnetic pull, the frothing waves of the tide were returning to their home in the depths of the warm ocean, and soon the cave's entrance would open, sucking the small speedboat out of its rock confines into the open water.

Jesse continued to discreetly examine part of the cave within her vision's reach, knowing that Jilly would be doing the same. The quiet sigh from behind her told her that her twin had found no help in that view of the terrain and Jesse echoed the sigh. How would they ever get free?

The Lieutenant had secured the boat by dragging it up onto the shelf, for otherwise it would have been smashed to pieces on the rock walls of the channel. When the tide reached its lowest point the waves would be calmed enough and he would drag the small craft back into the water.

It would be dark by then, and if he could escape without notice, he would leave the twins to rot. If he was discovered, on the other hand, he'd have some insurance. Without warning, Friedrick chuckled to himself, his hold on sanity a tenuous thing as that deceptive creature within him stroked his battered and twisted mind while it tenaciously gnawed at his soul. Maybe—if he had time—he would enjoy a bit of sport with the two girls. His vacant gaze raked over them with interest. Soon the cave would open and he would see.

*   *   *

"So when Jilly headed into the jungle, we just thought she—you know—needed a break. About ten minutes later, Jesse looked at the jungle and just kind of followed her. I could show you where they went in, Dad."

Kathy looked at the woven mat that covered the rock floor of their cozy cavern home. She felt somehow that it was her fault. Her mother had told her to watch the twins and she had let them wander off. It was easier to let them do their own thing than to be constantly nagging them to behave. And she had been so busy passing buckets of water that she didn't notice for quite some time that they were missing. She and Maria had left the beach and gone looking, but when they weren't sighted right away, the two had headed for Rachel immediately and then returned to search the beach.

Looking out at the fading daylight, the teen felt the knot in her stomach harden.

"I'm sorry, Dad, I should've paid closer attention. It's my fault."

Hawk pulled his fifth child into a bear hug, his silent strength reassuring her of his love. And then he sat back and studied her face with his dark eyes.

"Tell me every little thing you can remember. Who was on the beach with you? Did anyone leave before the twins? Did they argue with anyone? Tell me everything."

*　　　*　　　*

There was no shifting of light as the final swoosh of water opened the cavern to the fresh air. The sky was as black as the small cave opening. Calming almost instantly, the water settled its tortured foaming and lapped at the lower half of the channel, mirroring the flames that continued their demented choreography across the small bundle of driftwood.

The Lieutenant puffed and panted as he dragged the streamlined craft off of its rock cradle and into the dark froth at the channel's edge. Securing it with a rope, he wiped at his sweat-beaded forehead and swung his attention to the two captives propped against the far wall.

"Don't go far ladies, I'll be back, I'm sure." His eyes were empty, but the lips bore a twisted and tight grin, and the two girls shuddered with a newer, darker fear. They watched as he stepped into the cool waves, ignoring his water-soaked pant legs. He waded deeper, pulling himself into the lightly bobbing boat, and allowed the craft to be drawn with the calmer current. He eased out of the cavern, ducking beneath a clump of stalactites, shivering under their slow shower of lime-rich water droplets. Using the safety oars, he walked them along the cave's walls, protecting the boat's outer shell from the unforgiving granite outcroppings. And then the man was gone, leaving the girls with nothing more than the meager firelight for their company.

Jilly ignored her own ropes and wiggled herself closer to Jesse, seeking out the ropes that bound her twin. After a few minutes of determined groping, she located the knot situated at her sister's wrists. Her fingers tingled with numbness, but she moved quickly, working at the bindings while Jesse waited. And then her sister was free and she could feel fingers digging at her own ropes. Soon, she, too, felt the rough hemp loosen, and then she was up and slipping along the rock wall, Jesse mirroring her movements.

We need to get into the water, fast. Jesse nodded at the unspoken command and the two slipped into the cool, murky depths, both pushing thoughts of sharks and other saltwater predators and unsavoury things from their overwrought minds. Jilly opened her mouth to call out a warning and a small wave slapped at her face. She gagged and spat at the foul-tasting surf. Without warning, a hand clamped onto the top of her head and pushed her under the lapping waves.

Normally, Jilly would have fought the hand that held her by her shiny black hair, but she relaxed, conserving her energy until she felt her lungs would burst. And just as she was about to pass out, the hand was gone and she was gasping in the fresh night air in great, huge gulps.

Before her bobbed a duplicate face, concern etched into the young features. Eyes glittered from her sister's shadowed face and she turned every which way to get her bearings. A voice snarled across the waves, bouncing and echoing from the rock cliff behind her, and she drew in another lung full of the sweet air before plunging under the black waters again.

The two girls swam hard, working to use the currents and undertows to their advantage without being sucked into the tentacles of seaweed that swayed below them. Their strokes were steady and slow, as they both had no desire to draw attention from underwater company or their captor above them.

They heard the roar of a motor nearby and stopped all movement, drifting to the surface to draw more of the sweet night air. The twins floated quietly, their faces half submerged as they watched Friedrick zigzag the boat across the rocking waves. If they didn't find a way to hide very soon, he would discover them.

Jesse slowly moved her head, looking at everything around her that was mutely revealed by the faint starlight. To their right, she could just barely make out the dark-against-dark of the cavern mouth, and she groaned inwardly at how little progress they had made. The Lieutenant had just tipped the boat's nose to cover a wider arc in their direction when the thought came to her—the tide was returning and the cave mouth would be covered again.

Under the pull of the shifting currents, she felt her sister clasp her hand. *He wouldn't expect us to return to the cave, would he?* Jilly gave Jesse a gentle tug to show that she had acknowledged the thought and together they drew in a large breath and sank beneath the surface again, struggling to take advantage of the steadily increasing movement of the water.

The pressure was incredible as the waves began to surge and tug about the two girls. They could see nothing and were at the mercy of the fickle ocean. Churning hard, they worked as a team to propel themselves with the driving tide, occasionally brushing against clusters of rocks. They worked hard to avoid the slimy swaying claw-like fronds that reached at them from the blackness below, and finally broke the surface again, panting hard to refill their oxygen-starved bodies.

From a greater distance, they heard the shout of voices and the flickering of small torches jostling along the far shoreline like drunken fireflies. The cave mouth loomed above them and the girls worked the waves hard with their limbs as one final swell lifted them and bounced them between the rocks that sheltered the small opening, pushing them into the gaping maw of gloomy blackness.

The speedboat's engine roared suddenly, revealing that the Lieutenant had been closer to them then they had realized. As the girls scrambled for the safety of the rock shelf, the droning grew distant until the only sound they could hear was the crashing and roaring of the incoming tide and the occasional snapping of the smoldering embers nestled atop the scorched rock.

21

HAWK PLOPPED HIMSELF DOWN on the cool, damp sand, ignoring the waves that lapped about his legs. He screamed then, in frustration, as the roar of the boat's engine died away with the increasing thunder of the incoming tide.

Dropping his head in his hands, he played over in his mind the piecemeal story that told him where his twin daughters were. He couldn't remember what had prodded Isabella to mention the Lieutenant's response to the young lad earlier that day, but she had. That led to the question. *Where was the Lieutenant?* And they all began to search their minds to recall when they'd last seen him.

One of the mothers in charge of the children had seen him grow angry at the lack of obedience. She had heard him talk about being a god and ruling the islanders. She had even enjoyed his look of shock when he found out that his pestilence had been stopped. And then she had watched him run down the road that led to the beach. It didn't take a lot of imagination for Hawk to put it all together. They now knew the owner of those larger footprints. And they also remembered his penchant, like a monarch of old viewing his vast holdings, for cruising around the warm waters surrounding the island in the small speedboat. Somehow, he had seen Jilly enter the jungle and taken her. Jesse would have known and followed.

He lifted his head and glared out over the water. His daughters were in that boat and he had no way of getting to them. For the first time since he was a boy abandoned on the island, Hawk allowed tears to flow unchecked. What would he tell Rachel?

He looked up to the stars as many thoughts ran through his mind. *Was this what it felt like for Rachel when her family was destroyed by the wickedness of men? How did she ever get past the doubt of a loving God's existence?* As he continued to search the velvet blackness and its glittering diamond array, he looked deep within himself, realizing that he had never truly faced persecution beyond that first week on the island.

Throwing his thoughts to the firmaments above, he cried out all the doubt and anger, pouring his heart's frustrations out to his maker, waiting, hoping for a miracle. And when the boat's engine faded into the gentle lapping of nighttime's waves, he grew silent and morose. It was the second time in his life that Hawk had felt the sting of abandonment.

He stood slowly to his feet and turned to his sons. They waited for him, their own grief written on their faces as they shifted awkwardly against the swelling waves. He shook his head in sorrow and waded out of the water, dropping his torch as he began the trek back to his home.

*   *   *

The fear was completely gone. They were alone and safe, and Jesse and Jilly took advantage of the situation to pile more driftwood onto the fading coals. The girls shivered in the dampness as salt water streamed from their clothes and hair, dreading the sticky feeling that would come as they dried.

Removing their clothing, they giggled suddenly as though it was some great adventure, and laid the articles near the fire to dry. Jilly's stomach grumbled its protest at being ignored for so long and Jesse's echoed a reply. They'd had nothing to eat or drink, and twelve hours was a long time to wait, so the two set off to explore what had been forbidden for so long.

Together, they felt their way along the smooth rock wall that arched up and over them. The room had an oblong shape to it, its ceiling arching high above them, decorated with many varied stalactites. At the far end of the cavern, a large pile of rubble disrupted the even symmetry of the smooth walls. It sat in darkness, the small fire unable to pierce the shadowed distance, and they stopped short of it, feeling uncomfortable exploring further in their unclothed state.

Returning to the warmth of the crackling fire, Jesse added more wood from the diminishing pile of washed-up branches and debris, and then she turned the clothes as one would flip an egg in a steaming fry pan.

The stone floor was cold as the two huddled down by the fire to wait. Stomachs voiced their protests one last time as the girls leaned back against one another, hoping their clothes would dry soon.

*   *   *

The water lapped at the hull of the craft as it cut its way through the water. He had gotten away. So he didn't have hostages—or playthings—but he was free to start again. He looked at the small compass and made a minor adjustment in his direction. If all worked out, he could disappear into the crowds of mankind in whatever port he landed at.

He could feel the anger building in him, and he took a calming breath, forcing his mind to plunge into the presence that soothed and comforted him. Oh yes. They would pay for ruining his plans. He would complete what Hitler had begun and the world would remember him as the next Noah—or perhaps the next Messiah.

He smiled as the smoky fingers of that other essence stroked his agitated emotions. *Be patient. All will come when the time is right. Continue filling yourself with my presence and you will reap the rewards of prosperity.* He would begin again and those fools who thought they could push him from the seat of power would suffer his anger.

*   *   *

The murmur of many voices hummed and buzzed through the night air, punctuated by the soft sounds of weeping. Prayers mixed with one another, each voice discerned by Heaven's ear. Time eased its way past the darkest hour of night and still the island community pressed on, pleading for the safe return of two young souls.

*   *   *

Jesse awoke with a start. Shivering, she licked her dry lips, groggily eyeing the tumultuous waves. She was thirsty. And cold. She sat up and turned to face the red and orange coals of the dying fire. The wood was almost gone and she was sure they still had a long wait before they could escape the cave. She shuddered as she thought of entering the water again.

Sitting up, she reached over and felt her clothing. It was still damp, but she didn't care, and she slipped into the salt-crusted garments after giving them a brief shaking out. She was stiff and sore from the mauling they had received at the hands of the tides and she stretched to ease her aching muscles. Jilly slept on, exhaustion dominating the need for food and water.

Jesse stood slowly and crept away from her sister, curious to explore the cluster of rocks stacked against the cavern's far end. The darkness clung to her with a persistence that made her skin crawl, but she felt her way along the wall until she reached the jumble of boulders.

One by one, she rolled the smaller ones from the wall, allowing them to plop into the foamy water that slapped violently against the end of the channel. The sound evaporated in the splash and roar of each swell and she continued her mindless exercise, filling the moments with purpose.

"What are you doing?"

Jesse jumped in her fright and stumbled back against the large mound, letting out a yelp as her ankle turned. It wasn't often that the twins could catch each other off guard, and she massaged the slight injury as Jilly sat beside her, slipping on her own shirt and shorts.

"I'm sorry I scared you. I thought maybe you had found something, since you were working so hard."

"I was just bored and hungry and thirsty. I figured I'd kill time by throwing rocks. Want to join me?" Jilly smiled and nodded as she helped Jesse to her feet again. Scrambling to the top of the pile, the two worked together to roll the top boulder off its perch, watching as it tumbled and crashed down the mound and into the foam below.

*   *   *

"Are we going to be able to keep a lid on this whole thing?"

"I think so. Does it really matter? Once we have Austerlitz as our scapegoat everyone will forget."

"Aren't you worried about the subjects breaking their word once they're back into the society?"

"Not really. As I said before—does it really matter?"

"I guess not. I just can't help but remember his last screw-up and the mess we had to clean up."

"If it'll make you feel better, we can start releasing some conspiracy theory articles in the local newspapers and get a few novels out about government interference and Big Brother and all that."

"What will that do?"

"Saturate the market. Eventually the people get bored with it and forget. Once these people are integrated back into the population, no one will care about rumours of a secret society of power. If we do only that, it'll die quietly."

"So what about the spoiled samples? I'm still not sure I believe the scientists who claim the atmospheric pressure in the plane ruined them. That's nearly forty years of work down the drain. Are we going to start again?"

"We don't need to."

"What do you mean?"

"Think about it. We have all of our specimens leaving the island tomorrow morning. The DNA is combined the way we wanted it. We have a pure species of humans. Who do you think will survive?"

"I never thought of that. Aren't you worried about their children mixing with the polluted genetics of society?"

"Not really. Essentially we've done what we, *The Committee*, initially started out to do. We've given mankind's genetic code a healthy boost. Even if the children do mix, they'll only strengthen the weaker human DNA. Nothing has been ruined in the long run. "

"I suppose you're right."

"Yes. *The Committee* has succeeded once again. Perhaps it wasn't to the extent we would have wished, but it is better than it could have been. And there are other things that have been accomplished that I'm not at liberty to talk about at this time."

"Oh really?"

*   *   *

Friedrick screamed out a curse once again as he shook the empty fuel can. The boat's motor had chugged to a stop moments earlier, leaving him adrift with the ocean waves. He'd forgotten to bring fuel. Pitching the empty can out over the vast water, he fell off balance and plunked into the boat's bottom where he lay, working his mind through possibilities.

Taking a calming breath, the Lieutenant tried to meditate. He always thought best after a session with his guide. Sitting up, he positioned himself and closed his eyes, allowing the rocking of the craft to soothe his mind as he plunged into the emptiness of his own psyche to search for the voice.

Come to me. Come to my aid. I have been a faithful follower. You must help me.

A cold chuckle echoed through his mind, and he shivered.

Why should I rescue you, Friedrick? You've failed. Perhaps it is time to finish my work with you. Perhaps it is time to move on to someone else—someone more obedient and competent.

Friedrick's body jerked suddenly as he felt a cold hand clamp upon his brain. Pain shot through his head and he began to scream anew. Horrific faces and creatures flitted through his thoughts as the curtain of falsehood was torn away and he saw his guide for the demon it truly was.

His last conscious thought was strung together in a series of overlapping sentences. *I was fooled! Don't hurt me! Stay away! You lied to me!* And then his mind snapped and the man who had once used all his intellectual skills to manipulate those around him was suddenly rendered a blathering idiot.

Flopping back into the bottom of the boat, the old German officer—friend of Hitler, leader of power brokers, ultimate planner and schemer—began to convulse. Spittle dribbled down his chin and his eyes rolled back in his head. For a full five minutes the man shook and flailed. And then he was still.

He stared vacantly at the ribs of the small craft, unable to identify his surroundings. His mind was blank. An overwhelming sense of loss and loneliness covered him and the Lieutenant curled into a fetal position in the boat's center, popped a thumb into his mouth and pulled an oil-covered cloth to his cheek. Lying there, he waited, letting the sun's warmth and the light waves comfort his feeble and childish mind.

*　　　*　　　*

Flopping with exhaustion on the stone floor, the two girls gave up their game of rolling boulders. No longer did it hold back the thoughts of hunger and thirst. They were tired, but couldn't sleep for the dryness of mouth and sharpness of hunger pangs. They lay side-by-side, staring at the slightly reduced pile of rubble before them and the ceiling above it.

At some time, it was apparent, there had been a cave-in and part of the ceiling had dropped, rendering the canopy into a series of juts and rough edges. Jilly traced the veins of jaggedness with her eyes, trying to form patterns out of their randomness.

Suddenly, she bolted upright, noticing a darker spot near the top of the rock pile. Not taking her eyes from the small shadow, she reached over and patted her sister's shoulder, pointing to what she saw.

"What is it? What do you see?"

Without answering, Jilly rose to her feet and scrambled toward the very top, where the rubble met the uneven and broken ceiling. Jesse remained seated, throwing a quizzical look after her sister.

"What is it, Jilly?"

The twin reached the top and looked back at Jesse, a huge smile on her face. And then she turned again and plunged her arm into the shadow before her, confirming her suspicions.

"There's a tunnel back here!" She shouted in her excitement and felt her heart jump as her own voice rattled and echoed through the darkness ahead. Jesse was quick to scamper up the collection of rocks to join her sister, and together, they worked feverishly to broaden the opening.

"It looks like the cave-in closed a tunnel. So what do we do now?"

They sat and turned to momentarily watch the churning of the sea below. And then Jilly smiled.

"We still have awhile to wait. Why don't we explore it? We'll likely never get another chance."

Jesse scratched at her chin, turning her eyes to the remainder of the driftwood.

"I'll make a torch like Dad showed us. There's enough small stuff to do that with. Why don't you snap some of the bigger pieces into sticks? We'll take as many as we can carry to leave a trail. When we run out, we'll follow them back here to get more. What do you think?" An eager nod was all the answer she needed, and the two set to work.

*   *   *

It was the largest prayer letter of its kind, bearing the signatures of hundreds of people worldwide. Janet Stillwater-Gray Bear smiled and wiped at her eyes as she scanned the list of names filling page after page. Her husband, Andrew, had thought of the idea when they held their first meeting of the families of the lost children. Neither of them could have imagined something as powerful and ongoing as the single page prayer letter.

She returned to the beginning and reread the words they had penned so many years earlier, noting absently that she must copy it onto a fresh sheet before sending it again. Some of the ink was smudged with much handling and many tears, and the paper was crinkled and worn. She would file this original away as a reminder of God's faithfulness throughout the years. It was a simple letter.

To all of the families of missing children:

We have chosen to petition the God of creation in the name of his son Jesus for the freedom of our children. Below, you will find a prayer that we ask you to offer on their behalf. Once said, please sign your name and forward this to another who will pray as well. If you don't know of any others, return it to Andrew or Peter Gray Bear at the address below. Thank you for your time.

Lord and Mighty King,

You are awesome and deserving of all creation's worship, for everything belongs to you, Oh God. We don't understand your purpose behind the abduction of our children any more than we understand why you have called us to wait for so long. But now, Father, we see your hand beginning to move and we petition you for the sake of those same children. Please bring them home to us. Bring them safely. Let the world see your hand in all of this. May you be glorified. And give us patience for the final test of endurance. In Jesus' name we ask you. Amen.

> *Andrew Gray Bear*
> *Janet Stillwater*
> *Peter Gray Bear'*

And the list went on. Dozens of pages were filled with name after name of those who had repeated the prayer, pleading for their children, grandchildren, siblings, or cousins. Many names had been signed twice as the letter began its second circulation across the globe. Every nationality was represented. Every language was etched into those names.

For the first time since it all began, Janet Stillwater-Gray Bear began to see what she had not seen before. The world—a place of divided ideals and opposing beliefs—was being unified under the banner of Christianity. Believers worldwide were drawing together to call upon the God of the universe. For the first time, praise and worship was being lifted by representatives of every nation, and God's word was spreading rapidly in languages that had never before known the voice of Jehovah.

After so many years of darkness she finally understood the "why."

* * *

"I can hear crying."

"Me too."

"I know this sounds dumb, Jilly. But I think we've been in this cave before. It feels real familiar."

Jilly nodded her answer, realizing as an afterthought that her twin wouldn't see the gesture in the dim torchlight. It felt like they'd been in the narrow cave for hours, but she still had plenty of sticks in her arm with which to mark their path in the chance that they came upon other tunnels.

Jesse stopped suddenly and held her torch high, allowing the meager and pathetic glow to illuminate more of their confines. And then she began to laugh. Jilly dropped her bundle and stepped over to the wall, touching it as recognition hit her with full force, and then she, too, joined in on the laughter.

They left the twigs, carrying only the torch, and linked arms as they headed for the strange sound ahead, giggling over the unbelievability of the situation.

*   *   *

"Is the media ready?"

"Yes, Sir."

"What about the families?"

"Each government has offered to fly them to Miami to meet the subjects."

"It's too bad that the reporter quit. It would be interesting to see her article in tomorrow's paper."

"Maybe she can be persuaded to do one last piece."

"It doesn't matter. There will be enough coverage. Have we found Austerlitz yet?"

"Yes, Sir. It was strange though. The Coast Guard found him drifting in a small speedboat off the coast. He was delirious. It was odd."

"Why do you say that?"

"Well, he's only been on the water for less than a day. He should have been fine. But…"

"Yes?"

"Well, Sir, it's like he's gone backwards. He acts like a child. We found him…uh…sucking his thumb, Sir."

"Really?"

"Yes, Sir."

"See that the media finds out about his present mental state. This could turn out better than we'd hoped. Have him committed to our asylum until the families can bring formal charges against him. Make his face the most viewed media image in recent history. The people will want a criminal. Let's give them one."

"Yes, Sir."

"How are the subjects being retrieved?"

"We have representatives from each country approaching the island as we speak. They are aboard one of our luxury cruise ships. The islanders will be transported in tenders and will be welcomed with much fanfare. We have elements of the media onboard ship to cover the event. Between that and the reunion in Miami, it should be quite the show."

"Have you heard anything on the chosen one? Is the child well? Do you think he will fit the criteria?"

"By all of our tests and observations he's the one, Sir."

"That's perfect. Fine. Okay then; let's get going on the arrest and confinement of Austerlitz. We need the people angry and ready for the release of his captives. Get that on the news A.S.A.P."

"Yes, Sir."

*   *   *

The first scream echoed through the cavern and pulled the small crowd's attention to its harsh and piercing sound. Others echoed it as some were sure they saw what could only be ghosts. And then two dirty, bedraggled eleven-year-old girls stepped from the back of the Gray Bear home into the large opening that was so familiar to them.

Pandemonium broke loose as Rachel rushed to her daughters, crying and laughing at the same time. Broken sentences poured forth as each spoke overtop the other, explaining, filling in missed details, hugging and crying.

Hawk heard the screams from his lonely post outside the cave's mouth. Turning in fear and pent-up rage, he stormed into his home, knife drawn, killing instinct honed by the pain and frustration of losing his children.

Across the room, he saw the crowd gathered and his mind slowly absorbed that which was the focal point of their attention. He dropped his knife, not hearing the heavy clatter of metal on stone, and rubbed his eyes with meaty fists, disbelieving the sight that was before him. And then he loosed a whoop of joy and pounced upon his wife and two daughters.

The rest of their children stepped back, allowing their parents to reunite with Jilly and Jesse. Happy grins plastered the faces in the room and tears streamed freely as all rejoiced with Hawk and Rachel at the return of their precious girls. And then, when the raw emotion had passed, and the truth and reality of their reunion had settled on them all, calmer, more detailed questions were passed back and forth.

"I think you both had better start from the beginning." Hawk pulled back and eyed his twin daughters, noting every detail from the damp and wrinkled clothing to the salt-encrusted hair.

"What happened?"

Jilly looked at her twin and stepped forward, willingly taking the responsibility of leadership on her own small shoulders.

"Mom sent us all to the beach to help pass water up the line to put out the fire, but I didn't really want to help. I waited until everyone was busy and I slipped away into the jungle. I only planned on resting for a little while, but Mr. Austerlitz came crashing into the clearing and saw me.

He said he was hurt and limped toward me, asking for my help. I fell for it and he grabbed me by the hair and told me—he told me he'd break my neck if I made a noise."

Jesse jumped in with her part of the story then, and Jilly waited.

"I knew where Jilly was so I followed. I was so mad when I saw him grab her hair that I just ran at him and punched at him. I should have gone for help, but I didn't. I'm sorry." They both dropped their gazes and waited.

Hawk tipped their chins up and looked from one to the other soberly.

"I'm assuming you've learned that disobedience and impulsiveness are wrong since the consequences you've faced far outweigh any discipline I could have given you." The girls nodded.

"Ok, so we'll consider that dealt with. Go on with the story."

"He dragged us to the beach near the cliffs where he had his boat pulled up on the shore. It took a lot of work, but he made us drag it to the water and get in. The tide was still out enough that we could slip into that cave you told us not to ever go in to. We got inside and got the boat up onto this rock shelf just in time 'cause the tide suddenly gushed back in and the hole closed.

He tied us up and built a fire with some old driftwood. I don't know how long we were there, but it was dark when he put the boat back in the water and left the cave. He said he would come back for us..." Jesse looked away, fear and horror clouding her eyes as she remembered the threat, and Hawk's jaw muscles clenched at what his mind concluded. Jilly picked up the conversation as she touched her sister's arm gently.

"We were able to get untied and we jumped in the water just before he came back. We saw your torches, Dad. He probably would have found us if you hadn't arrived when you did.

"While he was searching, we could tell the tide was coming back in again. We waited until the last minute and went back into the cave, hoping he wouldn't see us. We went exploring and saw a big rock pile at the back of the cave. We were bored, so we started rolling the rocks into the water.

"That's when we realized that there used to be a tunnel and it was buried when the ceiling caved in. We made a torch and followed the tunnel."

A smile crept across Jesse's face, and she interrupted her sister's tale.

"You should have heard us laugh when we realized it was the dead end tunnel in our own home. We could hear you guys crying and just followed the sound." She raised her voice a bit. "Sorry we scared you guys. We were so glad to be home, we didn't think about what you'd think when you saw us come out of the tunnel."

Those who had screamed chuckled at their previous reaction, and their mild laughter sought for competition with the chatter that sprang up at the conclusion of the girls' amazing tale.

Hawk cleared his throat then, and pulled his girls closer.

"I, too, have a confession to make."

Two sets of curious eyes stared up at him as he continued on.

"When I saw the boat pulling away, I thought you were on board. I was so angry at God for not getting me there quicker. I doubted him—his love for me—his power to do anything about the situation. It was a real struggle to hold onto my faith in his ability to control all of it in spite of what I understood and saw. And then you two appeared in my very own home and I must confess I'm ashamed that I ever doubted him. So you see, we all have something to regret from this—and much to be happy for."

Again, he hugged them, his tear-filled eyes meeting his wife's own exuberantly moist gaze.

"Where did the Lieutenant go, then?" Yngve brought a serious note back to the relieved and happy group. "He is a danger. We must watch through the remainder of the night."

Hawk nodded his agreement, and the small crowd headed for the burned-out clearing to pass the word that the girls were home.

22

THE SOUND OF THE CAMERAMAN'S VOICE was lost in the crisp breeze that whipped around the hardwood deck of the large cruise ship. It didn't matter. The brown-haired woman knew that her cue had come simply by watching the light atop the camera. It was too late to make a final adjustment to her hair and she just hoped that the wind wouldn't cause her eyes to water like the last time. She had barely finished her report and gone off the air when one fat teardrop had tracked a streak of mascara down her otherwise flawless cheek. She ignored a stubborn strand of the straight fine hair as it swished back and forth across her forehead with the wind's erratic pulse. Pulling in a deep breath, she dropped her voice into the lower more professional tones of a newscaster and pressed on.

"This is Sandra Heffing, with NACB news. I'm standing on the deck of this beautiful luxury cruise liner, but instead of whisking wealthy vacationers off to a romantic frolic in the Caribbean sun, this great ship is on a mission of mercy. Never before has an event like this taken place as the ship *The Collingford* churns its way toward the mysterious tropical island that holds the victims of three decades of genetic experimentation.

"Representatives from every country around the globe are on board with me as we wait for the rendezvous with the first tender load of victims from the Austerlitz experiment.

"To recap: these people, some of which were kidnapped by the recently institutionalized ex-Nazi Lieutenant Friedrick Austerlitz, will be brought aboard and officially welcomed home by their own country's diplomats. Austerlitz continued experiments fostered by Adolph Hitler during World War II and has recently been admitted to The Genington Foundation's Institution for the Mentally Disturbed with extreme schizophrenia and other nervous disorders.

"Many of these victims have been born in captivity and will require processing and social integration courses in order to allow them to join their relatives in their homelands. Each government is being encouraged to come to some sort of agreement, as many of these people were forced to marry outside their culture. Some unions are between countries having hostilities against one another.

"Hold on a moment please...yes...I've just received news that the United States, Canada, Great Britain, France and Australia are offering asylum to those who do not wish to return to their countries, and I'm certain that other nations will follow suit in the near future.

"As to Mr. Austerlitz? According to the UN, he will be facing charges of crimes against humanity. Until then, he will remain in protective custody at the institution. This is Sandra Heffing reporting—NACB news."

The camera clicked off, the light went out and Sandra slapped at the restless hair with annoyance. Then she turned her attention to the waters below her, silently begging the ship to cut its way through them in order to reach the island quickly. She was determined to be the first to make a name for herself documenting the rescue of the islanders.

*   *   *

Andrew Gray Bear and his wife Janet stood silently, Andrew's younger brother Peter acting as a wall of muscle while the crowds of reporters, diplomats and spectators surged around them. They, like the families of the rest of the victims, waited dockside while the massive ship weighed anchor and prepared to off-load its passengers. Too much time had passed since the initial rescue. Quarantines had been set and completed. Medical assessments had been processed.

Forms had been filled. And through it all, the families who had hoped and prayed through the decades for the return of their children continued in their restless patience. But this day would see it all end and Andrew smiled broadly at that thought.

A large crowd of adults and children gathered along the rail of the liner's open deck, marveling at a world that many of them had never seen before. A stray thought flitted through the Native man's mind as he eyed the simple peasant-style clothing the rescued people wore. They reminded him of the pictures he had seen as a boy of some of the first pilgrims who landed on his country's coastline so many years before, and he pondered the parallel.

More of *The Projects'* families poured out of the ship's vast collection of lounges and rooms, and the crowds shifted and murmured as they viewed their offspring for the first time in three decades. And then they grew silent, tears of joy mixed with the anger and heartache of lost childhood. Many sobbed openly, oblivious of the TV cameras that swept the scene, capturing their grief for the newscasters who were eager to display their sorrows and joys to the event-hungry world.

Great ropes dropped onto the massive cement dock, and men scurried to secure them onto the tree-sized posts which would hold the great ship against the rubber padding that ran along the water's edge. More men struggled to maneuver a series of heavy metal walkways up to the one empty space in the ship's rail, and the crowds surged forward as the ship began to expel its occupants one at a time.

Police and security personnel stepped in—human shields incorporated to keep all but the immediate families from the roped off clearing around the bottom of the stairs. A slim, older man stepped to the head of the staircase—the first to be released—and the crowd hushed. He was blond with much grey in his thinning hair. Reaching out, he took the hand of a younger, dark-haired beauty, and together they walked down the stairs to the waiting crowd. They were trailed by a small covey of children of various ages—shy and nervous creatures who peered at the great throng with fear and curiosity. And then the stream of people flooded down the steps behind the man, spreading out and mingling with those waiting.

Camera shutters clicked and chattered, and the voices of reporters blended together in a loud cacophony as each man or woman tried to document their slant on the momentous occasion. TV cameras zoomed in on individual faces, capturing for eternity the range of emotions scattered across the crowd. Children clung to their mothers' skirts and fathers hovered close to their families with cautious protectiveness as the wall of people closed in around each small cluster of refugees.

A woman broke from the masses and waddled toward that first couple, assaulting the air with her high-pitched Italian. And then she wrapped the younger woman in a rib-crushing hug and bawled out her joy. Isabella smiled happily as she introduced her mother to her husband. Small faces peeked from behind her legs, awed by the loud exclamations of the woman they were told to call Grandmother.

Andrew, Janet and Peter continued their silent vigil, searching the various figures that milled about on the distant deck. The wind lifted a long strand of white hair and Janet was immediately drawn to a face that so clearly resembled her own. Unable to restrain herself, she let out a squeak of excitement. Grabbing Andrew's shirtsleeve, the agitated woman pointed to the masses and bounced up and down a few times in her eagerness.

And then her hand clamped onto the large paw of her Native American husband and, dragging him with her, she eagerly elbowed her way to the collection of people gathering on the dock within the confines of the police circle. Peter chuckled at the dainty bulldozer and trailed his brother and sister-in-law.

Janet heard her name echo faintly over the heads of chattering people and she watched, overwhelmed, as the older version of her sixteen-year-old daughter threw herself against the opposing crowd, pushing and elbowing her way into her mother's arms.

Andrew and Eric smiled shyly at each other and introduced themselves as Peter huffed his way to their sides. The two women, crying and hugging and laughing, pulled them into their embrace and it was as though the lost years didn't matter.

*   *   *

Representatives from two very hesitant nations stood off in another cluster. Chinese words overlapped by an English translation overlapped by a Russian translation made for a confusing conversation to overhear. The children of Charlie and Natasha watched as the linguistic ball bounced from nationality to nationality while their own parents acted as the middlemen. And then, one by one, each child was presented—first to a Russian diplomat, then to a Chinese diplomat—and back and forth they went until the last to be presented were a diminutive couple of vintage years.

Charlie's parents stood with tears streaming down their faces as they waited for the formal welcome and introductions that tradition demanded. They stood as tall and straight as their aging bodies would permit and their faces wore the solemn mask common to their society. And yet, they could not hold back the tears that spoke so eloquently of their true feelings.

Charlie approached his parents wearing the same stillness of face and bowed low, a gesture of honour. The bow was returned with as much dignity as could be mustered. And then Natasha was introduced and she, too, bowed low and offered a greeting in Charlie's native tongue, drawing a small smile on the lips of her father-in-law. Each child, as taught to do, bowed before their grandparents, and when the formalities were finished, Mr. Chang threw tradition to the wind and caught his son in a fierce embrace as he openly praised and thanked God for the return of his child. The action was duplicated as his tiny wife sidled up to her tall daughter-in-law and, grinning happily, reached for her.

*   *   *

Amidst the crowds of milling people a Tillie hat collided with the massive structure of a Hawaiian male chest and was swept from its moorings on the top of a gray head. Michael whooped with joy as he swung his mother-in-law in a circle. Never mind that he hadn't even met her yet. So great was the large man's joy that he immediately passed her off to Pamela and repeated the gesture with his wife's father, who laughed with great humour at being so easily manhandled. Beyond that, a large cluster of stockily-built Hawaiians waited impatiently for their turn, huge smiles outshining the loud colours of their brightly flowered shirts.

*   *   *

A shrill whistle pierced the air, bouncing its echo off the concrete walls, drawing a silence from the crowd. Andrew knew that whistle. He had taught a small boy to whistle in just such a way. Raising himself to his full height he returned the call and stood amazed as the hushed crowd suddenly parted between the two sounds. His eyes clouded with tears as he watched a giant of a man in his mid-years directing his steps toward him.

The man with the face that so resembled his long-dead wife approached in the emptiness of sound as the crowds held their collective breath. He was flanked by a woman, four strapping lads, and four beauties, and never once did the younger man hesitate in his step but, upon approaching, wrapped his arms around the aged shoulders of his father. Andrew—stoic Andrew—cried like a baby in the embrace of his only son.

On the deck of the great ship, a small family stood off to one side, away from the stairs that led to America. Adam and Eve, bearers of the hideous project's name, had no one to greet them, but they smiled happily for their friends. Their children huddled around them, their sameness unimportant to the couple who loved them so much. They waited. There was no rush. Soon enough, the five of them would cross the mighty Atlantic Ocean to reclaim a small tailor shop in the heart of London, England.

*　　　*　　　*

"So it's finished?"

"Yes, I think so. Although, I must admit, it's been a long haul."

"I never thought it would take so many years for them all to settle."

"What did all of you expect? Most of them have completely forgotten their culture and its religions."

"I must say, I find it rather unusual that so many have taken to the Judeo-Christian beliefs. Why do you suppose that is?"

"I don't really know, but I've been informed that it's become a rather popular ideology in the strangest of places. I've heard it's begun to sweep through China and Russia, of all places."

"Do you think we should do something about it?"

"I suppose we should wait and see."

"Shall I propose a toast to the overwhelming success of *The Project*, gentlemen?"

"Why would you do that?"

"Because the *true* purpose behind the Adam and Eve Project *was* completed."

A stunned silence filtered through the room.

"But I thought we agreed it wasn't completed—unless there was another purpose that this group of men knows nothing about?"

"Oh, but there was." He savoured the moment and smiled.

"Our primary purpose was to create the perfect man. The perfect world leader. Someone who would have the intellect, stamina, longevity and presence to lead the world—under the committee's directive of course. The old man told me that just before he died. The saving of the human genetic code was a secondary—but equally noble purpose. But it was also a vast and cumbersome cover for what we were truly hoping to accomplish."

"And you say we succeeded?"

"Oh yes—we succeeded immensely. Several times over. It's just a matter of waiting for him to grow up. But right now, we have another pressing problem."

"Oh?"

"Yes. It seems the one we've set in place in Iraq has begun to enjoy the taste of power."

"How is this a problem?"

"He's becoming abusive in his treatment of the people. He's also threatening to shut down oil supplies to the free world."

"That won't do at all."

"No. It won't"

"What will you do?"

"I'm not sure. Perhaps some nice little drug. Or maybe a takeover."

"What if you could bring democracy to that corner of the world? Would that help?"

"Perhaps. But that would require a war. I'm not sure I'm ready for that just yet."

Vengeance

It was a harsh land. A land created for survivors. Ruggedly beautiful in summer with sharp snow-capped granite peaks jabbing at crisp blue skies—their formidable structures providing a starkly contrasting backdrop to the endless carpets of wildflowers, moss and boldly coloured soil—to the brutal winters that sealed the land in a tight cocoon of glacial ice, numbing cold and darkness.

Far from the eyes of the governing authorities, it was the perfect place to experiment into areas that would otherwise be frowned upon. And it was, after all, only one Beluga whale. Even if the carcass was later found, it would be impossible for anyone to trace the elements back to the source.

The man watched as his subordinate's hand cranked the cable that ran from the small but sturdy crane to the net-encased mammal not thirty feet from the stern of the mid-sized fishing vessel. The boat rocked with the thrashing of the pathetic creature as it heaved its blanched hide in protest of the rough hemp. The erratic jerking and yanking was offset by the hypnotic rhythm of Hudson Bay's stiff tides and currents, and the man wanted the thing to be done and over so he could return to the safety of land.

He studied the whale as it was pulled alongside the ship. Alabaster white, it was a beautiful mammal. Almost a pity to destroy the thing. But like he had once been, it was an innocent at the hands of someone else's agenda. The whale stilled and, as instructed, the men kept it half-submerged. There was no point in stressing it any more than necessary.

He walked to the rail and reached down into a box lined with foam packing materials. Pulling out a large syringe, the man held it up to the grey skies and eyed the dose of clear fluid it contained. It should be enough to give them an accurate testing. If it could kill the whale, it would most certainly do its job on its other intended victims.

He patted the animal's streamlined smooth skin gently, almost apologetically. And then he plunged the syringe deep, emptying it of its contents. Surprisingly, the creature never moved. Its eyes were just above the waterline and it rolled the nearest one back to fasten on the man with the syringe. As though it knew its own fate. Returning the instrument back to its case, the man settled back to wait. He figured maybe three hours at best and then the creature would begin to show signs.

Ignoring the quiet whale, the man filled the gradual passing of time by scanning the nearby shore, keeping an alert eye out for any human intervention. It would be awkward explaining what had just been done. Better that there were no witnesses. Along a rocky outcropping, a flock of long-tailed ducks waddled and fussed, pleased with the mild summer as they preened their young and themselves. The tundra was vibrant with unusual and persistent life in the short span of time allowed for the warm season.

The man knew all about the tundra. He had studied it with great detail. He knew every plant from the arctic cotton that swayed in the crisp winds to the lousewort and saxifrage that covered the ground in a tenacious blanket. He had followed the migratory paths of the caribou, seen the polar bear in action and felt his heart swell with the aerial ballets danced by the peregrine falcons, snowy owls and Sabine's gulls. This was a land he could truly love given a different life.

But he only had the life he'd been handed and he would make certain it counted for something. In spite of those who had shaped it brutally and unknowingly—*because* of them.

He turned his eye back to the Beluga. It had settled into the net after its first violent protest and continued to wait patiently for whatever it was meant to wait for.

The creature had earned his instant respect and again he felt a twinge of remorse. Glancing at his watch, he was surprised to find that the three hours had come and gone in his fascinated study of the landscape. He moved closer to the seized whale and examined every inch of its sturdy form. Nothing. A frown flickered across his brow and he turned to his associate.

"Are you certain the dose was right?"

The smaller, bespectacled man merely shrugged and nodded.

"I wonder what's gone wrong, then." He turned back to the whale and gave it another once-over.

"I don't understand it, sir. This compound is strong enough that it should have shown its mark long before now. Maybe I should draw a tissue sample and take it back to the lab to see what went wrong."

The man nodded and stepped out of the dainty man's path.

"Get it done, then, and we'll be off. I'll contact my chopper pilot and he can pick us up on shore. Don't dawdle." He gave his associate a knowing look and reached into his pocket for his two-way radio.

"We're ready." He barked the two words into the receiver, waited for acknowledgement, and then turned to the vessel's captain.

"We'll pick up my chopper on shore. I'll need your lifeboat to get myself and the doctor there. Would that be a problem?" The ten thousand dollars above the rental of the fishing vessel pretty much guaranteed that it likely wouldn't be, and the Captain shrugged his submission.

Finished with his ministrations over the patient whale, the doctor turned and secured the tissue sample alongside the empty syringe in the padded case. He rose and heaved the bulky case into his arms almost jealously and maneuvered across the open deck to where the lifeboat was being lowered to the water's rolling surface. Before long, the two men were settled, side-by-side, in the small wooden rowboat and heading for shore.

No one on board the ship heard the small burst of sound deep in the bowels of the vessel where the engine room was located. Otherwise they would have scrambled like ants at a picnic in order to repair the small but effective damage done to the resting engine. So absorbed in the approach of the sleek helicopter were they that they also missed the second muffled pop that punched a small hole in one of the lowest of the ship's seams. Their first inkling that something was wrong came as the ship tilted slightly more than it should have in the Bay's choppy waters. The Captain ignored his retreating passengers as he tossed orders to his men, and then he turned a wicked eye back upon them when a crewman stumbled up the stairs and shouted that the ship had sprung a leak.

The first mate scrambled to the bridge with the intent of turning the vessel to shore, but as he fired up the engine, the small damage ballooned into a loud explosion and black smoke roiled up from the stairway that led to the ship's center. The Captain clutched the rail angrily and shouted for his men to jump ship and head for shore. If the freezing water didn't kill them, they might find a way to civilization using the small rowboat. And then he watched that dream go up in smoke as the helicopter pilot handed a can of what could only be gasoline to the man who had funded the expedition.

From the port side of his floundering ship, he watched the man pour the can of liquid over the lifeboat, and then inwardly raged as tongues of yellow and red flame leapt from the wooden structure, consuming it in an instant conflagration. He knew his fate then. It was broadcast to him and his men in the heat waves and smoke that plunged skyward, shifting and gyrating with the increasing rotation of the chopper's blades. And then those who had lured him and his crew to this strange mission in the north were suddenly gone, leaving him with a crippled vessel and a dozen or more regrets.

He watched his men splash their way to the shore and he, too, stepped over the rail with the intent of dropping into the bitter cold waters. At least if they made it to the gravel beach, there was a fire waiting to bring the life back into their hypothermic limbs.

*   *   *

From the distant circling chopper, the man watched dispassionately as the crew struggled and splashed their way toward shore. Few of them would make it through the arctic waters and those who did would not likely survive in the harsh tundra. The ship sank quickly, its heavy diesel engine pulling it under the icy waves. Within minutes no sign of it remained other than a dark shadow beneath the churning surface of the Bay. One by one, the men of the small fishing vessel *The Swordfish* slipped beneath the waters as they, too, succumbed to the frigid waters.

The man nodded to himself and reached forward to tap his pilot's shoulder. He'd seen enough. No witnesses. That's what he had decided. That's what he got. The chopper tilted and sped off toward the south, leaving the land as it had been. Empty. Stark. Barren. Incredible.

Bibliography

Trivia-Library.com at www.trivia-library.com

Wikipedia, the free encyclopedia at http://en.wikipedia.org

The Aviation Zone at www.theaviationzone.com

Collections at http://collections.ic.gc.ca

Strategy Planet at www.strategyplanet.com

Historical Naval Ships Visitors Guide at www.hnsa.org

Kriegsmarine and U-Boat History at www.ubootwaffe.net

Scharnhorst-The History at www.scharnhorst-class.dk

www.jfk-assassination.de

American Presidents at www.americanpresidents.org

Bookrags at www.bookrags.com

World History and Cultures in Christian Perspective Second Edition

A Beka Book Copyright 1997, 1985 Pensacola Christian College, Pensacola, Florida 32523-9160

Printed in the United States
69597LVS00002B/226-315

9 781897 373019